# A MYSTERIOUS ATTRACTION

Mac's gaze settled on the cleft in his chin and, against her will, she traced the appealing mark with her fingertip. His whiskers gently rasped her skin, sending a tingle down her arm. She wanted to lean forward and kiss his chin, explore the indent with her tongue as she tasted him. Her blood thundered through her veins and heat settled between her thighs. What was it about this man that made her lose all level-headedness?

She was a reporter. Objectivity was a requirement for her job.

Hormones were to be ignored. She'd never had trouble ignoring them until Jared. Now she couldn't turn them off.

Drawing away from him, Mac searched for an excuse to decline his dinner invitation. But the reporter within her had her own reasons to accept. Mac had questions she wanted answered and Jared would be stuck with her for the length of the meal. It made perfect sense.

So why did her stomach do a slow roll every time she thought of sitting across an intimate table from him? She had a mystery to solve and Mac McAllister had never let her libido get the better of her.

Of course, she hadn't been faced with temptation in the form of Jared Yates before either.

Dear Romance Reader,

In July last year, we launched the Ballad line with four new series, and each month we'll present both new and continuing stories set everywhere from medieval England to the American West—the kind of passionate, romantic stories you love best, written by the most gifted authors. At the back of each book, we'll tell you when you can find subsequent books in the series that have captured your heart.

First up is the second entry in Lori Handeland and Linda Devlin's wonderful *Rock Creek Six* series. This month Linda Devlin introduces **Sullivan**, a half-breed bastard with no place in the world—until he finds his fate in a special woman's arms. Next, Maura McKenzie continues the *Hope Chest* series with **At Midnight**, as a modern-day newspaper reporter tracks a murderer into the past, where she meets a Pinkerton agent determined not only to solve the case, but to steal her heart.

The passioante men of the *Clan Maclean* return in Lynne Hayworth's spectacularly atmospheric **Winter Fire**, as a widow with a special gift meets the laird of the proud but doomed clan. Will her love bring about his salvation? Finally, Kelly McClymer offers the fourth book in the charming *Once Upon a Wedding* series, introducing **The Infamous Bride** who begins her marriage on a rash wager—and finds that her husband's love is the only wedding gift she wants. Enjoy!

Kate Duffy
Editorial Director

*Hope Chest*

# AT MIDNIGHT

## MAURA McKENZIE

## ZEBRA BOOKS
### Kensington Publishing Corp.
http://www.zebrabooks.com

ZEBRA BOOKS are published by

Kensington Publishing Corp.
850 Third Avenue
New York, NY 10022

All Kensington titles, imprints and distributed lines are available at special quantity discounts for bulk purchases for sales promotion, premiums, fund-raising, educational or institutional use.

Special book excerpts or customized printings can also be created to fit specific needs. For details, write or phone the office of the Kensington Special Sales Manager: Kensington Publishing Corp., 850 Third Avenue, New York, NY 10022. Attn. Special Sales Department. Phone: 1-800-221-2647.

Zebra and the Z logo Reg. U.S. Pat. & TM Off.

First Printing: October 2001
10 9 8 7 6 5 4 3 2 1

Printed in the United States of America

# ONE

*Virginia*
*Present Day*

Trish "Mac" McAllister hated being wrong, but this time she wished she had been.

"How long has she been dead?" Mac asked Deputy Dan Wilcox who stood beside her in the wintry Virginia night.

" 'Bout half an hour. A couple was out walking their dog when they heard her scream. They called nine-one-one right away," the lanky deputy replied. "I called you after I saw the victim."

She sent him a grateful smile. "I appreciate your bending the rules for me, Dan. I know you're risking your job letting me near the crime scene like this."

He shrugged. "I figure you know as much about this case as we do. Hell, you're probably a whole lot more likely to solve it."

Mac wasn't so certain about that, but she didn't dispute her friend's confidence in her. Growing up together, she and Dan had tried dating in college but came to the conclusion that they made better pals than lovers. Because of their friendship, Dan had been an anonymous source for more than a few of

Mac's news stories. If Dan's boss ever discovered he was feeding her information, the deputy would be out of a job.

She squatted down beside the murdered woman, the scene lit by two sets of headlights aimed at the body. Mac's stomach rolled, but she shoved aside her squeamishness. This wasn't the first time—though she desperately prayed it would be the last—that she looked upon one of the victims of the Piano Man Killer.

Mac switched gears to reporter mode and studied the woman's body with an impassiveness gained from six years of covering the news for the *Staunton Sentinel*. The profile appeared to be the same as for the previous four victims: female, between eighteen and thirty years old, pretty with light-colored hair.

Without touching anything, she pointed to a thin wire wrapped with two twists around the woman's throat. "I'll bet you a year's pay that's a piano wire."

Dan hunkered down beside her. "I won't take you up on that one, Mac." He glanced at the reporter. "You gonna tell me why you were in town this evening?"

Mac shrugged. "Victims number one and number three were killed near here on this same date the last two years. I suspected the murderer would follow the same pattern. I was right." She clenched her hands into tight fists as helpless anger thrummed through her. "If only I could've figured out the exact location."

Dan laid a hand on her shoulder. "It wasn't your fault, Mac." He stood. "I have to see what's taking the state forensics team so long."

Mac nodded and watched the deputy stride over
to a white Bronco with a lightbar on its roof. She
took a deep breath and brought her gaze back to the
young woman who stared with sightless eyes up at
the night sky. Drifting snowflakes feathered her eyelashes in an almost obscene caricature of undefiled
beauty. Mac swallowed the bile that rose in her
throat despite her attempt to convince herself she
was too tough, too jaded, to let another violent death
bother her.

"I'll make the bastard pay, even if I have to follow
him to hell," she said with a husky voice.

"Talking to yourself again, McAllister?"

Mac glanced up and spotted Sheriff Lou Longley,
Dan's boss. She bristled at the county lawman's ar-
rogance and didn't bother to hide her aversion to the
pompous son of a bitch. He was too much like a
stereotypical power-hungry sheriff, using his position
to do whatever the hell he wanted and not giving a
damn about anyone who stood in his way.

Pressing her palms to her jean-clad thighs, Mac
pushed herself upright and met his insolent gaze.
"What hole did you slither out of, Longley?"

The sheriff's lips thinned in irritation and a ruddy
flush spread across his pockmarked face. Mac sa-
vored a taste of triumph, but a glance at the dead
woman erased the childish moment of victory.

"How the hell did you find out about this?" he
demanded.

Mac crossed her arms and felt the backpack con-
taining her laptop shift its weight across her shoulders. "I heard the call on my radio," she lied
smoothly. She wasn't about to endanger Dan's career.

Longley narrowed his eyes. "Takes longer'n fifteen minutes to get here from Staunton."

"I was in the area." Mac glanced down at the woman who'd been in the wrong place at the wrong time and a shiver slid down her spine. "I had a feeling there'd be a murder tonight."

"Reporter's instincts?" The sheriff's sneer gave no doubt as to what he thought of her chosen vocation.

Fury pulsed through her, obliterating any diplomacy she may have had left. "Something called investigative procedure—you should try it sometime."

Longley's nostrils flared and he turned slightly, casting one side of his face in deep shadows and giving him an ominous appearance.

Damn, she'd done it again. Every time her path crossed the sheriff's, she swore she'd hold her temper in check and every time she failed to do so. Of course, she couldn't help that he was a chauvinist pig who thought women belonged barefoot, pregnant, and in the kitchen—three things Mac had no intention of being. Ever.

"Look," Mac began, trying to sound conciliatory. "I studied the files of the previous four victims. Two of the women were killed five days before Christmas in this general vicinity. I came down here hoping I could catch him in the act."

"Instead, you mess up a crime scene." Longley glared at her. "Get back behind the line, McAllister."

She opened her mouth to defend herself and Longley took a menacing step toward her. "One word and I'll toss your sassy ass in jail for interfering with a police investigation."

Mac snapped her mouth shut. Though she thought

Longley was an idiot, he had every right to do as he threatened. This *was* his jurisdiction, even though she didn't think he could find his way out of a paper bag, much less track down a serial killer. But she couldn't risk pissing off the lawman any more than she already had. This story was going to be her ticket to the top, a journey that would take her sailing past the man who had rejected her and her mother. National Cable News anchor Jefferson Jacoby would be forced to acknowledge that the bastard daughter he'd abandoned was a better reporter.

*"Now,* McAllister!" Longley's command broke into her grim thoughts.

Dan appeared beside her and took hold of her arm. "C'mon, Mac."

As Dan drew her away, Mac sent the sheriff a mocking smile and called over her shoulder, "Don't forget to take pictures before you remove the body."

"Get the hell outta here!"

Longley turned away and Mac sent him a one finger salute. "Whatever you say, Sheriff," she muttered with as much disgust as she could jam into the four words.

"Jeezus, Mac, think you could make him any madder?" Dan muttered under his breath.

Her temper cooled and she sighed. "I'm sorry, Dan, but your boss is a jackass."

Dan chuckled. "Tell me something I don't know." They stopped at Mac's ten-year-old Mustang. "You should get back to town." He glanced around cautiously. "The killer could still be nearby."

Excitement keened through her as she swept her

gaze across their snowy surroundings. "I'm betting on it."

"Hold on now, Mac. Catching the bad guys is *my* job."

"You haven't exactly been burning rubber to catch this one."

Dan's lips thinned. "Damn it, Mac, we're trying. You think we like seeing women killed in our jurisdiction?"

She laid her hand on his arm. "I'm sorry. It's just that this story means so much to me."

"It won't make him love you," he said quietly.

Hurt ripped through Mac, but she kept her face free of emotion. Dan was the only one who knew about her father and what this story meant to her. "Maybe not, but it will make him stand up and notice me."

"For all the wrong reasons. Let it go, Mac. He's a worthless son of a bitch who doesn't deserve a daughter like you."

Dan's vehement defense brought unexpected moisture to her eyes, blurring her vision. To cover her embarrassment, she looked over at the sheriff who was glaring at her and Dan. "If looks could kill, you and I would be dog meat. You'd best join your boss before he destroys all the evidence."

"Go home, Mac," Dan said sternly.

"I betcha Beth doesn't put up with being ordered around," Mac said, referring to Dan's petite, strong-willed, and very pregnant wife.

He merely shook his head, then walked over to the sheriff.

Mac leaned against her car to watch Dan keep his inept boss from messing up the crime scene. Longley glanced up and she met his censuring gaze. Renewed anger shot through her. She hated arrogant men who thought the world revolved around them.

A memory blindsided her as she recalled waking up one night to hear her mother crying in their tiny apartment. Five-year-old Mac walked into the living room where her mother sat on the sagging sofa with tears coursing down her cheeks. Through the cheap stereo speakers, a man was crooning something about trying to get some stupid feeling again. Mac didn't think her mother even knew she was crying until Mac asked her what was wrong.

Over twenty years later, Mac could still hear her mother's answer as clear as if it were only yesterday. *"Never give a man your heart, honey. He'll only break it and leave you with nothing but a hole in your chest that can never be fixed."*

Mac closed her eyes tightly to hold the unwelcome tears at bay. Her father had broken her mother's heart and Mary McAllister's unrequited love for him had eventually destroyed her.

Dan was wrong. Mac couldn't let it go. Once she got her story on the Piano Man Killer, she'd force her father to acknowledge her publicly as the daughter he'd denied.

Mac opened her eyes and raised her head, taking a deep breath of the wintry air. *No man's ever going to steal my heart, Mom,* she vowed silently.

Snow swirled around Mac as she scanned the surrounding darkness. A movement caught her eye and she focused on an area about fifty feet away. A few moments later, she was rewarded with another fleeting glimpse of a man pushing through the brush.

"Dan, over there," she hollered as the wind snatched her words away. She glanced back at the two lawmen who remained near the body. "Dan!"

Without looking to see if he'd heard her this time, Mac dashed into the brush. Her backpack thumped between her shoulder blades; thorns tore at her ski jacket and one caught her cheek. She swore but continued on, using her arms and hands to take the brunt of the bramble's attack.

Was this the killer? Or a witness? Either way, Mac was determined to catch him. What she would do when she caught up with him was something she didn't have time to contemplate. She only knew this man had the answers. She knew it deep in her gut.

Her left foot struck something and she stumbled to her knees, her palms slapping hard on rough wood. It took her only a moment to realize she'd tripped on a set of train tracks. She shoved herself to her feet, ignoring the sting in her hands and knees, and searched frantically for the man she'd been chasing. She spotted him running between the steel rails up the old spur and forced her bruised body to race after him.

The increasing deluge of icy snowflakes buffeted her cheeks. The incline grew steeper and Mac panted, her breath coming in wispy white clouds. She blinked often to keep her quarry in sight. A stitch caught in her side and she pressed her palm against it.

Suddenly the man stopped and she stumbled to a halt about ten feet from him. Unable to speak as she gasped for air, Mac studied him closely through the falling snow as he did the same to her. Although he wore a heavy coat, she could tell he was average height and medium build, probably in his late twenties.

Brown hair covered his head and his pale face held no extraordinary features.

Had this nondescript man murdered five women?

Her gaze lifted and she found herself staring into penetrating eyes that reminded her of a snake hypnotizing its victim. Dread shot through her veins. Why hadn't she made certain Dan had heard her call?

*Real bright, McAllister. This'll teach you to look before you leap.*

*Yeah, if I survive.*

"What're you . . . d-doing here?" Mac demanded in between breaths, hoping sheer bravado would make up for her temporary lack of sense.

He remained silent, his body taut, like a violin string. Or a piano wire.

She shivered, uncertain if it was from the weather or the fear that ballooned within her, growing until it felt as if the Goodyear blimp had taken up residence in her chest. "Did you kill those women?" she blurted.

*Jeezus, McAllister, you keep going like this and they'll find a wire around your neck, too,* Mac's reality check taunted.

Something flickered in the man's hollow eyes and he shook his head slowly. "Nobody, nowhere, no *when* can catch me."

The man was definitely firing on too few cylinders. "What're you talking about?" she demanded.

He lifted his wrist, glanced at the cheap watch and abruptly cackled. "Midnight. Congratulations. You've come the closest."

He spun around and leaped forward, vanishing like a curl of smoke in fog. Mac blinked, then searched for a sign of him. She ran forward to the place where he'd seemed to disappear. Nothing.

A shiver slid down her spine. How could someone vanish into thin air?

The snow whipped around her in ever-increasing fury, and she turned her back to the northwest gale. She had to find shelter until the storm eased and she could make her way back down the steep slope. The unused rail spur would take her up to The Chesterfield, a former resort long since abandoned. At least its crumbling walls would give her a modicum of protection from the storm.

Ten minutes later, Mac, with her teeth chattering, stumbled into the dark ruins. Much of the building's roof was missing, but a corner still remained and Mac hurried over to the area beneath it. She dropped to the debris-covered floor and leaned back against the wall, gulping in deep drafts of air as she wrapped her arms around her drawn-up knees.

A few snowflakes drifted and eddied around her, but at least she was out of the main force of the blizzard. As her heart settled down to a less-frenzied beat, she reached into her pack to retrieve her cell phone. It wasn't there. *Damn.* She had forgotten it in her car.

She pulled a flashlight from the backpack and sent the bright beam dancing around her refuge. Layers of dust and bits of plaster littered the interior, along with broken pieces of chairs and tables. Scraps of old newspapers fluttered with the arctic breeze that swept in through the generous gaps in the walls. There was no sign of the man she'd chased, and she breathed a sigh that was both relieved and disappointed.

The memory of him disappearing before her eyes

brought a new shiver, this one of fearful foreboding. Nobody could simply disappear like that, unless you believed the gossip rags at the grocery checkout. His magic act had to be merely a product of her exhaustion.

Convinced by her logical explanation, Mac glanced around the room and noticed a chest a few feet away on the floor. She frowned. She hadn't noticed it when she'd plopped down. It had been there, hadn't it?

"First, the suspect disappears, then a trunk appears. Pretty soon you'll be seeing Mulder's aliens," she muttered to herself.

She sighed and shivered anew. Moving around might help her keep warm. The trunk drew her nearer. She ran her palm across the surface, which was surprisingly free of dust and animal droppings. Had someone left it here recently?

With light fingers, she traced the faint indentations of carved letters. She aimed her flashlight at them. "EMS," she murmured to herself. A company or a person?

Kneeling in front of the chest, she lifted the lid cautiously as her breath roared in her ears. When nothing jumped out at her, she smiled wryly. "Where's a genie when you need one?"

She played her flashlight across the contents, which appeared to be antique items in mint condition. "What the hell?" she muttered.

On top of the pile lay a dueling pistol, gleaming in the single light beam. A brass nameplate was next to it, and a bright gold chain wrapped around one point of a shiny sheriff's badge. She touched each item reverently, sensing they were significant, but to whom?

At the bottom of the chest rested the only object that looked as if it belonged in this time-forgotten hotel: a rusty pair of handcuffs that lay in two pieces. There were some letters etched on one side of them, barely detectable beneath the layers of rust—EJY. Mac reached for the two cuffs and wrapped her fingers around the corroded metal.

A sense of weightlessness engulfed her, sending a wave of nausea through her. Suddenly caught in a black whirlpool, she was paralyzed, unable to move her limbs. Panic raced through her and she welcomed the silence that enfolded her as consciousness abandoned her to the whims of insanity.

# TWO

*Virginia*
*December 1892*

Jared Yates rubbed his brow, hoping to ease the headache caused by the close confines of the train car. He usually rode first class, but all those seats had been sold by the time he decided to spend Christmas at the Chesterfield.

He should be on his way to Harrisburg, where his mother and six sisters, along with their husbands and children, were gathering to celebrate the holiday season. However, the thought of being in their midst brought to mind vultures circling above their next meal.

When his father had died five years ago, Jared had lost his only ally among the otherwise totally female Yates contingent. And after Sophia had been killed, the women in his life had made it their mission to find him another prospective bride. He loved his mother and sisters, but he didn't want to be submitted to a rigorous interrogation about marriage prospects.

He propped his elbow against the window and squinted out at the darkness where snowflakes escorted the train the last quarter mile to the depot. Sophia Devon, his former intended, was the real reason he was headed to the Chesterfield instead of Harrisburg. Sophia had been brutally murdered two years ago near the resort. In his mind, he could see her swollen features, barely recognizable after she'd been strangled with a steel wire.

The killer had never been found, though he'd strangled three more women since that time. Sophia and one other woman had been killed during the last two Christmas seasons near Hope Springs, and Jared had a gut feeling the murderer would return to claim his next victim some time in the next two weeks.

*And when I catch him, I'll make him pay. I swear it.*

A disturbance behind him made Jared turn around in irritation to determine its cause. One glance, then another made him frown in disbelief.

"What's going on here?" the woman—at least Jared thought it was a woman—demanded. With blond hair almost as short as a man's and wearing a bright colored coat, she made a peculiar sight.

"Where's your ticket, lady?" Frank Wells, the conductor, asked in exasperation.

"What ticket? Where the hell am I?"

Her frantic gaze darted around the train car, and deep in her honey gold eyes, Jared detected fear. However, she was doing a damned good job of hiding it, except for the slight trembling in her hands that he doubted few people other than himself could detect.

The conductor's patience wore thin and he grabbed her arm, pulling her to her feet. "C'mon, lady. I'm goin' to lock you in the baggage car until I can hand you over to the law in Hope Springs."

Almost against his will, Jared rose and sidled past

the passengers between him and the aisle. "What's going on, Frank?"

The conductor paused and the woman's wide eyes latched on to Jared. "Seems we picked up a stowaway at the last stop, Mr. Yates."

"I'm not a stowaway. I don't know how I got on this . . . this antiquated Amtrak," the woman stormed.

"Then where did you come from?" Jared asked mildly.

She swept her bold gaze from his eyes down to his toes and back up. Jared's body reacted like an adolescent boy getting his first peek in a whorehouse. Flustered, he tugged at his jacket self-consciously. If a woman like this odd-looking creature could stir his blood, he was overdue for a visit to the discreet Flower Patch in Richmond. Long overdue.

"Who are you? James West?" she asked.

Her husky voice brought to mind sultry nights, the whisper of silk sheets and damp skin gliding across damp skin. Jared blinked aside the arousing image. He definitely needed to visit Violet or Hyacinth. Maybe both.

"No, it's Yates, Jared Yates," he said stiffly. "Now tell us how you got on this train."

Unease flickered across her features. "The last thing I remember is chasing after some guy in the snow." Though defiance rang in her tone, Jared noticed an undertone of puzzlement. "Next thing I know, I wake up here with *him* screaming for a ticket."

"That's my job," the conductor objected.

Jared ignored him and instead concentrated on the slender woman. After working as a Pinkerton detective for over ten years, Jared could usually read a person within a few moments of meeting him. Or her. This strange woman, however, had him completely baffled.

Blue denim jeans hugged her willowy legs and she wore an odd pair of blue and white cloth shoes with laces. Her scarlet, turquoise and green jacket was open, revealing a white shirt that caressed the curve of her breasts in a way that made Jared's palms yearn to do the same.

No decent woman—even a prostitute—would be caught dead or alive in such outlandish clothing. Yet, Jared sensed an innocence at odds with her indecent attire and coarse language.

Suddenly, she swung a large pack that had been slung over her shoulder at the conductor and he stumbled back, releasing her with a muttered curse. She shoved past him, running toward the rear of the car and Jared took off after her. Though he had longer legs, the woman was nimble and reached the end of the train car before he could catch her. She threw open the door and froze, giving Jared a chance to wrap his fingers around her arm.

He tugged her back and firmly closed the door against the cold wind.

"What the hell was that all about?" he demanded.

She turned and tilted her head back to look at him. Blond strands fell across her brow and into her eyes. "I have no idea how I got here, wherever *here* is."

Her simple declaration with no hint of hysteria convinced Jared of her sincerity. "Look, I think we can work this out. If you apologize to Frank, I'll buy your train ticket," he said gruffly.

Suspicion lurked in her eyes, but she didn't fight him when he steered her down the smoky aisle past rows of curious and disapproving onlookers. They stopped in front of the conductor who scowled as he rubbed his arm where she had struck him.

"That's it, lady. You're goin' in the baggage car," the conductor said.

Jared raised a hand. "Hold on now, Frank. She's got something to say to you."

Jared tightened his grip on her arm and she glared up at him, then turned to Frank. "I'm sorry for hitting you with my backpack."

Her grudging tone almost made Jared smile, but he held back the smirk. "How much for her ticket?"

"You're not goin' to help this hellion, are you?" Frank demanded.

"It's almost Christmas, time for giving and forgiving," Jared cajoled. "Humor me. Let me pay for her ticket and I'll make sure she doesn't give you any more trouble."

Frank shook his head in pity or skepticism. "Sure hope you know what you're gettin' yourself into."

"Me, too," Jared muttered.

The conductor told him the amount and Jared handed him a couple of bills. Grumbling, Frank continued on down the aisle of the slowing train car.

"Let's sit down," Jared said to the woman.

He led her to a bench with enough room for both of them. She perched on the edge of the wood, poised for flight like a deer that had caught the scent of danger, and rested the bag she'd called a backpack on her lap.

"Relax," Jared said. "No one's going to throw you off."

After a few moments, her shoulders slumped and she leaned back. Her thigh touched Jared's and heat exploded along the length of the contact. Blood made a mad dash to his groin and he shifted away from her before she noticed his unwelcome reaction.

The woman looked at him a long moment, then

swept her gaze across the train car's occupants. "Is this a reenactment?" she asked.

"A what?"

"You know, a reenactment, like they do at old forts and during powwow days."

"Powwow days?"

Mac turned to study him more closely, which she found wasn't a difficult task. Bewilderment filled his expression and she shook her head in exasperation. How could someone better looking than Mel Gibson be so damned dense? "You grow up in a cave or something?"

"Harrisburg," Yates replied stiffly. "My father owned a store."

"I figured you were raised on a ranch, pretending to be some kind of cowboy," Mac said. "But you're missing the tie-down holster and pearl-handled Colt." She tried to imagine a gunbelt around his slim hips, but instead noted his impressive bulge. . . . Her stomach clenched as her imagination took a dangerous curve. What was wrong with her? She'd always preferred a man's backside to the front view.

"Sorry to disappoint you, but I'm a Pinkerton," he said dryly. "And I don't even like horses. That's why I'm riding the train."

"Maybe you should get yourself a car. You strike me as the Volvo type, kind of square and boxy."

The man's eyes telegraphed his feigned confusion and Mac found herself enjoying reading the message. She'd never seen bluer eyes outside of a movie theater. The hero role was tailor-made for Yates, or whatever his name was. Hell, he'd even rescued the damsel in distress, though Mac preferred to think of herself as a very smart damsel surrounded by idiots.

She forced her attention away from Yates and

searched the smoke-filled passenger car, wondering if the man she'd followed up the spur was aboard. How had he disappeared? And how had she gotten aboard this train?

What if the man she'd lost *was* the killer? Was he even now stalking his next victim? Why hadn't she curbed her impatience and waited for Dan? If she had, maybe the Piano Man Killer would be behind bars and she'd be writing her Pulitzer Prize-winning story.

"What's your name?" Yates asked, disturbing her somber thoughts.

"Trish McAllister, but everyone calls me Mac."

He scowled, drawing her attention to the creases at the corners of his sexy lips. Was that a slight cleft in his chin? Damn, she'd always been a sucker for those Kirk Douglas chins.

"I'll call you Miss McAllister," he finally said.

"If you call me anything, it'd better be *Ms.* McAllister, buddy."

"All right, Miz McAllister," he said tightly. "What're you doing in these parts?"

Oh, yeah, he had that western nomenclature down just fine. This had to be some kind of weird reenactment in which everybody had been instructed to maintain their roles no matter what happened. She'd looked for a camera and director right after the stupid conductor had taken his part a little too seriously, but she hadn't found anyone faintly resembling a member of a movie crew or cast. Unless she counted the cute little brunette who kept eyeing Jared Yates as if he were a box of Godiva chocolates.

Mac surreptitiously studied Yates and found herself wanting to sample him, too. He had a strong jawline, lips that would put Leo DiCaprio to shame; an aquiline nose that had been broken once or twice, which kept it from being too perfect; and a high forehead, a sure sign of intelligence her mother had said. His thick reddish-brown hair, parted on the side, fell rakishly across his forehead and was trimmed over his ears but brushed his collar top. It was his eyes, though, that Mac would bet had been the downfall of more than one woman—so light blue they almost appeared translucent. When Yates looked at her, it was as if she were the only woman in the world. No wonder they'd chosen him to be the good guy in this little skit.

However, men that handsome knew it, and it didn't bother them to use their skin-deep charm to lure women into their beds. She pictured her father. Even at fifty-nine, he was still handsome enough to entice a fourth wife to the altar. That wasn't even counting the numerous women he'd seduced and cast aside.

Despite Yates's blue eyes and cleft chin, Mac trusted him as much as she trusted her father.

"Where's this train going?" she asked.

"The Chesterfield," Yates replied.

Mac recalled the ruins where she'd found shelter. It had been a high-class resort years and years ago. These reenactors were going a bit far. "And I suppose you're going to soak in the hot springs and play a round of golf, too."

"Maybe." Yates's voice sounded cautious, as if she were an imbecile who had just displayed a rare moment of intelligence.

"And I'm going to have lunch with the president, buddy."

Yates's expression told Mac he'd gone back to his original impression of her: that she was an idiot. "You should have more respect when you talk about our president, Miz McAllister."

Mac had the sudden urge to stand up and salute the

red, white and blue. In fact, she wouldn't be surprised if Maverick Mel Look-alike wore patriotic boxers. On second thought, maybe briefs—very brief briefs. The thought of checking her theory personally brought a tightening deep in her belly.

*Whoa! Time to get those galloping hormones back under control, Mac.*

She shook her head, unable to believe she'd let a gorgeous hunk sidetrack her thoughts. "Sheesh, you sure immerse yourself in your character. Get a life, buddy."

"I *have* a life," he replied, his voice filled with as much irritation as his expression.

"So what do you do when you're not riding around on old-fashioned trains spouting patriotic rhetoric? Not that I mind; your role fits you like a glove, though the trousers should be tighter. Makes the cowboy— excuse me, *Pinkerton*—appear more masculine." She winked. "If you get my drift."

Jared Yates actually blushed, giving him a boyish quality that Mac found too damned endearing for her peace of mind. She shifted mental gears and donned her reporter persona. "So what do you do in real life? Please don't tell me you're a wannabe actor—that would only be another strike against you."

"I told you, I'm a Pinkerton detective," Yates replied hotly. "Why don't you tell me which asylum you escaped from and I'll take you back before you hurt yourself?"

"Cool your jets, Mr. Pinkerton Detective. I'm not going anywhere until I figure out what the hell's going on here. If nothing else, I might get a decent sidebar from this little adventure."

Yates shook his head and rolled his eyes heavenward.

Enough was enough. For the umpteenth time, she wished she hadn't forgotten her phone. "Do you have a cell phone I could use?" she asked.

"You mean a telephone?" he asked, overacting his pretended ignorance.

"Enough already!" Mac stood and Yates yanked her back down to the bench. "Ow! What'd you do that for?"

"You're supposed to remain in your seat until we're stopped."

She rolled her eyes but remained seated. As soon as Mac disembarked, she'd call Dan and tell him about the man she'd seen. And if there was a god, Dan would catch the suspect, Longley would be fired and Dan would be promoted to sheriff.

*Yeah, and if frogs had wings, they wouldn't bump their asses on rocks.*

Take it one step at a time. First, she had to escape this group of reenactors before they expected her to join their little performance.

She glanced again at Pinkerton Detective Jared Yates. Too bad he was so fanatical about his make-believe world. It might have been fun to get to know him better. Her gaze flickered to his impressive virility. A lot better.

The train came to a stop and Mac jumped to her feet.

"What's your hurry, Miz McAllister?" Yates asked, displeasure creasing his brow.

"While you're playing your games, the rest of us have a job to do."

"And what job do you have?"

"Getting the scoop on a helluva story."

Without waiting for his reply, Mac shouldered her backpack and elbowed her way through the crowd.

This was worse than gridlock in L.A. She finally emerged from the train car and blinked in the dim light. Snow continued to fall, though the flakes had decreased both in size and intensity.

She glanced at the large wooden sign across the top of the building—The Chesterfield. That *was* the name of the dilapidated place where she'd taken shelter. Mac shivered with apprehension. Had the suspect she'd followed given her some kind of hallucinatory drug?

Passengers surged past her onto the wooden platform, shoving her aside. People dressed in turn-of-the-century costumes greeted those coming off the late-night train. A few women were even crying, as if they hadn't seen each other in years.

A woman dressed in a long black cape and wearing her brown hair in a tight bun at the back of her neck greeted the passengers with a welcoming smile and twinkling eyes. She wore a wide-brimmed hat with stuffed birds perched atop its crown, which would have been laughable if Mac had been in the mood.

Jared Yates stepped off the train and joined the woman. She gave him an especially warm smile as he took her hands in his.

*Probably one of his conquests,* Mac thought, not without a trace of jealousy. No, not jealousy, disgust.

It didn't matter. The woman appeared to be one of the organizers of this whole farce. With her typical long-legged stride, Mac approached her and Yates.

The "Pinkerton" glanced at her then tipped his hat to the Mary Poppins twin. "I'll see you later, Miss Sparrow."

Mac's gaze flickered to Miss Sparrow's outlandish hat again and nearly laughed. Well, if the bird fit . . .

Yates nodded curtly to Mac then strode away and she found her attention glued to his backside.

"Wouldn't you know it—he'd have nice buns, too," Mac muttered. She forced her admiring gaze away from the tempting distraction to address the bird woman. "I was wondering if—"

Miss Sparrow's eyes widened and a pale hand flew to her mouth. "Miss McAllister, how did you get here?" she asked with a definite British accent.

Mac blinked . . . twice. "How'd you know my name?" she demanded.

Her eyes wide, Miss Sparrow's mouth opened and closed like a landed fish. Maybe her name should've been Miss Trout. Finally, she managed to twist her lips into a benign smile that reminded Mac of a Disney movie and nearly sent her into a saccharine fit. "Mr. Yates told me."

Mac's reporter instincts screamed in protest. The woman was lying. "Bullshit."

Miss Sparrow's hard-fought composure crumbled. "Oh, dear. I had hoped you would be different, but I'm afraid you're even worse than the others."

The woman took hold of Mac's arm and Mac reacted without thought, jerking away from her. "Listen, lady, I want to know what the hell's going on, and I want to know right now. Or I will make a scene that puts Meg Ryan's restaurant scream to shame. Do I make myself clear?"

"No." Total bewilderment filled Miss Sparrow's face.

This time Mac didn't detect any subterfuge, only confusion. She pulled her attention away from the woman and surveyed her surroundings, cataloging the train, the depot, and the shape and number of buildings that surrounded them in the inky darkness. Her gaze fell on the so-called Pinkerton, who leaned against a post smoking a thin cigar. Yates could make the Marlboro man look like a city slicker with that loose-hipped, sexy-as-hell pose.

Something tickled the back of Mac's brain, something she didn't want to examine too closely. But she had no choice. She brought her attention back to the slender, very proper woman. "What's the date?" Mac asked.

"It is after midnight, so it is December twentieth," Miss Sparrow replied.

"The year?"

For a moment, Miss Sparrow remained mute. The feeling of dread grew, knotting Mac's stomach.

"Tell me what year it is," Mac demanded, using anger to hide her growing panic.

"Eighteen hundred and ninety-two."

# THREE

*This can't be happening.* People didn't just jump from one year to another like some *Quantum Leap* fantasy. Hell, even Sam Beckett couldn't go back to a time before his own birth.

Mac, mouth agape and not giving a damn, stared at Miss Sparrow. The woman appeared completely sane, which left only one explanation.

Mac paced back and forth on the now-deserted depot platform, her heart thudding in her chest and her fingers clenching and unclenching at her sides. Her breath misted in the cool air. "I must've fallen asleep and now I'm dreaming." She stopped abruptly and dragged a hand through her hair. "Or I have hypothermia and this is a fever-induced hallucination, which means I'm going to die if I can't wake up. Damn."

Miss Sparrow planted herself directly in front of her. "You must calm down, Miss McAllister," she said firmly. "The fact is you are not dreaming, you are not ill, and this *is* eighteen ninety-two. Deal with it."

The contemporary phrase caught Mac's attention and her eyes narrowed. "How do you know? Who are you? What's going on?"

"Please, Miss McAllister, do not be difficult. If you will come with me, I will endeavor to explain."

Mac stepped away from the Englishwoman. Her mind told her body to run fast and far, but Mac reminded herself she had no place to go. In spite of the cold winter night, she felt a trickle of sweat glide down her back. The last time she'd lost control of a situation she'd been a sophomore in college doing her first interview. She'd sworn it would never happen again and it hadn't. Until now.

"I'm not going anywhere with you, lady. Not until I get some answers," Mac said.

"Is something wrong, Esme?"

Mac swung around and came face to chest with Mister Pinkerton. She tilted her head back, catching the pungent scent of tobacco from his clothing, but instead of repulsing her as it normally did, she inhaled deeply. Mixed with the tobacco was damp wool and the man's own masculine scent. The tantalizing mixture brought Mac's hormones to the blast-off point, and if Yates so much as touched her, she suspected the rocket would ignite.

"We were only discussing Miss McAllister's plight," Miss Sparrow said.

Mac swung her gaze to the Englishwoman, but the eyes that met hers commanded Mac to remain silent. For once, she heeded an order. Besides, she wasn't capable of speech at the moment.

*Stay tuned for the next miracle.*

Yates's impossibly light blue eyes scrutinized her, making her feel like one of those monster beetles in an entomology collection. She lifted her chin and met his gaze steadily.

"Do you know her?" Though he continued to stare at Mac, his question was directed to Miss Sparrow.

"She is my third cousin twice removed on my mother's side. She is a Scotswoman," Miss Sparrow lied smoothly. "And we know how stubborn those Scots can be, don't we, Mr. Yates?"

His eyes flickered away from Mac to Miss Sparrow. "Will you be spending the holiday here?"

"Of course. Where else would I be? Especially now that I have family to spend it with," Miss Sparrow replied cheerfully.

Yates smiled and Mac forgot to breathe. His smile should be registered as a lethal weapon.

He tipped his narrow-brimmed hat to Miss Sparrow. "Good day, then." Turning to Mac, his smile gave way to suspicion. "Miz McAllister."

He didn't doff his hat to her, and the insult wasn't lost on Mac. As she fumed, her gaze followed him as his easy strides carried him off the depot and toward one of the waiting horse-drawn wagons.

*Horse-drawn wagons.*

Mac's doubts disappeared, taking her anger with them. "It's true, isn't it?" she asked quietly.

Miss Sparrow joined Mac and patted her arm. "There, there, Miss McAllister, it's not that bad. Perhaps you will even come to like it."

Mac pulled away from her solicitous hand and gave a short bark of laughter. "Don't push it. You have answers and I want them."

Miss Sparrow's lips thinned, just like Mac's third-grade teacher's after Mac had put a snake down Jim Taggart's back. Jim had deserved it for squealing on her after she'd eaten Lisa Harold's sandwich. Miss Sparrow deserved it for throwing her whole world into chaos. In fact, she deserved more, but Mac couldn't muster up even a small battery from her sarcasm arsenal.

"Come along," Miss Sparrow said.

She led Mac away from the now-deserted railroad

depot and down a path leading to a series of buildings. As they marched down the walkway, Mac took a deep breath of fresh crisp air. There was no hint of carbon monoxide or sulfur or any other manmade pollutant. The only light guiding them was the reflection of the moon on the freshly fallen snow.

Mac shook her head faintly. "I can't stay here. I have to get back."

"I'm afraid that's impossible."

Feeling as though she were caught in an *Alice in Wonderland* nightmare, Mac halted. "I don't know who you are, but you obviously know a lot more about what's going on than you're telling me. So give me answers, lady. Now."

Miss Sparrow continued walking, ignoring Mac's outburst.

"Shit," Mac muttered and hurried after her. This demure lady was far from a pushover and Mac would do well to remember that. She wouldn't underestimate a woman wearing a Tweety hat again.

Knowing she wouldn't learn anything yet from the obscure Miss Sparrow, Mac followed along silently, memorizing the details around her. They arrived at a large building and entered. After the complete darkness of the night, the dim lights made Mac squint as she stumbled down the wide, richly furnished hall. Numerous plants sat along the walls and the musty scent of soil and dampness tickled Mac's nose.

"This is the bathhouse," Miss Sparrow said.

Mac narrowed her eyes. "Men and women bathing in the same place? That's pretty radical."

"No, of course not," Miss Sparrow said indignantly. "There are separate facilities for our male and female guests. There is a swimming pool, as well as warm restorative pools, which the guests may use to soothe their minds and bodies. The doctor's office is also located in this building."

"That gives me a warm tingly feeling. Which pool does he keep his leeches in?"

Miss Sparrow suddenly halted and Mac stumbled, nearly running into the woman's back.

"Miss McAllister, your rapier sarcasm is quite unbecoming. Perhaps this time is not as advanced as your own, but you will find we are not uncivilized either. Kindly keep your comments to yourself or you will antagonize the same people you must live among." Miss Sparrow paused, then said quietly, "That would be a lonely existence."

Mac had been on her own for years and she wasn't about to become Mister Rogers now. A good reporter always remained objective and never let her feelings get in the way. She shrugged. "Whatever."

Miss Sparrow tipped her head to the side as she studied Mac. The affectation reminded Mac of the woman's namesake searching for a worm and she almost laughed. Instead, she covered her mouth and coughed. She must be losing it.

Hell, she *had* lost it the moment she found herself aboard the train.

Miss Sparrow spun on her heel and continued down the corridor and through another long walkway. Mac followed, memorizing every surrealistic detail. The interior changed, looking more like a hotel now with doors every twenty feet and steamer trunks set outside them. The garish wallpaper reminded Mac of the wall covering in her grandmother's one-hundred-year-old farmhouse, but not nearly as faded and timeworn.

*Gee, Mac, you think that's because it's new in this century?*

Finally, after more twists and turns, they stopped at

one of the indistinguishable doors. Miss Sparrow fished a key out of her coat pocket and unlocked the door. She entered the room; Mac, her suspicion meter rising even higher, followed slowly. Miss Sparrow flicked a switch and light flooded the room from a fixture in the middle of the ceiling.

"Since it is so late, I am afraid you will have to spend the night with me," Miss Sparrow said.

"Why can't I just get a room? Looks like you have plenty of them," Mac said.

"And how will you pay for it?"

The woman had a point, but Mac wasn't about to surrender. "My Visa. It's accepted everywhere that another card isn't."

Miss Sparrow rolled her eyes heavenward. "Are you certain you sent the correct one?" She returned her attention to Mac. "Tomorrow morning I will show you around the resort and I shall speak to the Major about a position for you. Perhaps you could become a maid."

"And clean toilets?" Mac shuddered. "Forget it. I scrubbed enough of those when I put myself through college."

"Then what would you like to do?"

"Go back home."

"Impossible. You must be flexible, Miss McAllister."

Mac threw her arms in the air and exploded, "And why should I be? I didn't ask to come here and I sure as hell don't want to stay here." Her trembling voice betrayed her fear. "Maybe it's time you tell me what's going on."

"Oh, dear, this is not at all what I expected." The proper woman perched on the edge of the bed. "Perhaps you should also sit down, Miss McAllister."

Somewhat mollified, Mac dropped into a straight-backed chair. "Spill it, lady."

"I do not have all the answers. All I know is that you were brought here for a reason, and you are not allowed to leave until the next solstice."

Mac calculated quickly. "That's in June."

Miss Sparrow bobbed her head up and down. "That is correct. There is some mission you must undertake to help someone. If it is successful, then you will be allowed to return to your own world, if that is your choice."

Mac's tentative control slipped and she came to her feet like a jack-in-the-box. She stomped over to stand in front of her jailer. "You're telling me that I was chosen by *whatever* deity to complete an *unknown* mission to rescue a *nameless* person who is in *unspecified* danger."

Miss Sparrow's face lit with a smile. "Precisely, Miss McAllister. That wasn't so difficult to understand, was it?"

Mac groaned and fell back into the chair she'd just vacated. She buried her face in her palms, frustrated beyond reason and afraid she was the insane one instead of Miss Sparrow.

A hand on her back startled her and she jerked her head up.

"Come, come, Miss McAllister. I thought you were made of sterner stuff."

"You thought wrong," Mac said petulantly.

"You have had a most shocking evening. After a good night's sleep, you will feel better."

"I doubt it." Mac stood and glanced around. "Where's the bathroom?"

"The water closet is up the stairs, down the hall and to the left. Twenty women share it."

"Great, I'm back in high school gym class."

Miss Sparrow folded her arms across her chest and gave Mac a withering look. Mac waited for the condemning words, but the woman's expression spoke louder than any verbal reproach.

Mac held up a hand. "All right, I'll behave myself like a good little girl."

"It's getting late, Miss McAllister, and I must get some sleep. My day begins quite early."

"What do you do here?" Mac asked curiously.

"I am the head housekeeper. I oversee the maids and waitresses who work here at the Chesterfield."

"How many toilets did you have to scrub to get that job?"

"None. I went to school for the position." She paused, clasping her hands in front of her in a demure pose. "You could say I have a B.S. degree in cleaning toilets."

For a split moment, Mac was stunned, then she burst into laughter. "Was that a joke, Miss Sparrow?"

The woman appeared affronted, but Mac saw the twinkle in her eyes. "In some circles, I am known to have quite a sense of humor, Miss McAllister."

"Would the Prissy Prudes of the Past be one of those circles?"

Miss Sparrow covered her mouth, but not before Mac saw her smile.

"I'm headed for the water closet." As Mac left the room, she muttered, "If there's corncobs in there instead of toilet paper, I'm outta here."

Mac managed to find the water closet without running into anyone and was gratified to find that there were no corncobs or even old catalogs. When she was finished, she pulled the cord hanging from the tank, glad to see a flush was still a flush in the late nineteenth century.

As she washed her face, the door opened and a woman about Mac's own age entered, but that was where the similarities ended. The woman wore a long Mother Hubbard gown that covered her from neck to ankle, as well as a white cloth cap on her head. Loose strands of reddish hair curled around her face and her cheeks were liberally sprinkled with freckles.

"Hi," Mac greeted.

"Hello. Are ye new here?" the woman asked with a lilting Irish accent.

"I just came in on tonight's train." Mac paused, considering whether to perpetuate the lie and shrugged inwardly. It would be a good cover. "I'm Miss Sparrow's second cousin once, uh, twice removed from . . . Hell, I'm related to Miss Sparrow."

The girl blinked in amazement or outrage. Probably both. "I didn't know Miss Sparrow had any relatives."

"It was quite a surprise for both of us," Mac said dryly.

"Are ye just visitin' then?"

Was this woman part of the welcome gossip wagon? Well, maybe she'd just give her some fuel for the fire. "I'll be hanging around until my dear cousin can find herself a man. I swear, the family had pretty much given up on her. They sent me as a last ditch effort to help put an end to her spinsterhood."

The stranger's eyes widened. "Miss Sparrow is lookin' to get married?"

Mac glanced around warily, as if there might be somebody about to overhear their conversation. "That's right. Poor woman just doesn't know how to go about catching a man. Maybe she could use some lessons."

The girl's eyes were now the size of saucers. "Goodness gracious, I didn't know. We all like Miss Sparrow and would hate to see her leave, but if she's unhappy . . ."

"If you really want to help her, you and the others can watch for eligible bachelors," Mac said in a low, conspiratorial voice.

"Aye, we could do that. I'll talk to the other girls about it."

"Thanks. What's your name?

"Erin Connolly."

"Thank you, Erin. And maybe we should keep this a secret from my cousin. Poor thing would be embarrassed to pieces if she found out everyone knew of her, shall we say, predicament?"

"Of course. I'll go speak to some of the others now."

Erin nearly ran out the door and Mac smiled. She turned, catching her reflection in the mirror. "You're evil, Mac, very evil." Her grin grew.

She finished washing up, feeling only a little guilty about her fabrication, and returned to Miss Sparrow's room. Though she was cleaner, Mac still felt subhuman and the sense of imbalance she'd had ever since arriving in this era remained. It was like being in a really vivid dream, complete with Technicolor and Surround Sound. Only more so.

She knocked on the door lightly and waited for Miss Sparrow's reply. The woman would probably go into an apoplectic fit if Mac saw her in her unmentionables.

"Who is it?"

"Mac."

The door was opened a few seconds later by Miss

Sparrow, who now wore the same getup the woman in the bathroom—no, water closet—had worn.

"I hope you don't expect me to sleep with that many clothes on," Mac said and added with an arched eyebrow, "In fact, I usually sleep in the nude."

Miss Sparrow rolled her eyes. "If you are attempting to shock me, you have failed. What you wear or do not wear in the privacy of your own room is your decision. However, in order to fit in this time period, you must be prepared to wear a dress and corset during the day." Before Mac could argue, the woman raised a hand. "You will do so if you wish to return to your own time."

Mac had definitely underestimated her. The hardest part about this incredibly weird situation was the loss of control. Never had Mac felt so helpless and it frightened her, but she'd be damned if she'd admit that to anyone.

"Since you're holding all the aces here, I don't have any choice," Mac said tightly.

"That is correct. Now, why don't you prepare yourself for sleep? You may share my bed."

"I sleep alone."

Miss Sparrow shrugged. "I must warn you, the sofa is lumpy."

"I've slept on worse." Mac bit her tongue. She must be more tired than she thought to reveal some of her long-hidden bitterness. Miss Sparrow, however, didn't seem to notice her slip.

"Very well. There are spare blankets in the chest at the foot of my bed. Good night." The woman turned away and buried herself under the thick comforter as she hummed a tune that sounded vaguely familiar.

Sighing loudly, Mac stripped down to her panties and bra. She gazed at the trunk a moment, thinking she had seen it before. But where? Shaking her head, she dug a few blankets out of the chest and made up a passable bed on the couch.

She spotted her backpack and suddenly remembered her laptop was ensconced within it. Dropping to the floor in a cross-legged position, she drew her computer out and quickly opened it. Turning it on, she waited impatiently for it to boot up. The time in the right-hand corner read 12:58 A.M. She positioned the cursor on it and double-clicked her mouse. The screen flickered once, twice, then blanked out completely.

# FOUR

"Time to awaken, Miss McAllister."

"G'way," Mac muttered to the annoyingly perky voice.

Blessed silence reigned once more and Mac snuggled deeper into the blankets. She wasn't due at the newspaper office until noon and the way she felt, she was going to sleep until the last possible moment. She shifted, her feet colliding with something solid.

She didn't have a wall at the end of her bed.

Suddenly, her covers were yanked off and Mac's eyes flew open. "What the he—"

"Miss McAllister, if you do not hasten, you will be late and the Major is a pedant for punctuality. He believes that a person's true nature is revealed by his or her timeliness, or lack thereof."

Mac, her mind hazed with cobwebs, stared at the veritable epitome of efficiency. "I'm in the army now?"

"Of course not," Miss Sparrow said, folding Mac's blanket with professional proficiency. "Major Payne is the overseer of all the employees here at the Chesterfield Hotel. Everyone must report to him at seven o'clock sharp."

Mac groaned and pulled her pillow over her head. "Shoot me now and put me out of my misery."

The pillow was unceremoniously tugged away and added to the growing pile of bedding on a nearby chair.

"That is not an option. Rise and shine, Miss McAllister. You have thirty minutes to perform your ablutions and dress."

Mac smiled, closing her eyes once more. "I can perform ablutions in fifteen, tops."

"Not when your apparel includes a corset and five layers of underclothing."

Mac feared few things, but a corset was one of them. She jumped to her feet, the last vestiges of sleep gone. "No way. No corset."

Miss Sparrow merely stared at her with that calm, self-assured expression that told Mac she didn't stand a snowball's chance in hell.

Fifteen minutes later, Mac sucked in her gut and her breasts jutted out in direct proportion.

"I can do this. I can do this. I can do this," she chanted. Then Miss Sparrow tightened the laces. "I can't do this. I can't do this." She tried to breathe in a lungful of air but couldn't. Her throat grew tight and the growing loss of control fueled her panic, threatening to turn it into a full-blown anxiety attack. "L-loosen them," she stammered. "Please."

The corset eased from around her waist and Mac breathed deeply to flush her lungs with fresh oxygen. The terrifying hysteria faded more slowly and she was disgusted by her trembling hands and wobbly knees.

"Are you all right, Miss McAllister?" Miss Sparrow asked in concern.

She nodded, hating the numbing fear that escaped from the niche where she'd buried it years ago. "I have this thing about not being able to breathe." She managed a weak chuckle. "To be honest, it scares the hell out of me."

Miss Sparrow studied her thoughtfully. "Thank you for sharing that with me, Miss McAllister."

Mac waved a hand, embarrassed. "Don't be thinking we're soul sisters or anything now."

"I would never presume such a thing." Miss Sparrow began to bind the corset, leaving it snug but not overly restrictive. "I shall leave it like this. Your waist will not be fashionably tiny, but I suppose cleaning water closets is not what one would call a glamorous job."

"Whoa, slow down. Didn't I tell you I wasn't going to clean toilets ever again?"

"Just as you told me you wouldn't wear a corset. Might I remind you that it is eighteen hundred and ninety-two and you must follow the rules if you are to return home?"

She again used the one threat that Mac couldn't combat. "That's hitting below the belt," Mac muttered.

Miss Sparrow's hands settled on her shoulders and turned her around. Her expression was contrite. "I am sorry, Miss McAllister, but I am merely stating the facts. Please know that I am not your adversary."

Mac stepped back, unsettled by the woman's comforting overtures. She wanted to be angry with someone and Miss Sparrow's sincere words shifted the anger to a more dangerous emotion. "Apology accepted," Mac said gruffly. "Where's the next layer of this sadistic uniform?"

Jared Yates yawned widely as he stepped out of his room and closed the door behind him. Out of habit, he turned the doorknob and reassured himself it was locked. Even in a hotel as illustrious as the Chesterfield, a person couldn't be too careful. Pickpockets and thieves could be found everywhere these days.

So could murderers.

He tugged at his coat's lapels and adjusted the shoulder holster hidden by the jacket. The revolver's weight brought him only a token measure of comfort. Four women had been killed near the resort in the last two years. The murders had worried the hotel owners enough that after the second victim was found, they'd gone to the Pinkerton National Detective Agency to hire a detective to find the killer. Murder was not the kind of publicity they wanted for their esteemed resort.

It wasn't that they didn't have confidence in Chief Garrett's abilities, but the fast-growing town of Hope Springs kept the lawman exceptionally busy. Jared had spoken with Garrett about the murders and the constable appreciated the Pinkerton's involvement, giving his full support and assistance in the investigations. Jared respected the man except for Garrett's permissiveness with his wife, who managed a restaurant as well as presided as chef. Whoever heard of a female chef who wore men's trousers? Of course, he had to admit that the food rivaled Chef Sashenka's here at the resort.

Shaking his head, Jared puzzled again as to why a man would allow his wife such independence. Women were supposed to keep a man's home neat and clean, and raise their children, not work outside the house.

His thoughts took him to his fiancée. Always softspoken and amenable, she had already proved to be a perfect hostess during their engagement party.

Now she lay in a grave, the first victim of the strangler.

Jared, with more personal than professional interest in the crimes, had argued, yelled, and cajoled his boss into allowing him to take the case. However, the killer seemed to disappear into thin air after each murder and Jared had simply run out of clues. If only he could ascertain the killer's motive, he might be able to come up with a suspect. Or was there no other reason than that the victim was a young, vulnerable woman?

Jared didn't like where his thoughts were taking him, but then he hated everything about this case. He hated feeling helpless while the killer was out there stalking his next victim, and he knew without a doubt that the man was out there now.

A shiver chased down his spine. If only he could warn the women, but he'd been ordered not to for fear that it would cause a panic and affect the resort's reputation, which in turn would decrease profits. Jared despised playing the game, but he had no choice. A good Pinkerton agent was a master of tact and politics, and Jared was one of the best.

He turned a corner and spotted a woman at the end of the hall. She was attempting to enter a room as she glanced nervously down the hall. He slipped into a recessed alcove in the corridor and carefully peered around a tall potted plant, pushing aside a frond that blocked his view.

Although the woman wore the dark gray uniform of a maid, her furtive motions suggested that she might only be masquerading as an employee. It was uncommon for a woman to become a criminal, but it happened occasionally. Female thieves tended to be widows or orphans who didn't have a man's firm hand to keep them on the straight and narrow path of law-fulness.

The woman finally opened the door and slipped inside, taking her cleaning pail with her. Keeping close to the wall, Jared soundlessly moved across the carpeted floor. He paused outside the door, which had been left open two inches. Determined to catch the thief in the act, Jared pressed the door back and stepped inside the plush room. His gaze immediately found his quarry.

A nicely curved backside was aimed in his direction, wiggling in time with her movements as the woman scrubbed the floor of the water closet. Heat arrowed through Jared's veins, warming his face and making his trousers uncomfortably snug.

Mortified, he began to back out of the room, but the sight of familiar short blond hair suddenly penetrated his previously occupied senses.

"Miz McAllister?" he asked, shocked to hear his voice had risen nearly an octave since the last time he'd spoken.

Much to Jared's disappointment, the derriere abruptly ended its little performance and the woman twisted her head around. Surprise and a touch of embarrassment flooded her face, but the emotions were quickly dispatched as a mocking smile curved her full lips upward. "So we meet again, Mr. Pinkerton Detective."

She was the only woman who could make him go from lust to irritation in a split second. "Jared Yates," he corrected stiffly.

She laid her palms on her thighs and tilted her head back to meet his eyes. "All right, Mr. Yates. What brings you to my little corner of the world?" Her eyes widened. "This isn't *your* room, is it?"

He glanced around at the elegant furnishings of one of the Tower rooms where the wealthy stayed and shook his head. "Hardly. Especially as I'm here on business."

"Really? What kind of business?"

This time there was no derision in her tone, only honest curiosity. Jared wasn't quite certain how to deal with this side of Miss McAllister. He leaned a shoulder against the wall and crossed his arms, hoping he gave the illusion of nonchalance. "Come, come, Miz McAllister, you can't tell me you'd be interested in something as tedious as detective work."

She grinned, motioning to her pail. "Like cleaning toilets is a thrill a minute?"

Though Jared hadn't known what she'd say, that wasn't even close. He had to ward off a smile that tugged at his lips, then cleared his throat. "Perhaps I stated it wrong. Detective work can be exciting, but for the most part it's fairly monotonous. Right now, there's not much I can do about the case I'm working on until something breaks." The thought of another woman, perhaps Miss McAllister, strangled by a thin wire made him look away from the maid's steady gaze.

"Hey, lighten up. It can't be that bad," she said.

Jared wished she was right, but she didn't know about the murders and he wasn't going to tell her the grisly details. He doubted even *her* feminine sensibilities could handle it without going into a swoon. Besides, he had his orders: no panic-inducing warnings.

He met her assessing gaze. "Some things *are* that bad, Miz McAllister."

Her eyes narrowed, reminding him of a cat's. She began to push herself to her feet.

Before Jared could stop himself, years of ingrained manners made him clasp her arm and aid her upward.

He was nearly seared by the warmth emanating through her sleeve. He quickly released her and stepped back, certain he would be scorched if he didn't.

"Thank you," she said, her voice husky, almost shy.

Shy? That was one word Jared couldn't use to describe Miss McAllister. At least not the woman he'd met on the train.

Still, the drab gray uniform did much to sober her appearance, though nothing to hide the curve of her breasts against the white apron pinned to her bodice. In fact, the startling white kept drawing his attention to her full bosom. He had the insane urge to unpin the apron, leaving the dull gray of her dress to cover her so no other man's eyes would be attracted to those ripe breasts.

"So you're working here?" The moment the words left Jared's mouth, he wished he could retract them. He didn't have time to be visiting with a maid, especially one whose sharp tongue ought to be scrubbed with her supply of soap.

"No, I just clean water closets for the fun of it," she responded airily.

Jared gnashed his teeth. He knew better than to attempt to have a normal conversation with her. Normal and Miss McAllister were mutually exclusive.

She shrugged. "It beats living on the street. Besides my, uh, cousin, wanted me to stick around."

Jared was intrigued by her odd phrases and his detective instincts made him continue. "You don't sound Scottish."

"I've been in this country awhile."

He arched an eyebrow, surprised to see pink tingeing her cheeks. "So why did you decide to visit your cousin now?"

She narrowed her eyes. "You play detective with everyone you meet or do you just find me fascinating?"

Jared blinked at her audacity. When they'd met on the train, he had thought her behavior was caused by fatigue, or perhaps she'd been afraid to admit she had never traveled alone. But it appeared her bluntness was as much a part of her as her unusual gold-flecked eyes. It was a shame. Even with her short hair, she was attractive, in an eccentric sort of way. However, no man worth his salt would want a woman as outspoken as Miss McAllister. Perhaps she'd been sent here to have Miss Sparrow teach her manners and proper deportment. Yes, that had to be it. Miss Sparrow was a gentlewoman, unlike her Scottish cousin.

"I thought maybe we could have a civil conversation," Jared said.

She threw back her head and laughed. Not one of those simpering giggles, but an honest-to-goodness, straight-from-the-belly laugh. And damn, if he didn't find himself chuckling.

"Do you always strike up civil conversations with maids in strangers' rooms?"

She glided over to him and stood so close he could detect the sweet scent of her breath as she gazed up at him. His humor vanished as all the blood in his body rapidly shifted to south of his belt buckle. When he opened his mouth to reply, he realized he couldn't even remember the question.

Her eyes twinkled with mischief and something else he couldn't identify. She licked her bow-shaped lips and Jared's gaze followed her dainty pink tongue as it left behind a glistening path that could tempt the saints.

"Why did you follow me in here?"

Jared was wondering the same thing. If he'd known his suspected thief was Miss McAllister, he would have run in the opposite direction. "I thought you were a robber."

"Is that why you're here, to catch robbers?"

"No, but that doesn't mean I would ignore one if I caught him or her in the act."

"And you thought you caught me?" She smoothed his shirtfront with her palms and the light touch made Jared's erection press painfully against his trouser buttons. "If I didn't want to be caught, you wouldn't catch me."

Stunned, he realized she was playing a seductive game with him. Was Miss Sparrow's cousin a sporting woman? It would explain her bold behavior. No, his instincts told him she had never done that type of work. So what kind of game *was* she playing?

"You've never had *me* after you," he finally said.

The blond woman tilted her head to study him. "Does Jared Yates always get his man?" She paused. "Or woman?" Her eyes glowed with heat. The scamp knew exactly what she was doing to him.

His instincts could be wrong. No proper woman would speak so blatantly. How far would she go? "Sometimes I get lucky."

Her unabashed gaze slid from the top of his head down to his feet and back up. His tingling body would've sworn her hands made the same journey.

"I'll bet you do," she said with a husky whisper.

The air between them came alive, sparking like a wildfire and devouring everything in its path until no obstacles remained. The woman leaned closer, the tips of her breasts brushing his chest. The distance between their lips seemed both infinite and nonexistent.

Approaching voices in the hallway acted like a

bucket of cold water over Jared's head and he jerked away from temptation. What was it about this blond enigma that made his common sense fly out the window?

"I should leave you to your work. I'm sure the Major wouldn't look too kindly on me bothering an employee," Jared said, adjusting his jacket in an attempt to cover his arousal.

She wrinkled her pert nose, reminding him of a young girl, as she grumbled, "Major Payne is appropriately named."

Jared couldn't help but laugh and he noticed her smile was genuine instead of the usual sardonic twist of her lips. It brought a flush to her cheeks and a sparkle that lit her eyes from within. "I suspect all the other girls think the same way," he said.

Her smile shifted to the more familiar cynical one. "Yeah, but I suppose us *girls* need a man's supervision. God forbid what might happen if we try to think for ourselves."

Jared's humor fled and his eyes narrowed. "You aren't one of those suffragettes, are you?"

"What if I am?"

He groaned. "I should've known."

"I didn't say I was," she retorted. "I thought detectives weren't supposed to jump to conclusions."

Intrigued by her lightning-fast wit, Jared studied her silently.

"What? Am I drooling? Do I have a zit on the end of my nose?" she demanded.

"Nothing. No. And I have no idea what a zit is," Jared replied. Was he actually growing accustomed to her bizarre language?

She frowned and her brow crinkled, giving her a strangely endearing look. "I should get back to work.

Miss Spa—ah, my cousin said if I don't do a good job, there's nothing she can do to stop the Major from firing me, and then I *will* be out on the street."

Something flickered across her face, something akin to remembered anguish. The emotion seemed so out of character for the spitfire that Jared suspected the memory of what had caused the anguish had been unpleasant and too real. A wave of protectiveness crested through him, surprising him with its potency. Trish McAllister wasn't a woman who wanted anybody's help or protection.

"In that case, I'd better leave so you don't lose your job," he said.

She grimaced. "Such as it is."

Jared knew he should retreat, knew he should turn around and walk out the door, but knowing and doing were two completely different things. "Will I see you at the ball tomorrow night?" Why had he asked that? He knew the resort employees didn't come to the fancy dances.

"I didn't even know there was one," she replied, then shrugged. "I'm not much for these dam—darn corsets. I'd probably pass out on the dance floor."

"I'd be there to pick you up," Jared said gallantly, and realized he meant it. Though he didn't approve of Miss McAllister's boldness, he found himself challenged by her unique candor.

Startled, the woman glanced away. "Thank you, but I don't think I'll be going. Doesn't sound like my kind of thing."

Relieved and disappointed, he sent her a nod. "Have a good day, Miz McAllister."

"You, too, Ja—Mr. Yates."

Any of the other maids would have curtsied politely, but this woman merely kept her gaze locked with his.

Finally, he broke the heated contact and slipped out of the room. Once in the hallway, he forced himself not to look back. But he was certain Miss McAllister had stuck her head out the door and was watching him walk away.

He also had a sneaking suspicion that it wasn't his back she watched and he allowed himself a quiet chuckle.

Her shoulders aching, Mac groaned as she set her food tray on a long wooden table in the employees' dining room. She raised her skirt hems higher than propriety dictated and stepped over the plank seat with a decided lack of grace. At the moment, Mac didn't give a hoot about decorum and ladylike behavior. She was too tired and her head was throbbing.

Plopping her elbow on the table and her chin in her palm, she stared at the unappetizing lumps on her plate. She would've given anything, including her traitorous laptop, for a pizza delivery.

Before she could continue her fantasy of eating a pizza with pepperoni and extra cheese, three younger women dressed in the distinctive starched white blouse and dark blue skirt of the waitresses descended on her table. Two of them sat down across the table while the third, who looked familiar, lowered herself to the seat by Mac.

"We met in the necessary two nights ago," the woman beside Mac reminded her with a friendly smile.

Erin Connolly, the representative from the welcome wagon. Her friends must be the other members.

"Hi, Erin," Mac said with as much enthusiasm as she could muster, which wasn't a whole lot.

"These are my friends, Jane and Louise." She motioned first to the plain-faced brunette, then the plump blonde. Erin eyed her uncomfortably. "Ye didn't tell me your name."

"Oh, sorry. Trish McAllister, but everyone calls me Mac."

"That's an odd name for a woman," Jane said.

"You could say I'm an odd woman."

Erin smiled tentatively. "Ye are different, but that's not such a bad thing."

For some reason, the younger woman's approval lightened Mac's exhaustion. "That's what I always thought." She tasted the cream-colored mass on her plate—mashed potatoes. Edible. Barely.

"So how long have you all worked here?" Mac asked, anxious to take her mind off the unappetizing food, her sore muscles and being stuck in the nineteenth century.

"Eight months. It was either work or marry the husband my da chose," Erin said, then shrugged. "I left a note for Da givin' him my blessin' if he wanted to marry the dolt since he thought he was such a good lad."

Mac laughed, then glanced at the other two women. "What are your stories? How long have each of you been working here?"

Louise blinked puzzled blue eyes at Mac, but Jane launched into her tale. Ten minutes later, Mac shook her aching head to rid it of Jane's incessant buzzing. All she'd learned was that Jane had been at the Chesterfield for six months and she giggled after every other sentence.

It was a relief when Louise finally spoke her two words. "Three months."

Erin leaned close and whispered in Mac's ear. "Louise is shy."

*No kidding.* Mac had heard parrots with a larger vocabulary.

Erin glanced around anxiously, then spoke in a low conspiratorial voice. "We've been lookin' for a man for Miss Sparrow like ye asked and we think we've come up with one."

"Oh?"

"He and Miss Sparrow are already friends so all they'll need is some pushin' in the right direction."

Mac smiled, her exhaustion disappearing. This could be a whole lot more fun than she had anticipated. "I like this one already. Who is he?"

"I'm not sure if ye know him."

"Who?"

"Jared Yates," Erin said smugly.

Mac suddenly knew how Wile E. Coyote felt when the boulder landed on him.

# FIVE

"He'll eat her alive," Mac blurted out.

*Smooth. Real smooth.*

"Ye know him?" Erin appeared surprised.

Mac squirmed on the hard wood. "I kind of met him on the train when I came in."

"He's sooo handsome," Louise crooned, her eyes closed and her lovelorn expression spoiling the rest of Mac's appetite.

So Louise-of-few-words was a Pinkerton groupie. "He's all right if you like the macho type. Personally, I think he's more than Miss Sparrow can handle," Mac said, keeping her voice nonchalant.

Jane giggled. "You don't know your cousin very well. She could handle a lion without a whip."

The image of Miss Sparrow wearing her bird hat facing a snarling lion almost made Mac want to giggle like . . . like Jane. She groaned. She thought only her body had gone back in time, not her brain. Quashing the giggle, Mac studied her new "friends."

"Maybe she could handle a lion without a whip, but I think she'd need one for Jared Yates," Mac said.

That brought a round of laughter.

"My, you girls sound like you're having a jolly good time."

Mac glanced up to see a smiling Miss Sparrow standing above them. "Hi, cuz. How's it going?"

Miss Sparrow's smile wobbled, then righted itself. "Quite well, thank you, dear cousin. How was your day?"

"Unmemorable," Mac replied wryly. "What I wouldn't give for some Scrubbing Bubbles."

"Ah, well, of course," Miss Sparrow said with only the slightest hesitation. "I spoke with the Major and he's pleased with your work. He says you have a good future with the resort as long as you comport yourself as admirably as you have done."

Mac realized there weren't many careers open to women in the late nineteenth century, but if she could find something else—*anything* else—she would gladly leave behind her pail, corset and ugly gray dress. Recalling Miss Sparrow's explanation of why she had come back in time, Mac wondered if her mission involved someone connected to the resort. And if it was, then she couldn't stray far from the hotel. Getting back to her own time was the only reason she would continue to do her servile job like a dutiful little maid.

"I have finally procured a room for you," Miss Sparrow announced.

"My own?" Mac asked.

Miss Sparrow shook her head. "Of course not. All maids and waitresses are assigned two to a room."

Mac groaned and said in a monotone, "I'm ecstatic."

"At least you will be able to sleep on a bed and not a sofa."

"Whatever. Where is it?"

"On the second floor with the other employees. In fact, you shall be rooming with Erin."

The Irish girl clapped and smiled with genuine pleasure. "Good. I have been a wee bit lonely since Sheila got married."

If Mac had to have a roommate, Erin wasn't the worst choice. If it had been Jane, Mac had a feeling she'd end up sleeping in the lobby.

Erin clasped Mac's arm. "We'll be gettin' along just fine."

"I'm sure we will," Mac said with forced brightness.

"You can move your things up there when you are finished eating," Miss Sparrow said. "It is room number two hundred and five."

Moving would take all of two minutes. Mac managed a smile for all concerned.

"I saw ye speakin' with Mr. Yates today, Miss Sparrow," Erin said.

Mac glanced at Erin sharply, noting the sly look in her eyes. She should have known the Irish girl would take her task to heart.

Miss Sparrow turned to Erin, an eyebrow poised upward. "Yes?"

Erin's face reddened, but she plunged on. "Ye've known him a long time, haven't ye?"

"Perhaps three or four years."

"And ye like him, don't ye?"

Mac watched the interplay like a tennis tournament spectator, wondering if Erin was right. Prim and proper Miss Sparrow with stick-in-the-mud Yates actually made sense. However, the unfamiliar lump in her stomach didn't agree.

"We are friends," Miss Sparrow replied. "When he first arrived at the resort, he brought his betrothed. A beautiful young woman. They seemed so in love."

Mac sat up straight, her exhaustion disappearing.

He was engaged? It only made sense, a man of his age in this time period. A man that handsome wouldn't have any problems finding a woman to keep him company in bed in any century.

Miss Sparrow sighed. "But that was before."

"Before what?" Mac demanded.

The Englishwoman's eyes revealed sadness. "Before she died. Two years ago—December 30, 1890—while they were visiting this resort."

"How did she die?" Louise asked, her eyes like saucers.

"Murdered. The poor dear."

Mac's news instincts screamed at her to find out the why, when, where, how, and who. However, a wave of sympathy obliterated the automatic reaction, surprising her. She'd always been strictly professional, checking her emotions at the door while she pursued a story. But the Piano Man Killer's victims had slipped past that locked door. Only Dan had witnessed her moments of weakness. Everybody else thought she was a tough bitch and she was proud of it. She'd worked damned hard to make a name for herself in the predominantly male field of newspaper reporting.

Maybe she was chosen to be brought back to this time because of her reporting skills. Maybe this unknown task *was* to find the woman's murderer and expose him to the world.

*And maybe I've been sniffing too many cleaning fumes.*

Mac reined in her wild speculations. She wasn't a detective. Surely whoever or whatever had brought her back could have chosen someone more qualified to track down a criminal if that was the mission.

Still, curiosity was a strong motivator. "Was the killer ever found?" she asked.

Miss Sparrow shook her head slowly. "I'm afraid not. Mr. Yates was unable to procure enough clues to learn the man's identity. Poor man, he blames himself for her death."

Mac frowned. What if Yates had killed her? No, he appeared too principled. All he needed were a pair of tights and a cape. But then crimes of passion were often committed by people who weren't believed to have a violent bone in their body. She'd witnessed the aftermath of someone killing a lover in a fit of rage too often. Anyone was capable of murder if given enough provocation, including Jared Yates.

The thrill of a news story sizzled through Mac, but it was tainted with the subjective disbelief that Yates could kill anyone, much less a woman, in cold blood. So if Yates didn't do it, someone else did and that someone could be connected to the spa. It seemed that beneath the veneer of the polished brass and shiny wood floors of the resort, the Chesterfield might be hiding some dark, dirty secrets. And she was just the person to unearth them.

"Lois Lane, look out," she murmured.

"What was that, Miss McAllister?" Miss Sparrow asked.

Mac focused on her overly bright expression. Could this strange woman who knew too much about Mac's visit to the nineteenth century be a part of the conspiracy?

*What conspiracy, Mac?*

*A Pinkerton's fiancée is killed and you're seeing gray men hiding in the shadows.*

It wasn't any stranger than being teleported from 2001 to 1892, was it?

"Is something amiss, Trish?" Miss Sparrow reiterated.

Startled by the use of her first name, Mac stared blankly at the woman. "Uh, no, everything's fine, Esme." Turnabout was fair play.

The Englishwoman continued to study her for a few more moments, then nodded. "Quite right." She turned so her gaze encompassed the three waitresses. "Hurry along, girls. Chef Sashenka has been complaining that his meals aren't being served quickly enough." She lifted the gold watch pinned to her bodice so she could read the time. "It is nearly six-thirty. The dining room will be quite busy soon."

"Yes, ma'am," Erin said.

Miss Sparrow hastened away, her steps determined and her spine ramrod straight. If nothing else, Mac had to admire her unflagging energy. Compared to Esme Sparrow, Mac was a weakling. *I should have used that gym membership I bought last year,* she thought wryly.

Mac watched in morbid fascination as her three companions quickly cleaned off their plates. She glanced down at her now-cold meal and shuddered. Maybe it was time to start that diet.

Erin rose and her friends followed.

"I'll be off at ten o'clock so I'll see ye then," Erin said. "Good-bye."

Her two companions echoed their farewells and Mac lifted a hand, waggled her fingers and said, "Ta-ta."

Alone once more, Mac observed the employees coming and going in the dining hall. There was a constant stream of people—mostly women, with a smattering of men thrown in. She assumed they were the bellhops and groundskeepers. It didn't appear that there were any male waiters and definitely no male maids. Sexism was alive and well in the nineteenth century.

Her head continued to throb and Mac recognized the symptom as the start of a migraine. She rubbed her temples with her fingertips. With the madness of the last forty-eight hours, she was fortunate she'd made it this long without one. But she had no doubt the burgeoning headache would be a bad one. Hadn't Miss Sparrow said there was a doctor here?

She stood and carried her tray to the waste containers. As she walked to the door, a man around her own age fell in step beside her. He wore the navy blue uniform of a bellhop and appeared friendly.

"You're new here, aren't you?" he asked without preamble.

*Make that nosy.* "That's right."

"I didn't see you arrive." He opened the door, allowing Mac to precede him.

She smiled sweetly. "That's right, you didn't."

"Are you one of Miss Sparrow's special projects?"

Mac halted, an innate sense of caution and a large dollop of inquisitiveness nudging her. "What do you mean, 'special projects'?"

The man's eyebrows arched. "Sometimes she takes one of the new girls under her wing and helps her out more than the rest."

"Does she do this often?"

He shrugged. "Every year or two."

Mac crossed her arms, ignoring the incessant pounding in her head. "So you've been here long?"

The man grinned. "For nearly ten years, miss. If you have any questions, just come to me, Rupert Smith. Everybody knows I have the answers."

"But are they the correct ones?" Mac couldn't help but retort.

Rupert didn't appear slighted as his smile stretched even wider. "For the right price."

Mac laughed. "I should've known there'd be a catch. There always is."

He placed his palm on his chest. "You wound me, miss. I merely provide an informational service."

"Does the Major know about this little service?"

Rupert leaned close. "Where do you think he gets *his* information?" He winked.

Mac's eyes widened in mock astonishment. "You're a spy for the Major?"

Rupert put a finger to his lips and glanced around. "Don't you be saying that too loud. I wouldn't want to be run out of town on a rail."

"Your secret's safe with me," Mac assured him, then added slyly, "for a price."

"I could tell you were smart the first time I laid eyes on you," Rupert said with an admiring gleam in his eye. "So what's your name?"

"Mac," she replied and held out her hand.

After a moment's hesitation, Rupert shook it. "Yep, you're one of Miss Sparrow's special ones, all right."

Mac shook her head at his obvious flattery and the pounding between her eyes reminded her she was on the way to find the doctor. "Could you tell me which direction the doctor's office is?"

Rupert's expression immediately turned to concern. "Are you sick, Mac?"

"Just a headache."

"Dr. Ziegler should be able to give you some powders for it," Rupert said knowingly. He pointed to the left. "Just walk down this hall, then follow the signs to the bathhouse."

"Thanks, Rupert. I owe you one."

Rupert stroked an imaginary mustache. "That you

do, Mac. I'll be reminding you of your debt one of these days."

Mac smiled. "I'm sure you will."

She turned and walked in the direction Rupert had indicated. In spite of the bellhop's avaricious attitude, Mac liked him. He may be self-serving, but he was honest about it. She knew where she stood with him, unlike Miss Sparrow and Jared Yates. There was something going on here, something her sixth sense was detecting but unable to grasp, and it involved the Englishwoman and the Pinkerton detective.

Mac hated jigsaw puzzles when over half the pieces were missing. However, her only chance of getting back was to find those pieces and put the picture together. It would be a challenge, especially if her migraine refused to abate. She wished she'd thrown her headache medicine into her backpack instead of leaving it in her car.

Sighing, she focused on her objective and found the doctor's office ten minutes later. She knocked on the door and a gruff "come in" sounded from within.

"May I help you?" the man who sat behind the desk asked.

It was interesting to find a male receptionist instead of a woman in this era.

"I'd like to see the doctor."

"You're looking at him."

In 2001, she had to call her doctor's office months in advance to set up an appointment. The people must be as healthy as horses here.

"I was wondering if you had some, uh, powders for a headache," Mac said. *And please don't tell me you have to use leeches.*

"Are you suffering from the vapors?" Dr. Ziegler asked.

She shrugged. "Could've been, I suppose. I mean, the cleaning supplies here aren't exactly controlled by the FDA, you know?"

His bushy eyebrows drew together as he stood and came out from behind the desk. "What is the FDA?"

*Oh-oh, another slip like that and I'll be shipped off to the funny farm. Unless this is the funny farm.* "Just a figment of my imagination. Now, do you—"

"Do you often have these figments of imagination?"

The overly solicitous air made the hair on Mac's arms stand up. She definitely had to gag that smartass inside her. "Ah, well, not really. Only when I have these headaches."

Dr. Ziegler leaned against the desk and crossed his arms, scrutinizing her. "It's too bad Drake Manton and his wife, Gina, aren't here visiting or I would have you set an appointment with him."

"Who's Drake Manton?"

"A mesmerist. He can do amazing things using the powers of the mind."

Mac wasn't going to let some precivilized hypnotist make her cluck like a chicken. "No, thanks. If you could just give me some aspi—some powders, I'll be on my way."

He sighed heavily. "If you wish, but if these headaches persist, I do believe it would be in your best interests to speak with Drake." He moved back behind the desk and pulled out a piece of paper and a fountain pen from a drawer. "First I must get your name and a little information."

Mac rolled her eyes and rubbed her throbbing forehead. Even in the past she couldn't escape paperwork. Dropping into a chair, she proceeded to answer his questions as honestly as she could without sounding like a fruitcake.

Twenty minutes later Mac left his office, three packets of white powder in her hand, having already taken one at the doctor's insistence. She paused in the hallway as she squinted in the bright light. Damn, this was not a good sign. She hadn't had a headache this bad since she was in high school.

Moving like a drunk walking a straight line for a policeman, Mac traveled down the hall. She passed wealthy guests headed to the restorative pools, and she kept her head bowed. But she would have had to be deaf not to hear their comments—from "shameful" to "poor soul" to indignant hisses—but Mac was beyond caring. Her only thought was to make it to her room before she lost the contents of her churning stomach.

"Miz McAllister?"

Jared stared at the woman who little resembled the spirited hoyden whom he'd verbally sparred with earlier that day. Lines of pain etched her brow and her face was the shade of flour.

She stumbled to a stop and he barely restrained himself from reaching out to catch her.

"Hey, Pinkerton man," she greeted him, her voice slurred.

She tried to continue, but Jared gripped her arms, careful not to hurt her.

"Miz McAllister, are you all right?" he asked, concerned by her pallor and uncharacteristic manner.

She pressed her palms to her ears. "I'd be better if you wouldn't talk so loud."

Was she drunk? He leaned closer but couldn't detect the stale odor of liquor. His worry increasing, he lowered his voice. "Are you ill?"

"Just a headache. Migraine. The doctor says it's from stress." She snorted. "He wouldn't believe the half of it."

"Perhaps you should go lie down."

"That's what I was trying to do until you stopped me."

Jared smiled slightly at the return of some of her usual spunk. He noticed the translucent bags filled with white powder. "Is that for your headache?"

She looked at them like she'd never seen them before, then leaned forward and said in a conspiratorial tone, "Better than leeches."

Jared tried to smother a chuckle with his hand. "Miz McAllister, I think I had better escort you to your room to ensure you arrive unharmed."

She closed her eyes tightly. "Thanks," she said hoarsely. "I'm not feeling too well."

Jared's humor disappeared and he wrapped an arm around her waist, surprised to feel that her corset wasn't as tightly drawn as most women's. His fingers splayed across her waist, a fingertip accidentally brushing the underside of her breast. Without the confines of a snug corset, her breast had less support and he could feel the occasional graze of plump flesh against his knuckles. He reminded himself that she was unwell and he was a gentleman, but his lusty reaction didn't heed his admonitions.

"I appreciate this, Mr. Yates," she whispered.

The vulnerability in her soft tone made him want to enfold her in his arms and shelter her. It was the last thing he expected to feel toward Miss McAllister. She seemed to be the most self-sufficient woman he'd ever met. "It's nothing," he said, equally as quiet.

He half carried her up the stairs to the second floor

where the employees' quarters were located, then paused. "Which room is yours?"

Her body tensed as she scanned the hallway. "Le's see, ah, two hundred something."

Jared shifted her slightly in his arms as he glanced around nervously. "Two hundred what?"

"Bottles of beer on the wall, two hundred bottles of beer," she sang in a horribly off-key voice.

Jared clamped a hand over her mouth. "Miz McAllister, you must keep your voice down. Now, which room is it?"

Her forehead creased as she attempted to think and he removed his hand when he was reasonably certain she wasn't going to continue singing. Suddenly her eyes lit up. "Two hundred and five. Yep, that's what it is."

Breathing a silent thank-you, Jared found the door down the hall on the right.

"I've been staying in Miss Sparrow's room, but she said I had to move," the woman murmured.

"You aren't staying with your cousin?"

"There's only one bed in her room and the sofa seriously needs a Posturepedic mattress."

Jared opened his mouth, then abruptly closed it. He didn't want to know. He tapped lightly on the door in case someone was inside, but nobody answered and he turned the knob. It opened easily and he ushered Miss McAllister in ahead of him.

She froze a few feet inside, her expression lost. "I hate this," she said hoarsely.

Fearful of the intensity behind her too-quiet words and uncertain why his own heart was hammering in his chest, he gave her arm a reassuring squeeze. "You haven't been here very long and it's still all new to you. It's all right to be frightened," he soothed gently.

"I'm not scared," she stated, her chin jutting out stubbornly.

But Jared saw the lie in her eyes. Too proud to admit her fear and too exhausted to hide it. What was she afraid of? Why didn't she want anyone to see it?

She settled her gaze on him. "You did your duty. You got me here in one piece. I'll be all right."

Jared should just have heeded her words, but his concern remained. "Why don't you lie down? You look like you're about to fall flat on your face."

"Can't. Not until I get this damned uniform off. I can't stand the corset or the three slips or the butt-ugly shoes."

His gaze flickered to her feet. The heavy black shoes weren't the most fashionable he'd seen. "When your roommate returns, she can help you." He took the packets from her hand and set them on the dresser. "You've already taken one of these, right?"

She nodded dutifully. "The doctor made me. The light doesn't hurt as much, but my head feels like it's full of cotton." Her fingers fumbled with the pin clasping the apron to her bodice. "Gotta get this damn thing off."

Jared didn't like the way her hands trembled or the flush in her cheeks. He wondered what the doctor used in his headache powders. There were as many kinds of powder to treat headaches as there were doctors. It appeared this one had used opium in his and it was adversely affecting Miss McAllister.

"Why don't you just lie down with your clothes on?" he suggested.

She twisted the pin, trying to release the apron from her chest. "Can't get it."

Jared exhaled an uneasy breath. Merely being in her room unchaperoned was grounds for her dismissal and he remembered how she'd said she'd be out on the streets without this job. But he couldn't leave her alone in this condition.

He noticed she'd finally accomplished removing the apron and undoing her bodice. He could clearly see the stiff white camisole she wore beneath the dress, as well as the shadowed valley between her breasts. Closing his eyes briefly, he offered a prayer to the saint who guarded drunks and fools. And a woman's virtue.

One look at her ruffled hair and flushed face, and Jared knew he could never take advantage of her. She was a dichotomy of innocence and wantonness as she stood in the middle of the room trying to escape the confines of her dress.

Jared took a deep breath and moved over to help rid her of the uniform. His fingertips feathered across her arms as he tugged the dress off her shoulders, then slid it down over nicely rounded hips to land on the floor in a heap around her feet.

He leaned down. "Put your hand on my shoulder and step out of the dress, Miz McAllister."

She clasped her hands together then held them out in front of her in a pantomime of holding a weapon. "Put your hands in the air and step out of the dress, Miz McAllister." She giggled and dropped a hand to his shoulder. "Eat your heart out, Joe Friday."

Though Jared had no idea what she was talking about, he laughed at the sound of her giggles. Gone was the cynical woman and in her place was a girl-woman whose behavior was so artless, it lightened Jared's own heart.

As she kept herself balanced using his shoulder, she stepped out of the dress with only a few awkward motions. Jared picked up the dress and turned to the armoire. He opened it and found a wooden hanger to place the uniform on.

"Now you should—" His voice died when he saw three petticoats piled on the floor with Miss McAllister wearing only a corset, camisole and drawers. As she reached around to the back of the corset, Jared grabbed her arms. "Oh no, you don't. We're already in deep water here."

"I don't see any water." Her warm breath cascaded across his neck and she pressed her body flush against his, then wiggled her hips. Her face lit up with a bright smile. "I knew you liked me."

Jared groaned. There were some things a man just couldn't control and his body's response to a half-dressed woman, in spite of her condition, was one of them.

"Come on, let's get you into bed," he said, guiding her backward to one of the narrow beds. He lowered her unresisting body to the mattress but when he tried to rise, her fingers clutched his lapels.

"Join me?" she asked in a sultry voice.

Sweat beads formed on Jared's forehead and one rolled down his cheek. He clutched her hands, trying to work them free of the cloth. "Let me go, Miz McAllister. You need to rest."

"Did I ever tell you that you've got a nicer butt than both Mel Gibson *and* Harrison Ford?" she asked seriously.

Jared had no idea who the two men were and didn't care. "No, you didn't. Please release me, Miz McAllister. I should leave before someone finds me in here."

"Worried about my virtue?" The golden flecks in her eyes darkened to copper. "Don't be." She stared at him with a look that burned as hot as the fire in

Jared's belly. The pressure on Jared's jacket increased, drawing his face close to hers.

And when she raised her head and kissed him, Jared didn't have the will or strength to pull away.

# SIX

Jared slid his lips across hers, savoring the feel of her, the taste of her, like warm honey. She opened her mouth, teased him, invited him further into her sweetness. It was an invitation he couldn't resist. He followed and indulged in a game of hide-and-seek with her tongue, pursuing her like a lover long estranged. When he found her, he proceeded cautiously, suddenly uncertain.

She moaned deep in her throat and her fingers curled into his lapels, drawing him impossibly nearer. He braced himself on the mattress, a hand on either side of Mac's hot writhing body. Fire licked through his veins at her ingenuous abandon and he ached to plunge his fingers into her silky hair and kiss her sweet-salty skin.

He broke away to regain his breath and equilibrium. Mac's whimper of need echoed his own eagerness and he lifted one hand, intending to place it against her cheek. He froze a hairsbreadth from her flushed face. She was ill and under medicinal influence. He wasn't, and the responsibility to remain rational weighed upon his shoulders.

His gaze dropped to the swell of her breasts as

she panted in and out with unfulfilled passion. It would be so easy to take what she offered. . . .

He groaned. No, he had never taken advantage of a woman and wasn't about to start now despite the overwhelming enticement. Besides, his masculine pride demanded that if he made love to Trish McAllister, she remember it, and he wasn't certain she would in her condition.

He gently but firmly uncurled her fingers from one side of his jacket and rested her hand on the pillow beside her flushed cheek. Within a few moments, her other hand dropped to her side and Jared straightened awkwardly.

Gazing down into her slumberous eyes, he knew he'd done the right thing. She would hate him and herself if he allowed their dalliance to continue to its obvious conclusion. If only his straining masculinity agreed.

"You need to rest, Miz McAllister," he said softly.

Her lower lip trembled. "Wanna make love."

Jared's breath caught in his throat. "I want to make love to you, too, Mac," he whispered hoarsely, then spoke loud enough that she could hear. "You're not yourself. You're ill and under the influence of Dr. Ziegler's medicine."

"You don't like me." The childish pout that accompanied her words made Jared smile.

He brushed his hand across her silky head, surprised to find how much he enjoyed the sensation of her short hair against his palm. "I like you. Honest."

She met his eyes and behind the drug's effects, Jared spotted an abiding sadness. "Most people don't." Mac's eyelids fluttered, then closed completely. Her breathing grew regular and when she spoke softly, he almost missed it. "Like you, too, Jared."

His heart tightened and the thickness in his throat caught him off guard. How had this strange woman he had known for such a short time slipped past his defenses so quickly? She was nothing like Sophia; she was nothing like any other woman he had ever met. Yet with one kiss and a muzzy "like you, too, Jared," she'd touched something that had remained cold and barren for two years.

He tucked the blankets around her still figure, his hands lingering on the smooth skin of her arm. Slowly, he raised his hand and feathered the back of his fingers across one velvety cheek. "Sleep well, Mac."

He forced his leaden feet away from her bed and scooped up the petticoats lying in a pool on the floor. He clutched the intimate clothing to his face for a few precious seconds, breathing deeply of Mac's unique heady scent. Reluctantly, he piled the undergarments on a chair. He hoped her roommate would take care of them so they wouldn't be too wrinkled in the morning.

Crossing the room, he paused at the door and gazed at Mac's relaxed features. She appeared so vulnerable, so in need of someone to guard her and hold her in his arms, that Jared almost returned to her side. Almost.

He opened the door a crack to check the hallway. Empty. With no one to witness his exit and report his inappropriate visit, he slipped out of her room and clicked the door shut quietly behind him.

* * *

By the time the Christmas ball began the following evening, Mac had finally shaken off the lingering aftereffects of her migraine and the drugs Ziegler had given her. She'd awakened that morning to Erin shaking her shoulder and telling her it was six-thirty. Thirty minutes before Mac had to report to the little dictator and stand at attention.

She'd barely passed muster under the Major's discerning and disapproving eye. Could she help it if her petticoats weren't made of wrinkle-free material? She'd never ironed anything in her life and she wasn't about to start now.

She had only a faint recollection of how she'd gotten to her room the night before and what had happened after that. She wondered if the misty memory of kissing Jared and the residual tingling in her body were real or inspired by the erotic dreams that had haunted her throughout the night. She'd barely been aware of all the bathrooms she'd cleaned that day while her mind had sorted through the confusing impressions. Even now, leaning against a wall in the dining hall as she waited for her roommate, Mac felt her face grow hot as she recalled Jared's touch in those fevered images.

She hadn't caught even a glimpse of the Pinkerton detective all day. Mac told herself it was for the best, but she couldn't help but wonder if he was staying away from her because of embarrassment. The man didn't even like her. Why had he helped her to her room? And why had he kissed her if indeed that had been real and not another fantasy in her already too-weird world?

Mac rubbed her brow, but was relieved not to feel the familiar onslaught of another migraine. In spite of her "hangover" from the powders Dr. Ziegler had given her, the remedy had worked. The headache was nothing more than a nebulous memory.

*The erotic side effects notwithstanding,* she thought with a grimace. But if she was honest with herself, those weren't all that horrific. In fact, they were downright stimulating as her belly grew warm and mushy with pure unadulterated lust—something she hadn't felt in a long time.

"There ye are." She turned to see Erin joining her. "How're ye feelin'?"

Mac smiled at the younger woman, surprised to find she was growing fond of the Irish girl. "Better, thanks, Erin. Well, do you have to work at the ball tonight?"

"Aye and I'm so excited." She clasped her hands together and tapped a little dance on the polished floor. Her expression sobered and her feet halted their impromptu jig. "But I'm nervous, too, afraid I'm going to be spillin' somethin' on a lady's fancy dress or a gentleman's fine suit."

Mac smiled, trying to reassure her as she laid a hand upon Erin's shoulder. "You'll do just fine." She leaned close and spoke in a conspiratorial voice, "But if you do get flustered and start stuttering, just imagine all those fine gentlemen and ladies in their unmentionables." She waggled her eyebrows.

Erin giggled and pressed her palm to her mouth. "Ye're shameless."

Mac crossed her arms and tipped her head in acknowledgment of the compliment. "I try."

Erin suddenly grabbed her arm. "Did ye hear? Mr. Yates is goin' to the dance and Miss Sparrow will be there actin' as hostess."

Jealousy's talons gripped Mac and her smile faltered.

"I heard that ever since his fiancée was killed, he hasn't attended a single dance." Erin sighed. "He must've loved her more than anything."

*Sell it to Harlequin,* Mac thought bitterly. Love was grossly overrated.

"Then I guess he won't be interested in any other woman for a long time," Mac said. "Looks like he's out of the running as a husband candidate for Miss Sparrow."

"I'm not givin' up yet, Mac. Are ye goin'?"

"I couldn't go even if I had a dress, which I don't. You heard the Major. Resort employees attend only if they're working or are accompanied by an actual guest," Mac mimicked in the Major's precise voice.

"Ye could watch from one of the garden doors," Erin suggested, her blue eyes shining. "Just be rememberin' to put on a wrap before ye go out."

Mac straightened, excitement banishing her exhaustion. This resort was a playground for the rich and famous, the movers and the shakers. Politics and intrigue flourished in places like this. She might be able to get the scoop on a story and sell it to a newspaper. Could she do that? If so, she could quit her job here and do what she was trained to do.

"Is there a newspaper in town?" Mac asked.

Erin's brow furrowed. "Aye. *The Hope Springs Times.*"

Mac almost laughed. *"Times,* I should have known."

"What're ye thinkin'?"

"I'm thinking that I might have just found a way to get out of the toilet cleaning business." Or maybe not. Though Nellie Bly was well known in the annals of newspaper history, she was the exception to the rule. But hadn't Mac broken some rules herself? She'd taken the grittiest stories at the *Staunton Sentinel* and had done a damned good job reporting them. She had even watched an autopsy with hardly a ripple. Of course, she'd been unable to eat anything for a day afterward.

"Where can I get a copy of the newspaper?" Mac asked.

Erin shrugged. "The new one will be out tomorrow."

"Is it delivered daily?"

"Heavens no. Dailies are for big cities like New York and Philadelphia."

"So the *Times* is printed once a week?"

Erin nodded suspiciously. "What is it you're thinkin', Mac?"

"Don't worry. I promise I won't do anything too illegal." Mac squelched a grin at the sight of the Irish girl's red face. She glanced around. "Have you seen Rupert?"

Erin shook her head. "If ye're lookin' for Rupert, ye're lookin' for trouble."

Mac smiled. "Rupert and I understand each other." She gave Erin a gentle shove in the direction of the ballroom. "You'd better get going or you'll be late and the Major will throw a fit."

Erin cast Mac one more wary look, then skipped off with a quick wave.

Mac glanced down at her utilitarian dress and sighed. The only other clothing she possessed were her jeans and those would definitely shock the drawers off more than a few of the women. On second thought . . .

*Behave yourself, Mac.*

She would have to remain in this outfit and hope no one noticed in the darkness outside. Hurrying off toward the front desk where she expected to find Rupert, Mac tried to keep her feet at an appropriate pace.

"Where's the fire, lass?" a gray-haired man called out with a thick Irish brogue.

Mac recognized the bellhop uniform of the older man and paused. "I'm trying to find Rupert."

"He be carryin' a trunk up to a guest's room."

She wrinkled her nose at the stale liquor scent that wafted across her. "Starting a little early, aren't you?" she asked in a low voice.

His already flushed face deepened to crimson and he glanced around furtively. "A weak man, I am, lass. Ye wouldn't be thinkin' of tellin' the Major, would ye?"

Mac felt compassion for the man's obvious fear. "As long as you aren't driving or operating any heavy machinery, I won't squeal."

His body slumped in relief. "Thanks, lass. The name's Jack O'Riley."

"Nice to meet you, Jack. I'm Mac."

Jack aimed a blunt finger at her and leaned close, forcing Mac to breathe through her mouth to escape the worst of the fumes. "Ye're the one Rupert was tellin' me about. He said Miss Sparrow had another special one visitin'."

"You mean she has a lot of cousins visiting?" Mac asked innocently.

Jack's surprise was well worth the price of admission. "He dinna tell me that," he mumbled. He eyed her closely. "Ye wouldn't be lookin' like Miss Sparrow."

"I take after my mother's side. Poor Esme, she ended up with father's features, including that tiny little harelip." Mac felt only a fleeting sense of guilt—she was having too much fun. She studied the older man. "How long have you been here, Jack?"

"Years and years," he replied. "My daughter Bridget used to work here, too."

"Maybe you can help me then." Mac glanced around and lowered her voice. "Were you here when Mr. Yates's fiancée was killed?"

He nodded somberly. "Aye, I was here. Horrible thing. Strangled, she was."

Mac's breath tripped in her throat. No, it had to be a coincidence. Stranglings weren't an uncommon method of murder. "What was she strangled with?"

"Piece of wire. Not a pretty sight I was told by them that seen the lass."

Mac hardly registered Jack's comment. *A piece of wire.* The Piano Man Killer! No, he murdered women in her time, not in the nineteenth century.

*But if I'm here, he could be, too.*

"Are ye all right, lass?"

The bellhop's anxious voice penetrated her shock and Mac took a deep breath. "Y-yes, I'm fine, Jack. Have there been others killed like her?"

"Aye," Jack replied slowly as if afraid he'd say too much.

"How many?" Mac pressed.

His bloodshot eyes widened, then he searched the lobby. "They don't want us to be talkin' about this, lass," he said hoarsely.

Impatience made Mac want to shake the man's shoulders, but she managed to restrain herself. "Who are 'they'?"

"The resort owners. Said we shouldn't be scarin' the guests."

She closed her eyes and counted to ten. Then added another ten for good measure. "I'm not a guest. How many more women?"

"There's been four altogether in two years," he finally answered.

There'd been five in her time for a total of nine women strangled. *If* it was the same person who committed the atrocious crimes in both centuries. How could it be? She had come back in time . . . was it so impossible to believe he, too, had traveled through time? And he *had* seemed to disappear before her eyes. Yet if he was guilty of all nine murders, he'd have to be able to jump back and forth in time at will.

Icy-cold tendrils of fear snaked down her spine. It was too much to process, too much to believe in one gulp. Mac had never even believed in Santa Claus or the Easter Bunny when she was a kid. Now as an adult she was seriously contemplating a Boston Strangler-type killer who could cross time barriers.

She'd been looking for the story of a lifetime and she'd found it—in spades—and it scared the hell out of her.

"Ye won't be tellin' anyone I told ye now, would ye?" Jack asked anxiously.

Mac managed a weak smile. "Don't worry. I'll keep it between us."

The older man's relief showed clearly in his creased face. "Thanks, lass."

"Don't thank me. I have a feeling the shit is going to hit the fan one of these days and we're all going to be in the line of fire," Mac said quietly. She lifted a hand. "Bye, Jack."

She ignored the bellhop's confusion and walked out the main door, oblivious to the night's chill. Her feet carried her across the front walkway of the hotel and around the corner. She paused, feeling like Cinderella before her fairy godmother appeared, as fancy buggies disgorged their wealthy passengers farther down in front of the ballroom entrance. Jewels glittered beneath the gaslights and stiff crinoline petticoats crinkled as the women were escorted inside. They were obviously the crème de la crème of Hope Springs' society. In Mac's own time, she'd scoffed at such obvious snobbery; but dressed as these people were in elegant old-fashioned gowns and starched suits, she couldn't help but be impressed by the fairy-talelike atmosphere.

She was amused and disgusted by her lapse in cynicism. These people were no different than those in her time as they jockeyed for positions of power and sought to outdo their political and business adversaries. It was just the arena that had changed.

Wrapping her arms around her waist, Mac crossed the road and entered the formal gardens area. In the dark winter evening, the garden appeared devoid of life. She tried to imagine it green and filled with colorful flowers, but her mind refused to release the images of the strangled women from her time. The area's current desolation suited the horrendous memories.

She spotted a concrete bench and lowered herself to it. Her many layers of clothing insulated her against the cold slab, but the slight breeze brought gooseflesh to her arms. The outer frigidity, however, was minor compared to the iciness in her chest.

"C'mon, Mac, snap out of it. You're a reporter, trained to get to the bottom of a mystery and you have a helluva one here," she murmured aloud.

She closed her eyes and logically ticked off the facts. Five women were strangled within three years in her time and four women were killed in two years here. Jared's girlfriend had been the first in this time period and she was killed December thirtieth.

Her eyes flew open. What if there had been more than four killed in this century? There were more open areas and fewer law enforcement personnel so it was possible that a body could remain hidden for a long time.

"Stick to the facts, Mac," she stated firmly. "We have enough real weird stuff without adding rash speculations."

She had to learn more about the murders that had occurred here and compare them to the ones from her time. Rupert "The Answer Man" Smith would be the person to talk to.

*What if he's the killer?*

Mac scrubbed her palms across her face. Whom could she trust? Miss Sparrow? No, she was already hiding something, though Mac didn't think she had anything to do with the murders. Jared Yates? She wanted to trust him, but he was her prime suspect. He might have killed the other women as a smoke screen to hide the fact that his fiancée had been the intended victim all along. The thought of Jared's strong fingers wrapped around a piano wire as he tugged it against the victim's neck made Mac's stomach roil.

She bounced to her feet and began to pace. That wouldn't explain the murders in her own time, unless Jared was a time traveler. Mac hummed the *Twilight Zone* theme under her breath. This guessing was driving her to insanity, unless of course she'd already completed that journey.

Music from the ballroom, carried by the wind, danced lightly around Mac. The sound was beautiful . . . and completely out of place with her grim thoughts.

A prickling at the base of her neck made Mac freeze in place. An uncanny sense of being watched swept over her and her breath stumbled in her throat. Dead leaves rattled across the ground and the breeze whispered mournfully through the bare tree branches. Mac's mouth grew bone-dry and her heart thundered so loudly it overwhelmed the harpsichord notes that drifted out of the ballroom.

Was the killer using the cover of darkness to find his next victim? Had Mac unknowingly set herself up as number ten?

A sound foreign to the evening caused Mac to gasp and she spotted a shadow moving across the ground toward her. She had to run. Now. Quickly.

Her feet refused to obey her panicked commands.

A dark specter sailed over her head, hooting as it went by.

An owl! It was only an owl.

Mac's knees threatened to buckle and she cast out a hand, catching a tree's sturdy trunk to steady herself. Her breath came in quick short spurts of white vapor in the cold air. The adrenaline rush disappeared and her muscles felt like limp spaghetti.

Nearby, a twig snapped under a heavy foot and the terror slammed back.

# SEVEN

"Mac?" Jared stared at the woman who stood as still as a statue in the deserted garden. Even her complexion was like marble.

Her mouth opened, closed, then opened again. "Jared?"

He took a step closer and she backed away, her eyes wide and frightened. His hands fisted at his sides, wondering why this feisty woman suddenly seemed afraid of him. "What happened? Are you all right? Did someone hurt you?"

"N-no, I'm all right." Her expression eased and fire sparked her eyes. "Jeezus, Yates, you took about ten years off my life. What're you doing sneaking around out here?"

Now that was more like the Mac he knew. His lips curved upward as he relaxed and crossed his arms. "I was hardly sneaking and I could ask you the same question."

She glared at him. "I wasn't sneaking. I was just standing here minding my own business. Besides, you're supposed to be at the ball."

He shrugged. "I got bored. I thought I'd come out and get some fresh air."

"You got some, now go back."

Though Mac sounded back to normal, or as normal as Mac could get, Jared wanted to find out the real reason she had been so terrified. "So what were you doing while you were standing there?"

She lifted her chin. "Thinking."

He grinned, unable to resist baiting her. "Now that's what *I* call frightening."

She wrinkled her nose and deliberately raked her gaze up and down his body, leaving a scorching path in her wake. "Not as frightening as you in that monkey suit."

"Monkey suit?" Indignantly, Jared tugged at his turquoise brocade vest, hoping the motion also covered his unexpected erection. Just when he thought she couldn't confound him any further . . . "What would you know about a monke—" He held up a hand. "No, don't tell me. I don't want to know. And to return to my original question, what were you thinking about?"

He thought he detected grudging admiration in her eyes, but it was gone before he could be certain.

"Things," she replied, shrugging one shoulder.

"What kind of things?"

"You know, the regular run-of-the-mill things, like if men are from Mars and women are from Venus, how did we all end up on Earth? And why do so many people think that Elvis is still alive? And please answer me this one, how did Captain Kirk manage to get all those women, even the alien ones?" She shook her head in puzzlement. "He never did anything for me."

Jared stared at her, wondering how in the world she was allowed to be out on her own. He didn't think she was dangerous, at least not to anyone but herself. He closed his gaping mouth and narrowed his gaze. "Have you taken another packet of Dr. Ziegler's headache powders?" He hoped so since that was the only reasonable explanation for her nonsensical ramblings.

She held up her hands as if in surrender. "No, and I don't plan to." She paused, appearing uncomfortable. "I don't remember too much about last night, except that you helped me to my room. You *did* help me to my room, right?"

Jared nodded cautiously, wondering if there was an ulterior motive to her question. "I saw you in the hallway after you left the doctor's office and thought you could use a little help."

"Thanks," Mac said with heartfelt gratitude. "I was pretty out of it." Her gaze swerved away from him and unease once again slid across her features. "Did we, uh, kiss or anything?"

So she did remember something and Jared found himself teasing her once more. "That depends. What do you mean by 'anything'?"

Even in the dim moonlight, Jared saw the red blush blossom in her cheeks.

"You know, anything like . . . like getting naked together under the covers?"

She spoke so quickly, it took a moment for Jared to decipher the words. He nearly choked on his own embarrassment. "No!" Realizing he'd shouted, he forcibly lowered his voice. "No, we didn't. However, it wasn't for your lack of trying."

Mac covered her face with her hands. "Busted," she muttered. She dropped her hands to her sides. "I'm sorry. I usually don't let my libido take control like that. It must've been something in the powder."

Jared blinked at the rapid change in her demeanor. One moment her words could put a sailor to shame and the next she was concerned and embarrassed about the previous night. Teasing her when she was feeling so mortified would be like kicking a puppy. "I'm sure it was. You weren't yourself." He cleared his throat. "I settled you safely into your own bed. Alone. Then I left."

Mac smiled crookedly, but Jared could see her relief. "A detective *and* a gentleman. What a guy."

He couldn't help but laugh, releasing the tension the awkward conversation had created. "You have an amazing way of expressing yourself, Miz McAllister."

"Call me Mac. I mean, you did tuck me into bed."

Jared shifted his weight from one foot to the other, not needing the reminder that conjured up too many tempting visions. Of course, most women wouldn't even think about bringing the subject up in public. But then Mac tended to ignore the most basic rules of polite society. He glanced around though he was almost certain no one else had ventured into the cold night. "You didn't tell anyone, did you? Your behavior wasn't exactly proper."

"And yours was?" She snorted. "Get real, Jared. But don't worry. I didn't tell anyone about our little misadventure and I have no plans to do so." She eyed him closely. "So what's the real reason you're out here and not sweet-talking some dressed-to-kill woman?"

Jared tipped his head, hearing something other than the usual flippancy in her tone. Intelligence gleamed in her eyes, as though she was searching for something else in his answer. "I told you—I needed some fresh air."

He wasn't about to tell her he was checking the area to see if he spotted anyone suspicious. He had every reason to believe Sophia's killer was nearby. He could almost feel the coldness that emanated from his evil. Frozen fingers trailed down Jared's spine as he glanced around surreptitiously.

"Is something wrong?"

At Mac's voice, Jared blinked and returned to the present. He had to escort Mac back into the hotel or she could end up the next victim. "I'm fine, but shouldn't you go back inside? You're freezing." Though he'd used that as an excuse, he couldn't help but notice her teeth *were* chattering. He stripped off his jacket and draped it over her shoulders.

She appeared startled by the gesture and her fingers clutched at the material. It reminded Jared of how she'd grabbed hold of his jacket last night, urging him downward, closer to her lips, until . . .

"Thank you," she said. "I guess it was pretty stupid of me to come out here without a coat."

He chuckled, glad she distracted him from his inappropriate musings. "It seems we can agree on something."

"And of course it would be my stupidity." She laughed, but oddly, there was no cutting sarcasm in the sound.

Jared smiled, finding himself reevaluating her once more. Her ability to genuinely laugh at herself was something he hadn't believed she could do. It made her softer, more human.

His gaze latched on to her lips, which were parted slightly, and he remembered too well how those full lips had tasted. Her blond hair was gilded silver in the moonlight, beckoning his fingers to stroke the fine soft tendrils.

Slowly, he lifted a hand and was aware of Mac following it with a wide-eyed gaze. His fingertips brushed a quicksilver strand and it slid across his finger like delicate filigree. His stomach muscles clenched, telegraphing their tension to his masculinity, which in turn hardened with need. He stared into her fathomless eyes, transfixed by their mesmerizing glow. The air was cold, but Jared's body burned hot.

His gaze lowered to her lips and he moved in closer, intending to capture them, open them, so he could rediscover her taste. He raised his other hand to rest his fingers against the pulse in her slender neck.

"No!" Mac stepped away and pressed him back with her palms against his chest. "No, this isn't right, Jared. We can't do this."

"Since when?" Jared demanded, his unappeased hunger making his words curt. "You were the one who wanted me last night."

"I-I was sick. You said so yourself," Mac said, though her voice lacked conviction.

Desire boiled through Jared, making him clench his hands at his sides. She had a point, but he didn't like it. Not one damn bit. "I'm sorry," he ground out tonelessly. "I was under the mistaken assumption we wanted the same thing."

She swayed toward him, then straightened abruptly. Her expression dissolved into characteristic irony. "Maybe we do, but I'm not about to turn my love life into a spectator sport." She whipped his coat off her shoulders and thrust it at him, saying coolly, "Thank you."

Shocked by her rapid turnabout, he took his jacket from her outstretched hand. Then he was treated to the sight of her fetching backside as she strode back to the hotel, the view doing nothing for his slowly fading erection. He jammed his arms into his coat sleeves and her soft scent surrounded him, making him angrier. And more frustrated.

"Damned woman. Why do I even bother?" he growled to himself.

But he didn't move until he saw her safely enter the building.

He turned slowly in a small circle, searching and listening for the killer. The hair at the nape of his neck stood on end. The bastard was out there watching and waiting.

What if he had come out later and found Mac's dead body? He saw in his mind's eye her pale neck marred by a thin wire and her colorless face with wide unseeing eyes. A chill cut through his blood and he closed his eyes briefly to dispel the image.

His eyelids flew open, still aware of an evil presence. "Come out, you coward," he said in a low voice vibrating with rage. "Or is it only defenseless women you show yourself to?"

Silence except for the music and muted conversations from the ballroom answered. His anger fled, replaced by melancholy. Sophia was dead, as well as three other women, and there wasn't a damn thing he could do to bring them back. Despite all of Jared's efforts, the killer remained free to continue his reign of brutal murders. The only thing Jared could do was hope he could catch him before he claimed his next victim.

His footsteps leaden, Jared returned to the ballroom. The brightness and wave of heat from the mass of bodies made him pause at the edge of the crowd. He spotted the constable and his wife dancing close and smiled bittersweetly. Even though he didn't enjoy dancing, Sophia had liked to attend the balls. So he'd escorted her, done his duty with two or three waltzes and then had moved off to the side. He'd often stood at the fringes watching her move from one man's arms to another, her feet gliding lightly across the floor. She'd been so carefree and lovely.

And now she was dead.

"Jared, are you well?"

The soft-spoken English accent made him smile. "I'm fine, Esme." His smile wavered. "I was just thinking about how much Sophia had enjoyed attending the resort's balls."

"Yes, she did, didn't she," the diminutive woman said. She gazed up at him thoughtfully. "However, I often wondered why she made you attend every dance, knowing you didn't take pleasure in them yourself."

Startled, Jared turned to her. "What're you saying?"

She shrugged. "Forgive my bluntness, but although Sophia was a beautiful woman, at times she could be somewhat self-absorbed."

Jared's initial reaction was anger at Esme's presumptuousness, but a part of him realized she was right. Sophia had been spoiled by her wealthy parents and though she was the epitome of good breeding in public, Jared had been witness to three occasions when she'd thrown childish tantrums in private.

"Her parents doted on her," he said neutrally.

Esme only nodded. "You have only sisters, no brothers. Is that correct?"

"That's right."

"It must have been difficult growing up in a home where your sisters had to be escorted to every social engagement and chaperoned."

That was an understatement. Since his father had worked such long hours to buy all the gowns and gewgaws the girls wanted, Jared was usually stuck taking them to every gathering that came along. "It did spoil my appetite for things like this." He scowled as he motioned to their opulent surroundings.

"Then why are you here tonight?" Esme pressed.

He took a deep breath, knowing he could trust the

woman. "I'm afraid the murderer will strike again and soon."

She pressed her palm to her mouth. "Oh my," she murmured. "Isn't there any way you could possibly warn the women not to walk alone after dark?"

He glanced into her frightened features, then back at the sea of shifting colors and sparkles. "You know I can't do that."

"I cannot believe our employers would be so callous."

"Not callous, Esme. Greedy." Her troubled expression wasn't lost on Jared and he sought to reassure her. "I'll be patrolling the resort in the evenings, not just for the killer but to make sure there aren't any women out alone." He grimaced. "Like Miz McAllister was."

"She was outside?"

"In the formal gardens by herself. I sent her back into the hotel." Jared thrust his hands into his trouser pockets. "I know this is none of my business, but if she's your cousin, why doesn't she look or act like you even just a little?"

Esme smiled. "Trish has always been a bit headstrong. That was one of the reasons she was sent here. She may be somewhat abrasive, but her heart is in the right place. It's just that she allows few people to see it." She studied him with a penetrating look but didn't add anything more.

Last night he had caught a glimpse of the woman beneath Mac's brash exterior and knew Esme was right. "Why is she that way?"

"Her childhood was not the happiest, and she learned at an early age to protect herself by affecting a forward demeanor." Esme sighed. "The child is now a woman, but she has never learned to trust. That is the reason she has not yet married."

"No man in his right mind would put up with her," he said, then realized how boorish that must sound to Mac's cousin. "I'm sorry. That comment was uncalled for." He shifted uncomfortably. "I think I understand, but she doesn't make it easy for a person to become a friend."

"That's why she needs someone special." Esme turned away from Jared to scan the crowd. "I must return to my hostess duties. Good evening, Jared."

"Esme." He nodded respectfully.

He couldn't fault the woman for her family loyalty, but Jared wasn't about to make a fool of himself again. He had caught Esme's not-so-subtle hints that he might be able to help Mac. However, Jared intended to stay as far away from Miss McAllister as possible. The woman was a bundle of contradictions rolled into an attractive package, and she would drive him crazy if he spent any length of time around her.

Yes, he would keep his distance from her. That should be easy enough to do. He was more or less a guest and she was an employee. No fraternization there. They occupied different social levels. And his mother would have a fit if she thought her only son was lusting after a common maid.

He chuckled to himself. That would be the only reason he would pursue Mac—to shock his mother.

His libido mocked him. That wasn't the *only* reason.

Mac sat cross-legged on her narrow bed as she read the edition of the *Hope Springs Times* she had liberated from the lobby. The headlines were history to her, but it was odd to be reading it firsthand rather than perusing faded yellow editions housed in a museum. There was a story about the newly elected president, Grover Cleveland, and his vice president, Adlai Stevenson, who would be sworn into office next month. Another article told about George Ferris and his design for the Ferris wheel, which he planned to have on exhibit in Chicago the following year.

However, the one that grabbed her attention was a follow-up story about ten Pinkerton detectives who had been killed while trying to break up a strike at a steel plant. Mac's heart tripped in her chest as she read about how they'd been hired by the company's management to get the employees back to work. Had Jared been involved in this?

She noticed her hands were trembling and quickly laid the paper in her lap. From the moment Jared had announced he was a Pinkerton detective, Mac had treated him like a comic book character. She had failed to recognize the danger inherent in his line of work in this day and age. Reading the article slammed that knowledge home, and Jared's courtship with deadly peril bothered her more than she cared to admit.

"Get over it, Mac," she chided herself. "If—*when* you get back home, Jared will have long since been buried."

, Instead of reassuring her, the realization only increased her apprehension.

Mac thrust the depressing thought aside and reached for the paper again. This time she opened it up to the local news and began to read. She laughed at the small town anecdotes, from Mrs. Grantham Jacobs's announcement that her sister and husband were visiting from Richmond to the colorful description of the unfortunate Mr. William Edwardson whose wagonload of chickens overturned. Although through the grace of God, no one—not even a chicken—was injured. There were notes about a cooking group led by Corrine Garrett, a quilting society that met once a week, and a men's organization that had several openings.

This newspaper and those in Mac's time were light years apart in content and style. If she could only get a job at the *Hope Springs Times,* she could show them a thing or two about the future of reporting.

Folding the newspaper, Mac leaned over the mattress and tucked it under her bed where her backpack was hidden. She scooted out of bed and turned off the light, then returned to the warmth of her blankets. Lying down with her hands tucked beneath her head, she stared at the ceiling. Music from the ballroom was nearly indiscernible through the closed windows. Fortunately, the employees' quarters were far enough away from the ballroom that no one's sleep was disturbed. Unless that employee was listening for something.

What? A woman's scream? Jared's voice? A reason she was here?

Mac sucked in a lungful of air through her nose and exhaled slowly through her mouth. The breathing exercises were supposed to help relax her, but they were only making her dizzy. She must be hyperventilating.

*Calm down, McAllister.*

*Why should I?*

*Because you're having a conversation with yourself.*

Good reason, but it was better than allowing herself to dwell on the possibility that Jared, a Pinkerton detective, was a serial killer. If she were prone to listening to her heart instead of the facts, she wouldn't believe him guilty of such heinous crimes. However, she was a trained reporter, a person who dealt with facts and statistics—provable items—and those told her he *was* a suspect.

*Yeah, try to prove Jared has been in my own century.* Yet he had been aboard the same train she'd found herself on after making the leap back in time. Another damning mark against him.

She brought a hand to her throat, remembering the feel of Jared's cool fingers against her skin. The memories of the strangled women had ambushed her at that moment and she'd almost succumbed to hysteria—a first for her. She'd felt like such a fool, but her suspicions couldn't be denied.

Tomorrow morning she would start her investigation into Jared Yates. The first person she'd interview was Rupert. The young man had a pulse on the comings and goings around the resort—the perfect snitch. Her only problem would be to convince him to share his knowledge out of the goodness of his heart.

Then there was Miss Sparrow. She and Jared appeared to be more than casual acquaintances. Maybe she could shed some light on Jared's background as well as that of his late fiancée. She'd also have to find out about the other three victims to see if there was any connection to Jared or to the woman he'd been engaged to.

The newspaper office might also have information on the killings. In two days, it would be Christmas and she'd have the day off, but the editor wouldn't be in his office either. Her next day off was five days after Christmas. She would walk down to Hope Springs, drop in at the newspaper office and talk to the owner.

Weariness washed over her. She'd only been in the past a short time and already it felt like forever. How would she survive six months? Her knees ached from scrubbing floors and her back twinged from bending over toilets and claw-foot bathtubs. Her teeth had grown fuzz with the powder they called toothpaste, and her hands were chapped and cracked from the harsh chemicals she used for cleaning. She didn't even want to think about the rags she'd have to use when her period arrived.

She threw her forearm across her face and groaned. There wasn't one solitary thing she liked about the nineteenth century. Well, maybe one: her father didn't exist.

But Jared Yates did.

*Make that two things.*

Finally Mac fell into a restless slumber, her dreams filled with disturbing images of Jared and her father and the faceless killer.

# EIGHT

"But, Rupert, I don't have anything you'd want," Mac argued for the tenth time. She glanced around the polished lobby, relieved to see there were few guests loitering on Christmas Eve.

"I'm sure you can think of something." Rupert removed his cap and glared at it as he twirled it around a finger. "Why after eight years did they decide we needed to wear these stupid hats? We look like those little monkeys on the street corners in Philadelphia."

"Maybe it's because you act like one," Mac retorted, her patience nearly at its end. She'd worked twelve hours straight with only a quick break for lunch and was tired and irritable. She would eat dinner after she was done interviewing Rupert.

She snatched his hat away to still his idle motions.

"Come on now, Mac. I may hate the thing, but if the Major sees me without it, I'll be fired," Rupert said, reaching for it.

Mac thrust the hat behind her back. "Not until you answer my questions." She smiled a predator's smile. "You do that and I'll give your hat back."

He threw his hands in the air. "That's like giving information for free. If I do that, I'll lose my credibility."

Mac laughed at his feigned indignation. "Who says you have any credibility?"

Rupert pressed his hand to his chest. "You wound me, Mac, as surely as if you'd had a gun and shot me in the heart."

She rolled her eyes. Rupert was a master at melodrama.

Mac concentrated, thinking of what she had that might be of value. Her computer, but that didn't work and she really didn't think Rupert would be interested in it anyhow since he couldn't buy anything with it. Okay, what else?

*Knowledge of the future.*

She moved closer to Rupert and asked in a low voice, "Have you heard of the telephone?"

He gave her a look that told her he thought she was an ignoramus, with a capital *I*. "Who hasn't?"

Mac hesitated, hoping there wasn't some sort of otherworldly tribunal for people who gave away secrets of the future. "Go out and buy as much stock in the phone company as you can. Someday you'll be a rich man. Trust me."

"And why should I trust you?"

She frantically searched for a reason. "Because I have a crystal ball and can see into the future." *C'mon Mac, can't you do better than that?*

Rupert guffawed, slapping his thigh in the bargain. "Now that's a new one, Mac. I'll give you that."

She grabbed his arm, squeezing tightly. She had to get the scoop on Pinkerton Agent Jared Yates and to do that she had to convince Rupert she was telling the truth. "It's true. I swear. You buy that stock and in a few years, it'll pay for the information a thousand times over."

Rupert sobered, studying her intently. "Either you're

a better liar than me or you're like that psychic who was here a few years ago." He suddenly grinned. "And since it can't be the former, you have to be a psychic. All right. With one condition."

"What?"

"You give me back my hat."

Mac smiled sweetly and presented it to him with both hands, but snatched it back as he reached for it. "You won't go back on your word?"

Rupert rolled his eyes. "On my honor."

She wrinkled her nose. "That eases my mind," she said sarcastically, but gave him the round cap.

He planted it on his head at a jaunty angle. "First question."

"What do you know about Jared Yates?"

His eyes twinkled as he waggled his eyebrows. "Ah, so it's Jared Yates you're interested in."

Mac elbowed him in the ribs, eliciting a yelp from the bellhop. "Don't even go there. When did he first start coming to the resort?"

Rupert rubbed his offended side. "You're a hard woman, Mac." He paused. "Yates has been coming here for as long as I've been here. For the first few years he'd come with his family." He smiled dreamily. "Did you know he has six sisters, each one prettier than the last?"

"Men," Mac muttered, but realized the information might be important. "Are they all younger than him? Does he have any brothers?"

"Yes and no. The family wasn't very happy when he became a Pinkerton detective."

After reading the story in the paper about the ten detectives who had been killed, Mac could understand their displeasure. "How do you know?"

"I heard him and his mother arguing about it. She thought it was too dangerous a job for her only boy."

"So he grew up in a houseful of women and his mother was domineering." She rubbed her brow. "Damn. He fits the profile."

"What profile?"

Rupert's confusion startled Mac. She hadn't meant to speak aloud. "Forget it. What was his fiancée like?"

Rupert pantomimed the shape of an hourglass and emitted a low wolf whistle.

*Some things never change.* "I assume you mean she was pretty?" Mac asked dryly.

"More like beautiful, but as my dear sweet mother used to say, 'Beauty is only skin deep.' "

Mac's suspicions rose another notch. "So she wasn't a nice person?"

Rupert leaned close. "Let's put it this way. When I saw her coming, I'd make myself scarce. She had a tongue sharper than a butcher's knife, but she was always careful that Jared wasn't in earshot when she laid into us." He adjusted his cap with a grimace. "Love may be blind, but in Jared's case, love was deaf."

The more Mac heard about Jared, his family and murdered girlfriend, the larger the knot grew in her stomach. Maybe Jared had finally seen his fiancée's true colors and gotten tired of her tirades. When she wouldn't allow him to break off the engagement, he killed her, and then went on to kill the other women to cover his crime.

Good theory, but it didn't explain why—or how—he murdered those women in her century. That was provided the killer was the same person in both times, and her gut was telling her they were. But no matter how hard she tried, she couldn't bring herself to believe that the sexy-as-hell Jared Yates was a cold-blooded killer.

*I'm as bad as a man thinking with his dick instead of his brain.*

She massaged her throbbing brow and hoped she wasn't getting another migraine.

"Why all the questions about Yates?" Rupert suddenly asked.

"Would you believe simple curiosity?"

"Nope."

Mac sighed. "Someday I'll tell you, but not yet. There are still too many unanswered questions."

"You're not really a maid, are you?"

Mac narrowed her eyes and glanced around cautiously, pretending to search for someone. "That's right. I'm a spy for England and I'm gathering information for a planned coup. They're still pissed off that they lost the Revolutionary War."

Rupert's jaw dropped and he stared at Mac for a full minute before he clamped his mouth shut. "You're joking, aren't you?"

"Yes, Rupert, I'm joking. They're only slightly miffed." Mac laughed at the bellhop's disgusted look and backhanded his arm. "Relax."

Rupert rolled his eyes. "I should know better when it comes to Miss Sparrow and her special girls."

"That's the second time you've mentioned that. Who are Miss Sparrow's girls?"

"They show up here needing a little extra help to learn their jobs and Miss Sparrow takes them under her wing."

Mac groaned. "Ha ha. Do they still work here?"

Rupert shook his head as he grinned, obviously relishing his clever pun. "All of them married and settled down to raise children."

"That proves it. I can't be one of her special girls. I'm not going to get married, much less have a barrelful of rugrats." Mac dismissed Rupert's strange claim. "One more question. What do you know about the other three women who were murdered near here?"

Rupert's easygoing manner disappeared and he glanced around warily. "I'm not supposed to talk about them."

The owners had certainly made their position clear among the staff. Nobody was supposed to talk about the dead women; in that way, the killer would remain nonexistent. It was the old ostrich-head-in-the-sand theory. The owners probably figured if the killer showed up again, the death of one or two or three women was the price they were willing to pay to keep the Chesterfield's reputation intact. Furious, she curled her fingers into her palms and silently damned the arrogant men who determined the value of a woman's life.

"So you don't care that other women could die the same way?" She tried to keep her voice impassive, but sharp sarcasm bled into her tone.

"It's not that, Mac. I need this job." He glanced around nervously, then spoke in a low voice. "I send most of my money home to my mother and younger brothers and sisters. My father died twelve years ago, leaving Ma with nine children. Since I was the oldest . . ." He broke off, embarrassed.

Damn, the young man wasn't the hustler he let everyone believe. Wasn't there anybody in this time who was exactly as he or she appeared?

Mac patted Rupert's shoulder awkwardly. "Hey,

that's okay. I understand. It's just—" She shook her head. It wouldn't do any good to make the bellhop feel any guiltier than he already did. "Remember what I said. Buy stock in the telephone company and you'll be able to take care of your mother in grand style."

She turned toward the employees' dining hall, but spotted Jared Yates sitting in a plush lobby chair reading a newspaper. She debated joining him. After her abrupt retreat from the garden last night, he must think her crazy. If only he hadn't touched her neck, she wouldn't have freaked.

They had been alone in a deserted garden then, but here there were enough people that she felt safe. He already believed she had some screws loose, what was another one or two?

Glancing back at Rupert who was busy carrying luggage toward the south section, Mac veered off to join the Pinkerton detective. She plopped into a chair across from him and allowed her gaze to roam across his muscular legs and up his thighs. The man could be an underwear model. She could imagine the billboard in Times Square: Jared Yates dressed in nothing but a pair of black silk boxers and a smile. Now there was a stimulating picture.

Her scrutiny shifted to his hands, which held the paper in front of his face. His slender fingers didn't suit a detective, but rather an artist. A hazy memory from the night she'd had her migraine returned, and she remembered the gentleness of those hands when he'd helped her undress and again when he'd brushed her cheek with his fingertips. Her skin tingled with the need to feel those skillful fingers across more than just her face.

*Oh, yeah, a lot more.*

"Good evening, Miz McAllister," he said blandly without looking up from his paper.

Though startled, Mac couldn't help but smile. "What gave me away, the smell of cleaning solution?"

Jared lowered the paper and met her gaze steadily. "No, I glanced up and saw you coming this way."

"Gee, and here I thought you might be clairvoyant."

He rolled his eyes and his jaw muscle clenched, working its way up into his cheek. "Spare me the sarcasm, Miz McAllister. I've had more than my share of it."

She leaned back in her chair and searched his sour expression. Could she blame him after last night's fiasco? She knew he'd been as hot to trot as she had been yet she'd run like a shy virgin. Nobody had ever accused her of being shy before and her virginity was ancient history. But she couldn't very well come flat out and tell him she suspected he was a serial killer.

The only option was to take the offensive. It was what she did best. "So what's going on?"

Her question seemed to startle him and he blinked, then cast his gaze down at the newspaper. However, Mac could tell he wasn't reading it.

"Nothing is 'going on,' Miz McAllister. I am merely taking advantage of the quiet evening to read the newspaper."

Rupert had said Jared had a family, so why wasn't he with them over the holidays? Mac's instincts kicked in for another round of suspicion. Maybe he was searching for his next victim. "It's quiet because it's the night before Christmas and most people are spending the time with their families."

"So why aren't you with your cousin?" Jared shot back, his voice cool.

"She's working." Mac didn't know if Miss Sparrow

was or not, but she wasn't about to give Jared any more reason to question her. "So why aren't you with *your* family?"

He lowered the paper only slightly this time and Mac heard an accompanying sigh of exasperation. "Because I prefer to be here."

"If I had six sisters I'd feel the same way."

"How did you find out I had six sisters?" he demanded.

She shrugged. "Common knowledge. I also heard you were engaged to be married a couple years ago."

Pain flashed through his eyes, surprising Mac by the intensity of the emotion. But was it the pain of losing her or the pain of guilt?

"The Chesterfield's rumor mill is certainly efficient." Jared studied her with eyes as sharp as a hawk's. "Why are you so interested in my past, Miz McAllister?"

*Bull's eye.* Jared was no slouch when it came to hitting his target either.

She shrugged, hoping the gesture appeared nonchalant. "I also heard she'd been murdered, and I thought since you were a Pinkerton detective that maybe you had tried to track down her killer."

Jared sat up in his plush chair and pressed the newspaper to his lap. The rustling of the paper sounded ominous in the silence surrounding them. "I *did* try."

Rupert had failed to mention that little fact. Or maybe he hadn't known. "And?"

Bitterness twisted his lips into a caricature of a smile. "I wasn't able to crack the case or that of the three other murders that followed."

Mac's heart thumped against her ribs. She hadn't expected him to spill the information so easily. Maybe he didn't have anything to hide. Or was he merely pretending to be helpful to throw her off the trail? "There were a total of four women killed, right?"

He narrowed his eyes and his voice was dangerously low. "I didn't say they were all women."

Mac's breath caught. She was getting sloppy and that wasn't going to win her a Pulitzer. *Always pretend to know less than you actually do.* "I heard some rumors." She shrugged and managed a fairly believable laugh.

Jared leaned forward, his elbows planted on his thighs. His body language screamed distrust. This man was no idiot, no cartoon character. He was sharp. Too damn sharp. "Who are you?"

"I'm Trish McAllister, employed as a maid at the Chesterfield." A little humility might be just what the doctor ordered. "And a darned good maid at that."

*Humility never was my strong suit.*

Jared's gaze flickered to her mouth and lingered. Mac resisted the urge to lick her lips, but she couldn't stop the lust that raced through her veins to crash in her belly. It had been a long time since she'd slept with a man. There always seemed to be more exciting things to do, like washing the car or doing the laundry. But one look from Jared's light blue eyes and Mac was looking for the nearest motel room. She glanced around, noting where she was and rolled her eyes in disgust. She doubted if the Chesterfield rented rooms by the hour.

A chill swept across her, reminding her that Jared was still her number-one suspect. Sleeping with the enemy wouldn't be the wisest course of action in spite of her body's inclination toward treason.

The flare of passion cooled in Jared's expression and he eased himself back against the chair. Deliberately, he raised the newspaper so his face was hidden once more. "If you plan to attend church service in Hope Springs, you had better get ready. The last train goes into town at eight-fifteen."

"Are you going?"

"No."

"Why not?"

The paper retreated to Jared's lap again. "You sound like my five-year-old niece. She's always asking why."

Mac grinned. "Smart girl. She obviously doesn't take after her uncle."

An unexpected smile tilted Jared's lips upward. "She wants to be a doctor. I'm sure she'll grow out of it."

"Why not encourage her? It'd be better than cleaning toilets." Mac wrinkled her nose in disgust.

"She'll marry and become a good wife and mother," Jared said firmly.

"Oooh, such an aspiring dream. Leave Mom and Dad only to have another person control her life." She rolled her eyes. "You're such a chauvinist pig, Yates."

"Is that a compliment?"

She tilted her head, eyeing him closely. *"You'd* think so."

"Tell me what *you* used to dream about," Jared suddenly said.

"Being a newspaper reporter," she replied without hesitation, then added softly, "It's all I ever wanted to do for as long as I can remember."

"What did your mother and father think?"

Without warning, pain gripped her chest as memories bombarded her. She couldn't seem to keep her mouth shut as the words spilled out. "My father abandoned my mom when he found out she was pregnant. My mother died when I was ten. After that, nobody cared what I dreamed or didn't dream." She shrugged, affecting an indifference she didn't possess. Tears clogged her throat and she stood. Damn, this wasn't supposed to happen. Bygones were supposed to be bygones, gathering dust in some forgotten corner. "I have to go."

Jared rose, blocking off her escape route. "Are you all right, Mac?"

The concern in his voice nearly undid her precarious control, but old behaviors were hard to overcome. She pressed her shoulders back and lifted her chin. "I'm fine."

He gripped her arms, but his grasp was warm and inviting rather than restraining. "Have you eaten dinner?"

Mac blinked at the unexpected question. "No."

"Would you like to accompany me to the dining room?"

"I'm an employee. You're a guest." The words nearly stuck in her throat, but Mac had learned there was a definite division between employee and guest that she was expected to maintain at all times.

"Technically, I also work for the hotel," he replied with a crooked smile.

Mac's gaze settled on the cleft in his chin, and against her will, she traced the appealing mark with her fingertip. His whiskers gently rasped her skin, sending a tingle down her arm. She wanted to lean forward and kiss his chin, explore the indentation with her tongue as she tasted him. Her blood thundered through her veins and heat settled between her thighs. What was it about this man that made her lose all levelheadedness?

She was a reporter. Objectivity was a requirement for her job.

Hormones were to be ignored. She'd never had

trouble ignoring them until Jared. Now she couldn't turn them off.

Drawing away from him, Mac searched for an excuse to decline his dinner invitation. But the reporter within her had her own reasons to accept. Mac had questions she wanted answered and Jared would be stuck with her for the length of the meal. It made perfect sense.

So why did her stomach do a slow roll every time she thought of sitting across an intimate table from him? She had a mystery to solve and Mac McAllister had never let her libido get the better of her.

Of course, she hadn't been faced with temptation in the form of Jared Yates before either.

# NINE

Jared hadn't expected her to accept his dinner invitation, but he was pleasantly surprised when she did. The past two nights he'd come precariously close to tossing aside every gentlemanly courtesy that had been ingrained in him in order to ravish the exasperating and too damned intriguing woman.

Having grown up with six younger sisters, he thought of how he'd feel if some man forced himself upon one of them. Even if Miss McAllister didn't have a brother to protect her, she didn't deserve to be treated with less civility despite her uncommon candor.

"Shall we?" he asked, lightly resting his palm against her waist.

She nodded, but he felt a slight tremor course through her. Mac wasn't nearly as self-assured as she liked everyone to believe. Her expression when she'd told him about her dream and her parents had given him a glimpse of the woman who lay beneath the brash exterior. That tiny glimpse made her softer, more vulnerable. Even though she'd never admit it, she needed a man to care for her and bring out her femininity. However, the upbringing that had made her so tough would be difficult to overcome.

At the entrance to the dining room, Jared and Mac stopped to wait for the maître d'.

"Are you sure about this?" Mac whispered hoarsely. "I'm still in my uniform."

Jared hadn't even noticed. Cursing himself for his thoughtlessness, he leaned close to her ear. Silky tendrils tickled his nose and he pressed even nearer. Her womanly scent surrounded him, undisguised by the overpowering perfume most ladies seemed to bathe in. He inhaled deeply. He could get drunk on her scent alone. "Would you like to change into another dress?"

She stiffened. "No, that's all right. Maybe this is a bad idea."

Mac tried to back out of the room, but Jared planted himself directly behind her. Though she might be right, he didn't want her to leave. Besides, it gave him an excuse to keep her in sight and safe from the killer.

Guilt twinged Jared. He should be outside scouring the grounds for anyone who didn't belong, as well as women walking alone. The foreboding that the killer would strike soon was growing. But the other two murders that had occurred around this time of year had been committed after Christmas, not before.

He hoped the killer, if he was going to strike again, wouldn't change his pattern. Turning his attention back to Mac, he asked in mock disbelief, "Are you scared of me?"

With her back almost touching Jared's chest, she turned her head to gaze up at him. Her face was inches from his. "Should I be?" Her tone was too somber in response to his teasing.

Instinctively he realized his answer was important to her, too vital to be laughed off. He didn't understand why, only that it was.

He feathered a fingertip across her delicate eyebrow

as he studied the copper specks in her dark eyes. He
could fall into her eyes and be lost, wholly and will-
ingly. "No. You never have to be frightened of me,"
he said quietly but with an intensity that surprised
them both.

Mac tried to swallow, but all the moisture in her
mouth had disappeared. Trish McAllister, who'd made
cynicism a religion, believed him. Jared Yates was not
the Piano Man Killer, nor had he killed his fiancée
and the other women. In his compelling eyes, she met
true integrity, not the bottled commodity that was
bought and sold by politicians and CEOs in her time.

Mac was vaguely aware of someone clearing his
throat.

"Table for two?" came a man's too precise voice.

She quickly turned away from Jared, so he wouldn't
see her confusion.

"Yes, please," Jared replied to the maître d'.

The man led them through the nearly deserted room
to a small table laced in shadows in one corner.

"Is this acceptable?" the maître d' asked.

Jared smiled. "Perfect."

He held Mac's chair and she lowered herself into it
carefully. He took the seat across from her. The maître
d' handed them menus, then returned to his post at
the front of the dining room. However, Mac didn't
miss the disapproval in his weasel-like face.

As she stared at the menu with unfocused eyes, she
was aware of Jared's baffled gaze. He was probably
wondering why she wasn't running off at the mouth.
Silent lulls were rare between them since they had
stumbled into each other's lives.

She had five months and twenty-six days to figure
out why she'd ended up here and what she was supposed to do to gain her ticket back. So why wasn't

she concentrating on that instead of the spicy scent of Jared's aftershave? Were the two—Jared and her predicament—related? Or had her hibernating hormones decided the long winter was over and the spring mating ritual had begun?

*C'mon, Mac, tuck it in. Mindless sex has its place, but it's not here.*

Jared watched her closely, wondering what was going on in her too lively mind. She was too quiet. Startled, he realized he wanted her to talk. He'd become accustomed to her ramblings and peculiar words and actually missed the sound of her voice.

Before he could ask her about her strange mood, she broke the silence.

"I wonder if anyone calls him Rat Man."

Jared nearly choked. "The maître d'?"

Mac leaned forward, her eyes dancing. "Did you notice his little mouth and beady eyes? And I swear his nose was twitching." She shook her head. "He should've gone into the extermination business—he'd have an inside track."

Jared closed his eyes, fighting the urge to laugh. Mac had the diminutive stiff-rumped man pegged right. Definitely a rat man. He gave up the fight and chuckled. "Have you always been so . . . forthright?"

"The word is obnoxious." She plopped her elbows on the table and clasped her hands. She gazed at him over the candle and the flickering flame was mirrored in her black pupils. "That's all right. I'm proud of my ability to antagonize everyone I meet within the first five minutes."

"I didn't know you were so talented."

"Aw shucks, Jared, you're such a flatterer." A smile twitched her full lips.

She shifted her attention to the menu and Jared did

the same, though he was aware of every movement she made, no matter how minute. A slender finger tapped her chin and her nose wrinkled like a child who had just tasted cod liver oil. Her short blond hair, though a bit wild, framed her oval face perfectly. He couldn't imagine Mac with long hair. She was too unique and the odd hairstyle suited her.

"Would you like me to order for you?" he asked.

She affected a helpless pose. "Oh my, there are just so many choices. Little ol' me couldn't possibly decide, so I'll just have the big strong man do it for me." She batted her eyelashes for good measure.

Jared laughed and held up a hand. "Point taken." He grimaced. "And understood."

"Who says you can't teach an old dog new tricks?" she asked with a smirk.

Jared resisted the urge to wipe the smirk from her face with a well-placed kiss.

A waitress approached them. "Are you ready to order?" She glanced from Jared to Mac and her mouth fell open. "Mac?"

"Hello, Jane," Mac said calmly, though Jared noticed her grip tightened on the menu.

The plain-faced waitress leaned close to Mac. "What're you doing with Mr. Yates?"

"What does it look like we're doing?" Jared broke in irritably. He didn't like being talked about as if he were a piece of furniture.

Mac tossed him a scowl and turned back to the girl. "Mr. Yates and I are having dinner."

"But I thought we were going to get him and Miss Sparrow together," Jane whispered, though Jared heard every word.

"Miss Sparrow?" he exclaimed.

Mac cast him an innocent look that appeared so

incongruous on her that he would've laughed if he hadn't been so dumbfounded.

"We thought you liked her," Jane said with wide eyes.

"Miss Sparrow?" Jared reiterated, knowing full well he sounded like a parrot but unable to say anything more intelligent.

"It was pointed out that you two have been friends for a few years and that you're also quite compatible," Mac explained. "Esme Sparrow is the epitome of feminine deportment and compliance, while you're a pillar of masculine supremacy and chauvinism. Seems to me you two were made for each other."

He opened his mouth to deny her claims, but the mischievous twinkle in her eyes stopped him. Instead, he turned to Jane. "I'll have the chateaubriand. We'll also have a bottle of cabernet."

The waitress appeared puzzled, but remained where she was, waiting for him to give Mac's order as well. Jared smiled to himself. He wasn't about to incur Mac's wrath again.

"I'll have . . ." Mac began, then glanced at Jared. "You're picking up the tab, right?"

He didn't like the sound of that, but he had invited her. He nodded cautiously.

She grinned. "In that case, I'll have the largest steak in the kitchen, done medium well."

Jane blinked in confusion, but wrote down the order. She took their menus and scurried away.

"You shocked the poor girl, Mac," Jared said. She'd also surprised him, but she didn't need to know that. Mac had shocked him enough in the past four days to last a lifetime.

Had he only known her four days? It felt longer, like a lifetime, maybe two or three. Though he knew little about her past, he had the uncanny feeling that he saw what mattered. With a start he realized he was seeing what Esme had wanted him to see.

"It's good for her," Mac said. "Besides, it's the first time I've seen Jane speechless." She grinned unrepentantly.

Jared steepled his fingers. "So what's this about playing matchmaker, with Esme and myself as the match in the making?"

"I tried to talk Jane and her co-conspirators out of it." Her eyes glittered. "I told them you were too much man for Miss Sparrow."

Jared almost smiled, then caught the underlying inference. "So who do you think could handle me? You?"

The dare lay between them, sparking as hot as the awareness that suddenly sang through the air. The lust was undeniable, the attraction equally so. Jared had trouble breathing the heavy air. Hell, he had trouble remaining in his chair when all he wanted to do was toss Mac over his shoulder and carry her off to a more private setting.

Mac narrowed her eyes and leaned forward, placing an elbow on the table and her chin in her palm. "Who says *you* can handle *me?*"

Jared's breath caught in his throat as his gaze dropped to follow the rapid rise and fall of her breasts. The motion hypnotized him, thickened his blood as well as points south. Her body, soft and curvy in all the right places, begged for his attention, though it didn't have to plead much. He remembered too well the feel of her skin and the taste of her lips. He pictured her as she lay in her bed, her fingers wrapped in his jacket and tugging him closer . . . closer.

His erection throbbed against his trouser buttons

and the ache to possess her was fast becoming an itch he couldn't ignore.

"Here's your wine."

The waitress's voice brought him out of his sensual haze and he shifted, drawing his jacket over the outline of his rigid shaft.

"Thank you," he said, his voice a shade higher than normal.

Jane poured a small amount into Jared's goblet and he lifted it to his lips and drank. "Fine." It could have tasted like sour apples and Jared wouldn't have noticed.

After both glasses were filled, Jane left them alone.

"Well?" Mac prompted. "Do you think you could handle me?"

"Is that a rhetorical question?"

She sipped some wine. "For now," she said, almost purring.

"Yes."

Mac tipped her head slightly in acknowledgment. "I guess we'll have to wait and see if you have a chance to put your money where your mouth is."

His mouth only wanted to be one place right now—on Mac's body. It didn't matter where, as long as he could taste her, devour her until she was writhing and moaning beneath him.

He raised his wineglass with a decidedly unsteady hand. "To rhetorical questions."

After a moment's hesitation, Mac clinked her glass against his and her eyes twinkled dangerously. "And answered challenges."

Jared lifted the wineglass to his lips and drank the contents in one gulp.

* * *

Three hours and two bottles of wine later, Mac and Jared strolled out of the dining room. She was getting old—she couldn't even handle a little wine anymore. Pathetic. The only good thing to come out of her nearly drunken state was a reason to lean on Jared. Even if she hadn't been tipsy, she would've found a reason to stay close to him, maybe to demand sympathy for a hangnail.

During the course of the evening, she'd grown more and more certain that her gut instinct was right. Jared was no killer. With that doubt gone, she allowed her other instincts to guide her. The only problem was those instincts weren't connected to her gut and definitely not to her brain.

She wrapped both her arms around his, relishing the hard bicep and his equally hard body. She pressed her nose to his sleeve and inhaled the scents of wool, tobacco and Jared.

How long had it been since the mere scent of a man brought a languorous pulsing between her thighs?

"What're you thinking?" Jared asked.

She glanced at him and nearly pooled to the floor in a boneless heap at the smoky warmth in his eyes. "I'm thinking that your eyes ought to be outlawed."

*No doubt about it—I'm pathetic.*

His lips curved upward in a slow sexy smile that would put Brad Pitt to shame. "Is that good?"

"Definitely good. Maybe too good."

"Why's that?"

"Your eyes do things to me that would be illegal in most states," Mac said.

His arm slipped around her waist, drawing her nearer. "It's hard to know the difference between your insults and your compliments."

"I like being mysterious." She winked, enjoying his momentary discomfiture.

"Enigmatic," he drawled.

"Baffling."

"Puzzling."

"Complicated."

"Paradoxical."

*He didn't know the half of it.*

Mac glanced up at him, which wasn't easy considering she was close enough to his side to be considered an appendage. "Oooh. You win. Most certainly a paradox."

They paused in front of the doorway to the Garden Room. It was dim, illuminated only by the moonlight that shone through the windows, but Mac could make out the chairs, tables and plants that were strategically placed so people could visit without being crowded by their neighbor. The room was empty. It was Christmas Eve; everybody had someplace to be.

Everybody but Mac and Jared.

"Would you like a tour?" Jared asked softly.

In spite of Mac's somewhat intoxicated condition, she recognized the invitation. The kind of exploration Jared intimated would involve a much more personal tour.

She lifted her gaze to tell him she wasn't going to fall for his cheap line, but one look at the sexy tilt of his lips and she was caught.

Hook, line and libido.

"I'd like that." Was that velvety tone hers?

Jared ushered her through the doorway and down the two levels of steps with an arm around her waist that scorched through her multilayered skirts. Mac clasped her hands in front of her, afraid if she touched him, she would rip off his shirt and jacket to run her palms along his sculptured pecs and abdomen. She knew the muscles were there. She had felt them tense, as if he, too, were holding himself back.

"The waters here at the Chesterfield are heated by an underground hot spring," Jared was saying. "The man who discovered it sold the land to a group of investors. It took five years to build everything you see here at the Chesterfield."

*My God, he was actually giving her a tour, complete with factual tidbits.*

Was this his form of a cold shower? If so, it wasn't working. The rich timbre of his voice curled through her, making her nerves sit up and take notice. Not that they needed much incentive.

Maybe Jared had no intention of making love to her. Could she blame him? She wasn't exactly a model of Victorian womanhood.

He led her to the floor-to-ceiling windows that lined one side of the room. She looked out into the night draped with broken moonbeams. A smattering of snowflakes fluttered down from the sky, reminding Mac of the cheap snow globe her mother used to drag out every year with the rest of the Christmas decorations. The scene inside the plastic dome was of a sleigh with a woman, a man, and a child inside. It was pulled by two black horses through a forest made of ugly green spikes that were supposed to be trees. She used to turn the globe upside down and shake it until her arm felt as though it would fall off, then she'd set it on the coffee table and watch the white flakes twirl around and around until they settled on the bottom. Mac had spent hours shaking the globe and watching the winter scene, imagining the people in the sleigh were her mother, her father and herself.

Five years ago she'd bought herself a snow globe

and shook it until the snowflakes whirled dizzily inside. She had stared at it, trying to find the magic that had been in the one from her childhood, but she could no longer see a loving family within the sleigh, only a cheap plastic ball with a tacky winter scene inside. The globe had ended up in the garbage on Christmas Eve.

Her breath hitched in her throat and she concentrated on the warmth of Jared's palm on her back. She leaned back against his chest, and his arms came around her waist, his hands clasped beneath her breasts. She rested her palms on his hands, feeling the light dusting of hair across his knuckles and the play of tendons beneath the skin.

"A perfect Christmas night," Jared said softly.

His breath fanned her neck and sent goose bumps scurrying down her arms.

*So maybe the tour was his idea of foreplay.*

For a woman who prided herself on her independence, Mac liked the security and comfort of Jared's strong arms around her and the solid chest she leaned against. She could get addicted to his steadfast presence, but she knew better than to do so. If she looked at this liaison as more than a romp in bed, she'd be opening herself up to heartache.

He bent forward and kissed her nape where her shoulder met her neck. She gasped and closed her eyes to lose herself in the overpowering feel of his lips upon her sensitive skin. The heat spread to her belly and settled lower. She shoved away the melancholy her memories had brought and focused on the erotic sensations he created, allowed them to fill her thoughts and thicken her blood.

Sex was good for a lot of things—burning calories,

relieving stress and allowing her to forget what needed to be forgotten.

Sex with Jared Yates would be better than good. She turned her face toward his and moaned, searching for his lips. He made the search easier as he accepted her invitation and met her halfway. Kissing Jared was like a birthday, Hanukkah and Christmas present all rolled into one. Masculine and gentle, sweet and tangy, hard and soft. He tasted like wine and . . . like Jared.

His fingers wove through hers, holding her a willing captive. She felt his engorged penis resting along her buttocks and she thrust back against its welcome hardness.

Her breasts ached to be stroked and her pebbled nipples strained against her bodice. If he didn't touch her soon, she would explode. She didn't give a damn if it was the wine or her lust that made her so forward, but she needed the release with an almost frightening intensity.

She lifted Jared's hand to one of her swollen breasts. He sucked in his breath between a mating of their mouths and rolled her nipple between his thumb and forefinger.

"Harder, please," Mac managed to say between gasps.

He obeyed and her knees nearly buckled. "Yes," she murmured through a sexual haze.

Jared brought his other hand up to tease and stroke her neglected breast, nearly driving Mac insane. He rocked his hips forward and he found the inviting groove of Mac's backside.

She groaned with want and need and plain old lust. Except with Jared the lust was anything but plain and old. It was new and electric and mind-numbing.

And suddenly she didn't care about indoor plumbing or microwaveable popcorn or espresso machines or the Internet highway.

All that mattered was finding a dark corner, preferably with a bed—although that wasn't a requirement—and hope that Jared let her have her way with him.

# TEN

Jared was going to do something he hadn't done since he was fifteen—he was going to stain the front of his trousers.

He should have realized that no matter what it was, if Mac was involved, it would be . . . different.

Exciting.

Amazing.

Extraordinary.

His body had flat-out dismissed his brain and was working on primal instincts. The soft flesh of Mac's backside against his hard length and the softer flesh of her breasts in his palms combined to take him past the point of rational thought.

But then around Mac, his thoughts were rarely rational as it was.

His goal was clear, and if Mac's movements and moans were any indication, their goals were one and the same.

A thread of sanity remained, reminding him they were in a public place where anybody could walk in and see them. It wasn't very likely on Christmas Eve, but Jared needed to protect Mac's reputation even if she was past caring at this point.

She clung to him, moving with him as he maneuvered her into a darkened alcove in a far corner. As they shuffled over, she turned within his arms and her breasts flattened against his chest. She grabbed his lapels in her hands, but he wasn't about to complain about the wrinkles.

He wrapped his arms around her waist and slowly lowered her to the cushioned wicker sofa. It was wide enough that he could straddle her thighs with his knees. Her eyes glittered, so bright he could see the naked need within their depths.

Jared's conscience attacked him without warning. The wine had released Mac's inhibitions and he was taking advantage of her. This was just like the night she'd taken the headache powders. He had no right to do this in spite of the electricity that hummed and sparked between them.

He drew back, his breath coming out in harsh gasps as he tried to regain control of his rampaging lust. He was in the elegant Garden Room at the Chesterfield rutting like a bull.

*What am I doing?*

Then Mac jerked him back down by his shirtfront and her busy fingers undid his buttons. Her fingernails grazed his chest as she worked the buttons free. "Damn it, Yates, don't you go all noble on me. I know exactly what I'm doing, and believe me, I want this." She paused and gazed up at him with heavy-lidded eyes that blatantly showed her arousal. "I want *you.*"

The last of Jared's reservations disappeared. Though he'd known Mac for only a short time, the fire that burned within him to possess her was like a conflagration, obliterating everything in its path.

Mac managed to open his shirt and slide her fingers through his curling chest hair. Jared threw back his head, biting his lip to control himself at her uninhibited touch. His erection throbbed and he knew he wouldn't last much longer. He shifted around and grasped the hem of Mac's skirt. Sliding his hands up her stockinged calves, he lifted the layers of skirts.

Her legs were willowy, and her muscles flexed and unflexed as he moved over them. She was beautiful, desirable, unrestrained—everything a man could want in a lover.

Finally her skirts were bunched around her waist, and he could smell her heat, her readiness for him. Her legs moved apart and she raised her hips, urging him to enter her.

"Not so fast," he whispered hoarsely.

In spite of his overwhelming need, Jared wanted to pleasure Mac first. He wanted her to scream out his name as her release washed across her.

Jared dipped his head toward hers and nuzzled her lips as he caressed her breast through the cloth. She moaned into his mouth and he increased the pressure on her nipple, thumbing it to a hard nubbin. He moved his hand down to her split drawers and to the springy hair surrounding her sex. His fingers skimmed across her mound and he felt the heated moisture at her entrance. He stroked her velvety flesh for a few moments as Mac's breathing grew more shallow and rapid. She arched upward, urging him to delve deeper.

"Does that feel good, Mac?" he whispered as he stared down into her flushed face.

"Oh God, Jared, yes. Don't . . . stop or I'll—" She was barely coherent.

"You'll what?"

She opened her eyes and reached for him, grabbing his head and yanking him close so she could kiss him with bruising intensity.

Every single muscle in Jared's body tightened and

he groaned deep in his throat. No woman had ever kissed him as though he were the only man left on earth.

He clamped down on his need to bury himself within her and continued to work his way farther into her dampness, opening her with his fingers. He found her swollen flesh and concentrated on that. Mac's motions became frantic as she bucked against his touch. She was moaning and panting, whispering his name over and over.

Then suddenly her entire body lifted off the couch. She cried out and throbbed around his fingers as she climaxed. Her passion spent for the moment, Mac fell back to the cushions, panting.

Jared nibbled her earlobe, then murmured, "Now we're ready."

He removed his hand from her pulsing center and unbuttoned his trousers to release his aching penis from its imprisonment. Leaning forward, he planted his hands on either side of Mac's shoulders to ready himself to enter her.

Then he looked at her and his breath caught in his throat. Her lips were slightly parted and the moonlight slanted across her, gilding her hair with silver. Her eyes were half closed as if she were caught in some world halfway between reality and a dream. A very erotic dream.

He'd never seen a woman so sensual, so desirable.

He took a deep shaky breath. He wanted to go slow, to spin out the enjoyment between them, to have them spiral out of control together.

She reached up, grabbed his arms and squeezed them desperately. "I need to feel you inside me."

Forget slow. This would be hard and fast. They both wanted it too badly.

He bent down to capture her lips with his while the lower part of his body sought their completion. Then Jared felt her fingers wrap around him and he nearly lost his tenuous control. He gritted his teeth and allowed her to guide him inside her.

She was drenched from her orgasm, yet her tunnel was tight as he entered her inch by inch. He wasn't surprised to discover she wasn't a virgin. A woman as bold as Mac would hold little regard for convention.

Finally he lay completely encircled by her snug heat. His breath rasped and he smiled to himself as her gasps sounded equally as harsh. She rotated her hips, letting him know she was ready. More than ready.

He withdrew slowly then plunged into her in one eager motion. She gasped, but it was a sound of rapture, not pain.

She wrapped her hands around his neck and pulled him close once more. Their kiss was almost feral as they nipped at lips and tongues. They wrestled and danced in a frenzy that matched the frenetic tempo of their mating.

Jared lost all track of time and place as her hips met his lunge for lunge. His world diminished to the sound of her fast shallow breathing, the smell of her aroused sex, the sight of her flushed face in the silver moonlight and the taste of her honeyed mouth.

He rotated slightly, and suddenly Mac was screaming and gripping his arms tight enough to leave bruises. She throbbed, clutching and releasing his hardness until his own orgasm was ripped from him. He arched, his mouth opening in a soundless cry as he emptied his seed deep within her.

Sated, Jared bonelessly draped over her heaving chest as he struggled to find the air he'd lost. He gath-

ered her in his arms and buried his face in the curve
of her neck and shoulder. Sweat dampened her skin
and plastered her hair to her forehead, but her relaxed
expression gave her a softer, more feminine appearance.

If her two climaxes had been half as incredible as
his, it was no wonder she lay so limp.

As his heartbeat returned to normal, doubts and re-
criminations began to appear. He'd behaved abomina-
bly toward a woman who had entrusted him with her
well-being. Although she hadn't been a virgin, his
guilt wasn't any less persistent. He'd courted Sophia
for a year and even after they were engaged, he had
only given her chaste kisses.

But then Mac wasn't anything like Sophia. Nothing
at all.

"Not bad, Yates." She opened one eye. "So how
well did I handle you?"

Any other woman would be wailing about her indiscretion, but not Mac. He couldn't help but smile.
"As well as I handled you."

She laughed softly. "And that wasn't half bad."

Her easy acceptance of their tryst shouldn't have
startled Jared, but it did. Unless she was expecting a
marriage proposal.

No. Any other woman would be planning a wedding, but not Mac.

He shifted off her, adjusted his disheveled clothing
and tried to make himself presentable. He turned away
as Mac stood unselfconsciously and shook her skirts
down. The smell of sex—salty and tangy—drifted
over to Jared, and his body reacted to the musky sensual odor, sending blood racing back to his groin.

Jared clenched his teeth. He should have been sat-
isfied, but it felt as if his body were regressing back

to the time when he first discovered how good women could make him feel. Only it wasn't just any woman, it was Mac.

The object of his distraction yawned widely and belatedly covered her mouth.

"Sorry," she said with a wry grin. "After fantastic sex like that, I could sleep like a baby."

Jared had talked himself out of believing Mac was crazy, but now he couldn't help but wonder again. Still, her drowsy eyes and artless appearance crept into his chest to lie beside his heart. Her swings from tough-talking lady to vulnerable sleepy child tantalized him and made him wish this was more than a temporary liaison. But that was out of the question.

In a week or two, he'd head back to the Staunton Pinkerton office where he was stationed. Unless there was another murder.

The bell began to toll.

"Midnight," Jared said.

Mac's gaze dropped, then returned to him and in her golden eyes he thought he detected moisture. "Merry Christmas, Jared," she said without the toughness to which he was accustomed.

He stared at her silently, wanting to discover the reason behind her sadness and knowing he wouldn't. They'd shared their bodies but his heart belonged only to himself, just as he suspected she tenaciously clung to hers. Besides, even if he would be willing to give his away, it wouldn't be to a brazen woman like Trish McAllister.

"Merry Christmas, Mac," he said. He barely stifled a yawn. "I suppose we should go to bed."

Mac grinned with familiar impudence. "Yours or mine?"

Jared's gut clenched as his gaze automatically

moved across her breasts and lower, his body having no trouble remembering . . . He swallowed hard and said firmly, "We'll each go to our own. I don't believe a repeat of tonight's indiscretion would be wise."

"You didn't enjoy it?"

He speared her with a sharp glance. Did she think he was made from stone? "It's not that." He shifted his weight from one foot to the other awkwardly. "What we did shouldn't have happened. It was the wine."

Mac crossed her arms and raised her chin. "Blame it on the wine if you want, Yates, but it wasn't that and we both know it."

Why couldn't she see that it had been wrong? Society didn't tolerate assignations such as theirs. "What if you get with child?"

Mac caught her breath. She'd never before forgotten about the pregnancy issue, as well as safe sex. Jared had been the first man to totally overwhelm her senses, the first man she'd had unprotected sex with since she had lost her virginity.

He had been the first man to put her pleasure before his.

Her world spun and she flung out a hand that latched onto a nearby chair. He was right. They could not have a repeat performance of tonight's mistake. There was too much at risk.

Including her heart.

*Where had that come from?*

Mac straightened her shoulders and glared at Jared. It was his fault this had happened. *He* had asked her to have dinner with him. *He* had kept refilling her wineglass. *He* was the one who suggested a tour of the Garden Room.

Damn him.

A faint train whistle sounded.

"Everyone's coming back from Christmas services in town," Jared said. "We should leave before someone spots us."

He reached for her to usher her out, but Mac hurried ahead before he could touch her. She might be mad as hell, but there was still something between them—a spark or pheromones or karma. She didn't want to know. All she wanted to do was get as far away from him as she could.

They walked down the hall silently, keeping a yard's distance between them. Mac had just experienced the most incredible sex in her life, and Jared had turned it into something tawdry. This was the first time in her handful of sexual encounters that it *hadn't* been tawdry . . . until he'd ruined it.

Her anger grew. How dare Jared treat it like some cheap affair.

*Isn't that what it was?* Mac's conscience taunted. He'd wined and dined her, then laid her.

*Jeezus, Mac, get a grip.* It wasn't as if she hadn't been going for the gold herself.

The lobby loomed ahead. It was as crowded as it had been empty earlier in the evening—people talking and laughing and exchanging hugs. Mac almost gagged. It looked like the final scene in *It's a Wonderful Life.*

A scream rose above the din and the buzz of conversations abruptly halted. Mac spotted one of the other maids she'd met her first day. Molly stood in the doorway, her red face streaked with tears and her snow-flecked hair falling out of the bun at the back of her neck.

Jared raced toward her and Mac followed without thought. She might only be a cleaning maid here at the Chesterfield, but she was first and foremost a reporter.

She dodged the startled guests and employees as she darted between them, keeping close on Jared's heels. She stumbled to a halt behind the Pinkerton as he grabbed hold of the hysterical girl's shoulders.

"What is it, miss?" he asked, keeping his voice steady and low.

The girl hiccuped between sobs and opened her mouth to speak, but no words came out.

"Relax. Take your time," Jared soothed.

Mac was impressed by Jared's composure and his ability to calm the frightened young woman.

"It's . . . L-Linda, my roommate." Another spate of tears interrupted.

Jared squeezed her shoulders gently. "It's all right."

"She's . . . d-dead. It's j-just awful." She covered her face with her hands.

Mac's heart leaped into her throat and her fingers curled into her palms. Though she had no logical reason to jump to a conclusion, her gut told her Linda had been strangled. Victim number five in the nineteenth century.

"Where is she?" Jared asked. His jaw was clenched, but his tone was gentle.

"B-behind the post office," the girl managed to reply.

One of the other employees reached out to comfort her and Jared released her into the waiting arms. His lips thinned and rage glittered in his blue eyes, then he ran out into the snowy night.

Mac started to follow, but a hand on her shoulder halted her. She turned to see Esme Sparrow's pale face as the Englishwoman held up her heavy cape.

"You'll need this if you are to accompany him," Esme said.

Startled, Mac nodded her thanks and accepted the warm garment. She donned it as she ran after Jared. The snow had diminished and Mac could make out the Pinkerton detective a hundred feet ahead of her. Oblivious to all but Jared's path, Mac hurried after him.

The walk was slippery from the snow and Mac's utilitarian shoes weren't made for running, but she wasn't about to abandon her quest because of an inconvenience or two. She was intimately familiar with the murderer's M.O. in her century. If she could examine the victim and crime scene here, she could determine if there was only one killer.

Her feet faltered. Did she really want to know? Wouldn't it be better if she just stayed out of it? This wasn't even her century. Why did she care?

*Because Jared cares.*

She shoved aside the little voice and increased her speed. Keeping her mind blank, she continued until she arrived at the resort post office, which she could barely make out in the darkness. She couldn't see Jared but did spot his footsteps in the fresh snow.

She followed them and found Jared and the corpse, which looked too much like the one Mac had seen five nights ago in her century. Snow dusted the dead woman's features, giving her a soft gentle appearance totally at odds with her violent death.

Mac took a deep breath and pushed her emotions into a far corner of her mind. A dark stain beside the girl's head and neck told Mac an artery had probably been nicked.

Jared glanced up from the grisly sight and spotted Mac. He rose to his feet in one smooth motion and stood between her and the mutilated body. "What the hell are you doing here?"

"I followed you," Mac replied. She sidestepped Jared's imposing figure and squatted down close to the body. "Was she strangled?"

"Damn it, Mac. You shouldn't be here."

"Was she strangled?" Mac repeated flatly.

His mouth pressed into a thin line and he nodded. "With a steel wire. It-it cut through the skin."

"Son of a—" she broke off. "Same as the other women?"

"Yes, except the wire didn't break the skin on the others." Jared stared at her, his mouth agape. "How do you know so much about the killings?" His scowl deepened. "Who the hell are you?"

Mac stalled by brushing her hands across Miss Sparrow's cape. What was she going to tell him? The truth?

*Not unless I want to be carted off to a hospital and spend the rest of my life banging my head against a wall.*

She would try to stay as close to the truth as possible without compromising her story. "I'm a freelance reporter. I covered another story involving the murders of five women, killed exactly like her." Mac pointed at the body. "The murderer was never apprehended."

Jared's mouth dropped open, then closed and opened again like a gaping fish. "Why the hell didn't you tell me?"

She crossed her arms, surprised to find her hands were trembling. "Because at first I thought you might be the killer."

"Me?"

Though Mac was shaking on the inside, she remained cool and composed on the outside. "It was possible. Your job allows you to travel."

Jared stepped close to Mac, invading her personal space, but she refused to relinquish an inch.

"But my fiancée was one of the victims. Why would I want to kill her?" His voice was low and angry, more dangerous because it was so controlled.

Mac's heart thundered as her palms dampened. She fought to remain still, to meet his furious eyes. "Men kill their wives and girlfriends all the time, Yates. Surely in your line of work you've seen it often enough."

His furious expression was enough to terrify the bravest of men, but Mac wouldn't be intimidated. This was too important.

She held his stare for a few moments longer, then turned away and moved closer to the body. Squatting beside it, she forced herself to examine the murder scene and body with a clinical eye. She leaned closer to the wire around the victim's neck. It appeared to be the same type the killer had used in her time—a piano wire.

"May I roll her over?" Mac asked without glancing at Jared.

Muttered curses met her ears, but Jared joined her and carefully shifted the woman to her side. Mac craned her neck to see the wire and found what she suspected would be there: two twists near the victim's nape.

The exact modus operandi the serial killer used in her time.

# ELEVEN

Just when he thought Mac couldn't shock him anymore, he found her doing it again. To discover she was a reporter following a story involving the murders of other women killed in the same manner had been a helluva surprise.

Now she was examining a dead body with the practiced ease of a seasoned Pinkerton. Even some of them would have been hard-pressed to look at this scene without losing their last meal.

She pointed to the wire at the back of the victim's neck. "See those two twists?"

He bent over and spied what she meant. "Yes."

"The victims from my, uh, from San Francisco had the same pattern—the steel wire twisted around twice behind the victim's neck."

She straightened but remained kneeling on the ground as Jared lowered the body to its original position.

"So you're saying the same man who killed those women in San Francisco is here now?"

Shoving her short hair back from her forehead with an impatient hand, she nodded. "If my theory is correct, he splits each year between here and there. The women in San Francisco were killed in late June and mid-December. Here they're murdered when?"

"Right after Christmas, then in June," Jared replied, marveling at how composed Mac appeared.

The woman who had been flushed with passion an hour ago had disappeared and in her place was an objective observer. Her analytical approach to this murder, as well as her aplomb when talking about the other victims, astounded him. There were female Pinkerton detectives who could contain their delicate sensibilities, too, but they had been trained to do so. Mac was a newspaper reporter. She should have been writing the latest social gossip column, not studying the bloody corpse of a woman who could have been her.

Jared struck back the rising fear that Mac *could* have been the latest victim of the insane killer. She had been with him so she was alive and well. But this woman was dead because he *had* been with Mac.

"Do you have pictures of the other victims?" Mac asked.

"Photographs?"

She nodded. "Though I'm fairly certain we're looking for the same killer, it would be nice to have my theory confirmed before we go off on a wild goose chase. If the wire was twisted in the same pattern on the other victims, then we'll have a validated match."

This person didn't even sound like the brash woman he'd come to know. Now her concentration was on the corpse, her mind sorting through the visual facts in front of her and whatever information she had gathered from the other murders.

"Did you know her?" Jared asked.

Her mask slipped, revealing a hint of grief through the exposed crack. "Yeah. She showed me where the cleaning supplies were my first day of work. She was a nice girl. Quiet. Shy."

She drew a hand across her eyes and Jared would have sworn he saw moisture glistening in them, but the sound of people approaching diverted his attention.

Chief of Police Garrett led a small group of men toward them but halted abruptly at the sight of the body.

"What's going on, Yates?" the policeman demanded, puffing in the cool winter air.

Mac rose unobtrusively and tried to melt into the background. Her lie might satisfy Jared, but she wasn't sure about the local authorities. She didn't want to have to deal with another Sheriff Longley.

"She was strangled with a wire just like Sophia and the other three women," Jared said.

"Son of a bitch," Garrett said, running a hand across his hair. "Anybody see anything?"

Jared shook his head. "I don't think so, unless that friend of hers—"

"Molly," Mac supplied automatically.

"Molly saw something," Jared finished.

Garrett aimed a sharp gaze in her direction. "Who are you?"

"Trish McAllister," Mac said, extending a hand to the lawman.

A smile touched Garrett's face as he shook the extended hand. "Miss McAllister. You remind me a little of my wife."

Mac frowned. She had only said a few words and shook his hand—why would he say that?

"What's your interest in this?" Garrett asked, his smile vanishing.

"She's a reporter," Jared replied.

Mac shot him a glare. "I have a voice, Yates."

The Pinkerton glowered and turned away to make a closer inspection of the murder victim.

"You're a reporter?" the law officer asked.

"That's right."

"And what does that have to do with this?" He motioned toward the body.

"That's my business." She quickly looked over at Jared who met her eyes and she repeated. *"My* business."

Jared's jaw muscle jumped into his cheek, but miraculously he kept his mouth shut.

Garrett's eyes narrowed as he seemed to sense the undercurrents between her and Jared. The lawman was sharp, sharper than the county sheriff she'd dealt with in the past. Future.

*Whatever.*

The constable nodded shortly. "I trust Yates to deal with it. And you." He walked over to Jared and hunkered down beside him.

Mac remained rooted in place, shamelessly eavesdropping on the two men's conversation.

"Same type of wire. Another young pretty unwed woman." Garrett cursed. "I hate this, Jared. No clues, nothing left behind as to who this son of a bitch could be."

Jared nodded curtly. "Yeah, I know. It's like he sneaks in, does his dirty work, then disappears."

*Which isn't too far off the mark,* Mac thought somberly. Had the man disappeared into the future again to continue his killing spree? She frowned, recalling the dates of the murders in her time. No, if the murderer kept to his pattern, he wouldn't kill there again until June.

How did he control his leaps in time? Though Mac, too, found herself stranded in the nineteenth century, she had to wait until she completed some task before she could return on the summer solstice.

Was the killer's task to murder women so he could return to the other time period during the solstices?

Mac's stomach rolled and she barely restrained the impulse to vomit. If her task was anything like the murderer's, she'd stay in the nineteenth century.

She returned her attention to the lawman and the Pinkerton.

"I wasn't expecting him to kill again until after the holiday," Jared was saying. "The last two holiday murders were between Christmas and New Year's." He fisted a hand. "Damn it, Garrett, I should've been out patrolling this area. Instead I was—" He broke off, clearing his throat.

Mac's insides froze. If he had been out patrolling instead of having hot and heavy sex with her, he might have been able to save this girl. Mac's eyes filled with moisture, but she bit her lower lip to hold back the tears.

*Don't you dare lay this on me, Yates.*

No, Jared wouldn't blame her. *She* blamed herself. If only she had pressured him more about the deaths, maybe they could have prevented this one.

However, the murderer was ruthless. Even if they'd deterred him from this killing, what about the next woman walking alone? Or if Jared saved that one, what about the next one?

No, the only thing that could stop this pathological killer was catching him. Or killing him.

In spite of the cape's warmth, Mac shivered.

Jared approached her stiffly. "You should go back before you freeze. We'll handle it from here."

"But—"

"No buts, Mac." His granite expression didn't bode well for her chances of winning this argument. "I'm sure you've gotten enough for your story."

His frigid tone startled her as did the fury blazing in his eyes. He thought the story was all that mattered to her.

Her conscience kicked her. Hard. Wasn't her goal to write a Pulitzer Prize-winning story? A sensational case like this, especially with the time-travel element factored in was bound to gain her what she coveted—worldwide recognition and her father's humiliation.

Let Jared think what he wanted. Her dream was within her grasp and nobody was going to stop her from grabbing the brass ring.

Drawing her dignity around her, Mac lifted her chin. "If I have any other questions, I'll ask Chief Garrett."

She whirled around to leave, but a strong hand latched onto her arm, spinning her back.

Jared leaned close, his mouth inches from her nose. Gone was the tender lover and in his place was an angry, desperate Pinkerton detective. "If you have any questions, you come to me, Miz McAllister." He made her name sound like a curse. "In fact, I'll be coming to talk to you tomorrow to get all the information you have about this bastard. And you *will* give me everything. Do you understand?" His eyes were shards of blue ice.

Mac shivered and nodded almost against her will. "I understand," she managed to say with a dose of venom.

He gave her a shove—not hard, but not gentle either. "Go on back and get some rest." He turned to one of the men who'd followed the town lawman to the crime scene. "Hailey, escort Miz McAllister back to the hotel."

Mac wanted to argue further, but her tongue remained stuck to the roof of her mouth. She turned around, Esme's cape spinning around her ankles, and marched away, vaguely aware of her "bodyguard" scurrying to catch up.

Back in her time, she never had a problem holding her own with a man. So why was Jared different? Why couldn't she tell him where to get off?

Why had she let him send her home as if she were a naughty child?

As she tramped across the uneven ground, Mac's temper cooled. She'd been complaining that nobody was who they appeared to be at the Chesterfield, yet she was guilty of the same pretense. Of course, she hadn't planned to tell Jared that she was a reporter or that she had been on the killer's trail for two years.

Hell, she hadn't planned any of this insanity—not falling back in time or getting it on with one of the nineteenth-century natives or letting herself feel something for someone.

She shoved the latter thought aside.

*Starving hormones.* That's all their sexual encounter had been. No maudlin emotions, no stupid fairy-tale ending. Nothing but pure unadulterated sex. Intercourse. Copulation. Whatever word they used in this stone age, it had only been animalistic urges.

By the time she and her silent bodyguard arrived at the Chesterfield, Mac had convinced herself of two things. First, from now on she would remain com-

pletely objective to pursue her story. No more hanky-
panky with the Pinkerton. And second, Mac was not
falling for Jared Yates because love was for fools and
she, by God, was nobody's fool.


The sound of voices outside her door awakened
Mac and she opened bleary eyes to see sunlight
streaming in the window. Erin's bed was neatly made
with no sign that the girl had been there, but Mac had
seen her sleeping last night when she'd returned to
the room.

More hushed voices from the hallway made her
wiggle out of her cocoon of warmth. It was a good
thing she had the day off or she would have been two
hours late for the Major's inspection.

The doorknob turned and the door opened far
enough that Mac could see Erin peeking in.

"Are ye awake?" the Irish girl asked softly.

Mac sat up and raked a hand through her tangled
hair. "As awake as I'm going to be until I get my first
cup of coffee."

Erin glanced behind her and Mac frowned, wondering who was with her. She didn't have long to
wonder as Erin entered, followed by her two shadows
Jane and Louise. Seeing Jane, Mac almost groaned.
She had a sneaking suspicion she was in for an in-
quisition.

"Did ye hear about Linda?" Erin asked. Before
Mac could answer, she went on, "She was murdered.
They say strangled." Erin shivered as dread filled
her face. "There are rumors that there have been
four other girls killed the same way in the past two
years."

Mac crossed her arms, eyeing her roommate. "It's

true. The killer's also murdered five other women in another place." *Another time.*

A trio of gasps greeted Mac's quiet announcement.

"How do you know?" Jane demanded.

*That was the million-dollar question.* Jared, Chief Garrett and the men who'd been gathered around the body all knew she was a reporter. It would be common knowledge before long.

"I'm a reporter. I trailed the killer from San Francisco," she said.

"That's a long ways away," Erin commented, her eyes wide.

*You wouldn't believe how far.*

"So you're not Miss Sparrow's cousin?" Jane demanded.

Damn. There were getting to be too many angles to cover.

"Actually we are. It was as good a cover as any." Mac shrugged.

"Are you and Mr. Yates working together?" Jane asked.

*That'll be a cold day in hell.*

"Not exactly. Last night at dinner, I was asking him questions," Mac said. *And then we got down and dirty in the Garden Room.* Her cheeks warmed with the memory of Jared within her, his body pleasuring hers in ways she'd only read about. She forced herself back to the present. "He's been investigating the killings since the first murder two years ago."

"It was his fiancée, wasn't it?" Erin asked softly.

Mac nodded solemnly. "She was the first victim."

Erin sank onto her bed and Louise, her face pale, sat beside her. Jane, however, remained standing.

"It could've been any of us, couldn't it?" Louise asked.

Mac glanced at the shy girl and saw that she understood more than the other girls. There was more to Louise than she had first assumed. "Yeah, it could've been." She scowled. "We have to let every woman here know what's going on. We have to warn them not to walk alone after dark."

"If this was the fifth victim, why weren't we warned before?" Erin asked.

"Because the men who own this place would rather risk our lives than sully their precious resort's reputation." Mac didn't bother to hide her fury.

The three girls exchanged anxious looks.

"We'll help," Louise said, an unfamiliar spark in her eyes. "I wouldn't be able to live with myself if another woman is killed because we didn't do anything."

"Louise is right," Erin said. "We have to warn everyone."

"We could lose our jobs," Jane spoke up.

Though Mac knew this, she was uncertain how Jane did. "Why do you say that?" Mac asked.

Jane's hands twisted in the folds of her skirt as she paced the room. "I've heard the rumors from other people who've been here longer. I didn't understand what they were talking about until now. The resort's image is to be protected at all times," she stated as if she'd been programmed.

Mac leaned forward, the blankets slipping to her waist to reveal the camisole she'd slept in. "At the cost of women's lives?"

"It's a small risk for the benefits of working here," Jane said flatly. "I've been broke and alone, doing what I had to in order to survive. I don't want to go back to that life."

She turned and rushed from the room, slamming the door behind her.

Mac could understand her position. She'd spent some time in the street herself after one of her foster parents had tried to beat her. She would never forget the fear and hopelessness she'd lived with for nearly two weeks before Social Services found her again.

"Do you think she'll tell the Major?" Mac asked.

"I don't know," Erin replied. She and Louise stood. "We're going into town later to attend church service. Would ye like to join us?"

Mac thought of her empty pockets and shook her head. "No, I can't." She aimed a forefinger at them. "Stick together, okay?"

Erin and Louise smiled.

"We will," Erin assured. "Don't ye go anywhere by yourself either."

Mac's throat suddenly felt thick. It had been a long time since anyone actually worried about her well-being. "I'll be fine. Go on and have a Merry Christmas."

Erin leaned over and gave her a hug, surprising her. "Merry Christmas to ye, too, Mac," the girl said.

Louise gave her a quick embrace, too, and wished her a happy holiday. Then the two younger women left Mac alone and wondering why her vision was blurry.

Jared paced the lobby for the fifteenth time as he watched the entrance he knew Mac would come through. But so far, he'd seen no sign of the woman.

The reporter.

Damn.

He'd gotten little sleep and had risen just as the

sun topped the horizon. While he had slept, visions of the five murdered women had crept into his nightmares. He had dreamed of last night's victim, only her face had transformed into Sophia's and he'd relived the pain and grief of his betrothed's death once more.

He scrubbed a hand across his face, belatedly realizing he had forgotten to shave this morning. No wonder everyone was making a wide berth around him. He probably looked like a vagrant who had come inside to beg for food.

He spotted Mac's familiar figure and a frisson of desire slid through him. Though she'd lied to him, she still had the power to affect him. There was no doubt she was a beautiful woman, even dressed in the same old uniform she'd been wearing ever since she began to work here. He recalled the denim trousers that she had worn when she'd arrived, how they had hugged her backside and legs. His blood rapidly heated.

"Down, boy," he muttered to himself. He had more important things to think about than Mac's long slender legs that had wrapped about his waist last night while he had—

Seeing Mac headed to the employees' dining hall, Jared hurried to cut her off before she could enter. He caught her arm just outside the entrance.

Startled, she blinked up at him and her surprise changed to anger. "Let me go, Yates."

"Not until we've talked."

"Not until I have my breakfast."

The equally strong-willed persons faced off and Jared couldn't help but admire her backbone. "Then we'll talk while you're eating."

She shrugged. "Suit yourself."

He released her and followed her into the dining hall, which was more utilitarian than where the guests ate. Jared had been in here before, but it hadn't been nearly as crowded as it was now.

"Why don't you find a place for us to sit and I'll join you after I get my coffee?" Mac suggested.

Jared eyed her suspiciously. An acquiescent Mac made him nervous. "You won't try to escape?"

A grim smile touched her lips. "Where would I go?"

"All right," Jared finally said. "I'll be right over there." He pointed to a corner where fewer people were gathered.

She nodded and strode to the front of the room.

Keeping his attention divided between Mac and his objective, Jared wove between the tables and benches. His gaze followed Mac as she moved with innate grace, filling her coffee cup and going through the line where the food was served. Once her plate was full, she maneuvered around her fellow employees to drop onto the bench across from him.

Her golden eyes danced with laughter. "Afraid I was going to slip out on you?"

"The thought crossed my mind," Jared admitted.

Mac forked a piece of biscuit and gravy into her mouth. "Have you eaten?"

He nodded impatiently. "Three hours ago."

"Then it's time for a snack." She handed him one of the muffins on her plate. "Here. Hope you like blueberry. The strawberry's mine."

Startled by her consideration, Jared accepted it without comment and took a bite. "It's pretty good."

"Yeah, they are."

Jared looked at her steaming coffee cup and wished she would've brought one of those for him, too.

"Have a drink," Mac offered as if reading his mind. She grinned and lowered her voice. "After all the bodily fluids we exchanged last night, I doubt that drinking from the same cup will hurt us."

Jared's face flushed hotly. "Doesn't anything embarrass you?" he asked in a barely audible tone.

Mac thought for a moment. "Yes, but if that comment bothers you, you'd really be mortified if I told you what did."

*No doubt about it, the woman had balls.*

He picked up her coffee cup, keeping his focus aimed at the rising steam instead of Mac's face and took a sip of the strong bitter brew. He set it back down. "Thanks."

Mac continued to eat as Jared watched her put away a plate filled with scrambled eggs, hash browns, two pieces of sausage, biscuits and gravy and the strawberry muffin. And that after a huge steak the previous night. He had never seen a woman eat so much.

"All right. I'm done. Fire away," she said and took a sip of coffee.

Her lips touched the cup where his mouth had been earlier. The memory of her lips opening beneath his ambushed him. He stared at her mouth, wondering what she'd do if he leaned over and kissed her.

"Haven't you ever seen a woman drink coffee before, Yates?" she asked.

Her sarcasm slammed him back to reality and he leaned back in his chair, affecting nonchalance. "Most women drink tea."

She snorted. "Just tally another mark for my scandalous character."

He couldn't help but smile. "You don't care, do you?"

"Why should I?" She studied him. "Let's cut to the chase and get to the question-and-answer part of our little soiree."

All right. He could play tough, too. "Who the hell are you?"

# TWELVE

*That's the million-dollar question.*

Mac had known without a doubt who she was five days ago, but that was before a bored supreme being decided to have a little fun at her expense: Trish McAllister, maid extraordinaire, whose specialty was scrubbing toilets.

No, she was still a reporter and had no intention of giving that up, especially now with the story of a lifetime at her fingertips.

"I told you, I'm a reporter," she finally replied. "I do freelance work for various newspapers around the country."

"You sell stories to them?" Jared asked.

She wrinkled her nose. "I'm not going to give them away. It's better than doing this." She made a sweeping gesture at her uniform.

His eyes narrowed. "Why haven't I heard of you?"

"I write under a pen name."

"What is it?"

Mac pushed her empty plate away, cursing the Fates who had put her between a rock and a hard place.

*A rock and Jared Yates.*

"T. A. McAllister," she finally said.

"I've never heard of it," Jared fired back.

She met his glare without flinching. "Do you know every reporter in the country?"

He scowled and his gaze faltered.

Mac pressed her advantage. "Tell me what you know about the murderer."

"And why would I do that?" Jared demanded.

Mac leaned forward and said in a low intense voice, "Because you want this bastard even more than I do and working together is the only way to get him."

She could tell she'd struck a nerve, but instead of feeling victorious, she felt guilty for using his guilt against him. But isn't that what made her such a good reporter? She found the soft underbelly of her adversary and went for it. Even though she'd slept with Jared, he was no different than any other source. So why had her conscience suddenly decided to lodge a complaint?

"Why are *you* so hell-bent on catching him?" Jared asked, his eyebrows drawn together.

Yates obviously used the same tactic, and Mac found she didn't like being on the receiving end. Not one damned bit. "It's a helluva scoop," she simply replied.

Jared stared at her as though she were something he'd stepped in while walking through a barn. "You're after a story. I'm after revenge and justice. If you get in my way, I won't hesitate to push you aside. Do you understand?"

The frigid tone of the Pinkerton's voice nearly froze Mac's blood, but she wouldn't give him the satisfaction. She lifted her chin. "I understand."

He glanced around. "Let's find someplace a little more private to talk."

"How about the Garden Room?" Mac asked without thinking.

Jared's lips thinned and his jaw muscle jumped. "If we had stayed away from there last night, a woman wouldn't be dead."

"Don't you dare blame her death on me." Mac's breath hissed in and out as she fisted her hands. "It takes two to tango, Yates."

She jumped to her feet and strode to the door, her hands clenching the tray tightly. She piled it and her utensils in their correct places, then stomped out.

Jared caught her wrist and yanked her into a secluded alcove. He grasped her upper arms and backed her against the wall, giving her no escape. His eyes sparked with fury. She had never seen him so angry and for a moment she feared he would strike her.

"I'm not blaming anyone's death on you, Mac," he said quietly, in direct contrast to his furious expression. "I take sole responsibility for my actions. If I hadn't been acting like a boy instead of a man, I would have been doing my job." Self-condemnation replaced his rage.

Mac had the insane urge to wrap her arms around him and comfort him. She could deal with a brash, angry Jared easier than she could this guilt-ridden man. She felt little tremors skating along his muscles and wondered how much longer he could hold himself together. Her own control was fading and she reached deep down inside herself to maintain her cynicism.

"And if I hadn't been acting like a love-starved old maid, we wouldn't have ended up where we did," Mac said without flinching. "So we can either keep kicking our own asses or we can start acting like adults and stop this son of a bitch before he kills another woman."

Jared's anguish transformed to reluctant admiration and his gaze settled on Mac's lips. She felt the beginnings of his arousal against her belly and her own desire flared. She closed her eyes, fighting the relentless attraction that scattered her brain cells to the wind.

"Only pheromones," she whispered.

"What?" Jared asked.

Mac opened her eyes to find Jared's confused expression inches away. She shook her head. "Nothing. Let's go find someplace where we won't be overheard."

Jared released her and took a step back. Without his hard-planed body pressed against hers, Mac could think more clearly.

"How about your room?" she asked.

"Are you crazy?"

She was on much firmer ground now and planted her hands on her hips. "Where else can we go where we won't be overheard by curious eavesdroppers?"

Resignation stole across Jared's features. "All right, but I don't think it's a good idea."

"Are you afraid we won't be able to keep our hands to ourselves?" Mac jeered.

He glared. "If you can control yourself, I can. What if someone sees us?"

Mac rolled her eyes. Sometimes she felt as though she were back in high school trying to make out with her boyfriend. "I think that people around here don't have enough to keep them occupied and out of another person's business."

Jared sighed and took her arm. "All right, but we can at least keep to the back stairs so there will be less chance anyone will see us."

"Whatever."

Mac allowed herself to be pulled up the smaller darker staircase that she used when doing her job.

They went up two flights and down a long hallway. Jared's room was at the end; he unlocked the door and then ushered her inside ahead of him.

Mac glanced around, impressed because she knew the maid hadn't been in, yet the room was neat and tidy. It looked like the Pinkerton detective was anal retentive about cleanliness in addition to his other annoying habits.

Jared motioned to one of the two chairs. "Sit."

She did so, then admired the rear view as Jared leaned over to drag out a suitcase from beneath the bed. She had to admit his tight buns more than made up for his annoying habits. She watched Jared unlock the bag and draw out a file of papers filled with handwriting.

"That's right, no computers," she mumbled.

Jared's head swiveled around to her. "What?"

She waved a hand. "Nothing. Are those all your notes?"

He nodded. "From the four previous murders. There are newspaper articles from the *Hope Springs Times,* too."

She reached for them, but he pulled them back. "I have one condition."

Mac rolled her eyes. "What?"

"This is completely off-the-record. There're some things in here that haven't made it into the newspapers." His gaze drilled into her. "And I want to keep it that way. Do you understand?"

"Then why are you letting me read it? I told you I'm a reporter."

Disappointment shadowed his features. "I thought the most important thing was catching the killer." He tucked the papers back in the bag. "I guess I was wrong."

"No!" Mac startled herself by her vehement denial. "You're right. Catching the man who's killing these women *is* more important than a newspaper story. But once he's captured, I have exclusive rights."

Jared studied her, his expression closed and forbidding. Mac didn't like feeling like a bacterium under a microscope, especially when the scientist was Jared Yates.

"All right," he finally said. "I have your word?"

She held up her right hand. "Scout's honor."

His lips eased into a slight smile as he withdrew the papers and handed them to her.

Mac uncrossed the fingers of her hidden left hand and accepted the pile of notes. She sat on the bed, tucking one leg beneath her, and leaned against the headboard.

In a few moments, she was engrossed in the notes and speculations about their killer.

Jared finished writing his notes about the latest murder and set aside the last piece of paper. He'd filled three sheets as Mac had studied all the information on the first four victims. His gaze strayed to her as it had often done during the past hour. Her puckered brow and the firm set of her full lips revealed her intense concentration as she perused the pages. It appeared that she threw herself wholeheartedly into whatever situation she was in, whether it was making love or doing her job.

She fascinated him. It had been a long time since anyone—man or woman—had confounded him like this. In fact, he couldn't think of a single person who had managed to surprise him as much as she did. It wasn't simply her energetic participation in making love, but her odd views on subjects he'd always taken for granted. Would his niece be happier as a doctor than a wife and mother? He hadn't even considered such a thing.

All he knew was that Mac kept him on his toes and he enjoyed their verbal sparring. Admitting that to her, however, was not an option.

"I see the previous December victims were killed between Christmas and New Year's. The first—" Mac paused and Jared caught her hesitant glance. He steeled himself for her next words.

"Your fiancée was murdered on the thirtieth, then the second woman was killed on the twenty-eighth."

Jared came to his feet to pace. "And the third on Christmas Eve. I was under the assumption that the killer would wait until after Christmas again, but I was wrong."

Mac shook her head. "There's no pattern, Jared, so you couldn't have known."

He stopped in front of her and leaned close. "Maybe not, but I suspected. If I had gone with my hunch, maybe that girl would be alive today."

"And maybe not," Mac said softly. Her gaze turned inward. "Even if you had guessed correctly, there's no guarantee you would've been in the right place at the right time."

He studied her pensive face, wary of her reflective tone. "What aren't you telling me, Mac?"

She blinked, startled out of her thoughts. At first he thought he'd pushed too hard as she retreated behind a stone mask. Then she spoke and though her tone was flat, her eyes were haunted with anguish. "I had my chance at saving a life, too. I blew it. I knew when, but not where." She stood and crossed her arms, then rubbed her chin. "The murders in June in my time were the twenty-ninth the first year and the twenty-fifth the second."

"Your 'time?' "

"My time in San Francisco," she said quickly as her cheeks flushed.

Jared's instincts told him she was lying, but why? She'd already confessed that she was a reporter working on the story. What else would she be hiding?

Unless she suspected who the killer was.

He squelched the thought. If she did, she would have told him. Wouldn't she? Another thought struck him and he leaned over to pick up the papers scattered across the bed and searched through them.

As if sensing his agitation, she moved up beside him and looked over his arm. "What're you looking for?"

"The dates for the June killings that occurred here."

Mac sucked in a quick breath, but remained silent.

Finally Jared found what he was looking for. "They were both killed the twentieth. I don't know what time, however. The bodies were discovered that day, but it was believed they'd been killed sometime during the previous night." His brow furrowed in confusion. "How the hell did he get from San Francisco to Virginia in four days?"

"Shit," Mac muttered.

"What?"

She glanced at him hesitantly, which was odd because Mac was rarely nervous. "Train?" she murmured.

"It's possible, but the killer would have to leave immediately after killing the women in San Francisco." He paused. "What about those women killed in December?"

Mac dropped her gaze to the papers spread across

the bed, though she knew the answers weren't there. "All of them were killed the night of the twentieth, somewhere around midnight."

"That only gave him four days to get here this last time." Jared stalked from one end of the room to the other, raking a hand through his hair. "How does he get from San Francisco here so quickly? Fly?" He glanced at Mac and saw downcast eyes and pursed lips. "Do you really believe the murderer you're after is the same one who's been killing here?"

She shrugged, strangely ambiguous for someone usually so forthright. "The method is the same, including the twists of the wire, but there could be two murderers working together."

Jared didn't want to think about two such killers walking around. It was difficult enough to believe that one person could be so evil. "I'll check out the train schedules, find out if it's possible for someone to travel across the country in four days."

Mac nodded, but didn't comment. Her expression was closed, not giving Jared a clue to her thoughts. He had become accustomed to her vocalizing her opinion and her silence bothered him. Maybe the murders had upset her more than she allowed him to see.

He stepped over to her slumped figure, intending to lay his hands on her shoulders, but stopped short of touching her. "Are you all right?"

She jerked her head up, surprised by his nearness. Some of her usual fire flashed in her eyes. "I was until you nearly scared the hell out of me."

Jared chuckled with relief. "Sorry," he said without contrition. He sobered and asked hesitantly, "Are the murders bothering you?"

She glared at him. "Back off, Yates. The only thing

we're sharing is information about the murders. You keep out of my head and I'll keep out of yours."

Both puzzled and angry, Jared couldn't decide which feeling was stronger. He forced his voice to remain calm and even. "I didn't ask you for your life history, Mac. I'm only concerned. Seeing the victims is enough to give me nightmares. I thought you might want to talk about it."

Her fingers tightened around her crossed arms and Jared knew they would leave red imprints on her golden skin.

"There's a psycho out there killing young women. He isn't raping or molesting them. He isn't torturing them. He's merely wrapping a wire around their necks and strangling them." She stared at Jared. "What's there to talk about besides finding a motive for this sick bastard?"

Not a single ounce of emotion colored her voice and Jared shivered inwardly. Was Mac that unfeeling that she could talk about these deaths as she would discuss the weather?

No, that wasn't fair. He had caught glimpses of agony in her expression, but if she didn't want consolation, who was he to offer it? Maybe this was her way of dealing with the horrific crimes and it would be best to respect her wish.

He nodded slowly. "Do you have any idea about a motive?"

She appeared relieved as she shook her head. "Maybe he gets off on the power of life and death? He decides who lives and who dies."

Jared caught the gist of her speculation, even though he didn't understand her exact wording. But, then, hadn't it been like that since the moment she'd fallen into his life?

"Something like being a judge?" he asked.

"Let's take it a step further—maybe he thinks he's a god." Something slid across her features, but it was gone before Jared could identify it. "Why a piano wire?"

He tucked his hands in his trouser pockets and began to pace anew. "It must have some significance for him."

Mac nodded, her lips twisted into a grimace. "Maybe his mother made him take piano lessons when he was a boy, so he punishes other women for what his mother forced him to do."

Jared halted and stared at her.

"What?" Mac demanded.

"Where did you come up with that?"

She shrugged. "I took a few psychology courses in college." A twinkle appeared in her eyes. "Just enough to make me dangerous."

Jared's mind reeled. "You went to college? Where?"

Mac groaned silently. Damn, she was getting more and more careless. She hated coming up with lies to account for things that defied explanation. *Keep it simple; less chance to get tangled up in the web of fabrications.*

"I told you I was a reporter," she stated as if that explained everything.

Jared neared her, stopping only a foot in front of her. His eyes were blue laser points aimed directly at her. "You show up on a train in clothes I've never seen on a woman before. You spout words I've never heard before and accuse me of being a liar. Then you change your tune when Esme Sparrow says you're her cousin, but there is little family resemblance. You become a maid when you are in fact a reporter doing a story on a murderer." He paused, searching, and Mac held his gaze, afraid if she looked away, he would see through her transparent deception. "What do you plan on becoming next? The queen of England?"

In that moment, Mac wished she could tell him the truth, but that would have been harder to swallow than being the queen of England. "I *am* a reporter, Jared. That is the honest-to-God truth."

"Why do I have this feeling you and the truth parted ways a long time ago?"

Mac's cheeks burned as she stabbed his chest with her forefinger. "The truth is all I have, all I believe in. It's the reason I became a reporter, to dig past the lies and facades to find the facts. I'd had it up to here," she drew an imaginary line across her forehead, "with people who showed one face to the world and another behind closed doors."

Pain jabbed her, striking behind her eyelids and slamming up into her brow. She had to get away from him before she lost it, before she blurted out things she herself would have to confront.

She twirled around and fled. In the hallway, she spotted Jane who was frozen like a deer caught in headlights. She stared at Mac, then her gaze shifted to Jared who stood behind Mac in his room. The shocked waitress spun away and hurried down the carpeted hall.

"Son of a—" Jared swore.

Mac turned to be caught in his murderous glare and her insides seized up. She pressed her arms into her belly. Could she blame him for not even wanting to be associated with her?

*That crazy McAllister woman.*

She could hear the mutterings as if they'd just been spoken, instead of being echoes from more than fifteen years ago. Before her mother had been institutionalized for her own safety and her daughter's.

Stifling a cry, Mac swept down the hall in the opposite direction. She heard Jared call to her, but she shut his voice out, hearing only the voices in her past.

She scurried down the back stairs and found herself in the kitchen. Chef Sashenka's Russian accent washed across her as she listened to him issue orders to his helpers. Before he spied her, Mac ducked out and forced herself to walk calmly through the guests' dining hall. One person called out to her asking for more coffee, but Mac ignored him.

Finally in the lobby, Mac found shelter behind a large potted plant and leaned her head back against the wall. Pictures and sounds from her childhood plucked at her tenuous control.

*She's crazy as a loon. Keeps singing these old songs.*

*He doesn't want you.*

*You are remanded to the court for placement within a foster home.*

*You have the devil in you, but don't you worry, I'll get rid of him.*

The belt descended and Mac jerked as if she could feel the leather lash against her back just as she had so many years ago.

"What're ye doin' there, lass?"

Mac's heart leaped into her throat. It took her a few moments to recognize the grizzled countenance of Jack O'Riley peering at her with something that resembled concern.

She drew a wrist across her cheeks and was shocked to find dampness on them. She hadn't shed a tear even when her mother died.

"Thinking," she replied. Stepping out of her hiding place, Mac eyed the sixty-something man's bloodshot eyes. "Too many Christmas spirits?" she managed to ask with a teasing note.

He smiled self-consciously. "Just a spot o' good Irish whiskey to celebrate the birth of the baby Jesus." His stale liquor breath washed over her and she automatically took a step back.

Mac waved a hand in front of her nose. "Must've been a helluva spot."

"Don't ye know there's nothin' small in Ireland?" He winked.

Mac laughed, the bad memories fading under the Irishman's joshing. "Be careful, Jack. I'll be thinkin' that you're flirtin' with me," she said with an affected brogue.

"Now ye're pullin' an old man's leg."

"Only your leg, Jack." Mac grinned.

He shook an admonishing finger at her. "You're a fresh one, Trish McAllister." A smile lit his liquor-flushed face. "I pity the lad who tries to court ye."

Mac grimaced. "Then there's no one to pity." She glanced around. "It's quiet today."

"Aye, but only till this evenin'. There'll be carols sung in the ballroom tonight. A tradition here at the Chesterfield." His chest puffed up like a robin who'd found a juicy worm.

"You keep doing that and you'll be popping those buttons off your jacket."

He sighed. "Then me Bridget will be nailin' my hide to the wall. Remember, I told ye she used to work here before she married. Now she's got a little one with another on the way." Pride filled his blood-shot eyes. "I used ta think she'd never wed, but finally my prayers were answered and I have wee ones to spoil."

When Mac had been young and foolish, she'd dreamed of meeting a man who would love her. A man who would be an equal in everything, from love-making and child rearing to housework and careers. But she had expected too much. Maybe that had come from reading "Cinderella" too often as a child.

That kind of fantasy was someone's idea of a joke, a very sexist joke. *Get a life, Cinderella.*

*Like you* have *a life?* a little voice whispered from deep within Mac.

# THIRTEEN

With a flick of her wrist, Mac brushed her unruly hair off her forehead and pressed her shoulders back. The other women had already been in proper formation when Mac stumbled in beneath the dark disapproving mien of the Major. Could she help it if the off-key carolers had kept her awake? When she had finally dozed off near dawn, she had consequently overslept.

As the Major began his inspection, Mac suppressed a shiver at the memory of the nightmare that had plagued her short slumber. A leather belt and a piano wire merged as the murderer had morphed into the devil from her own past.

"Did you sleep well, Miss McAllister?"

The Major's precise tones snapped her back to the present.

"Fine, thank you, sir," Mac responded with a plastered-on smile.

The man pinched his lips together in a cross between a grimace and a frown. He continued down the row and she sighed in relief. The Major's sharp look told her the sigh hadn't been silent.

If this were the army, she would be busted down to private without further ado. The image of the Major ripping the stripes from her sleeves made her snort. It also bought her another glare from the military mutant.

*My ass is grass and the Major's a big old bovine.*

That image threatened a bout of giggles, but she managed to contain them.

The Major completed his inspection tour and dismissed them. "Miss McAllister, you will remain here," he commanded.

"Shit," she muttered under her breath, her humor fleeing.

Less than thirty seconds later the room was empty, save for the austere Major and Mac.

He strolled over to her, hands clasped behind his back, and circled her slowly. Her heart skipped a beat and her forehead grew clammy. What was he thinking?

He stopped in front of her. "I have received some rather disturbing news."

"Hope it didn't spoil your day," she said flippantly, then wanted to bite her tongue. Her first editor had told her it was her mouth that would inevitably get her into trouble. Of course, he hadn't known her mouth would end up in the nineteenth century along with the rest of her.

"It did not. However, I believe it may spoil yours."

Did he know she was from the future? No, he couldn't. Only Miss Sparrow did and Mac suspected she was as adamant about keeping that secret as Mac herself.

The man's jaw muscle clenched and unclenched. "You were seen exiting the room of Mr. Jared Yates."

*Jane.*

For some reason, the girl had a beef with Mac and she'd found a way to punch below the belt.

"We were merely discussing the murder of Linda, sir," Mac said, her nostrils flaring with pent-up frustration.

"Why?"

Should she tell him about her reporter status? Mentally, she shook her head. He wouldn't care. His first and foremost concern was the smooth running of the Chesterfield, which included the enforcement of the stringent moral codes inflicted on the employees. The *female* employees.

"As you know, Mr. Yates has been pursuing the killer of his fiancée, a murderer who has also strangled several other women. I had a theory I wished to discuss with him," Mac replied.

"And that theory was?"

Mac stared at the imperious little man and considered the possibility that he could be the murderer. If she kept to the theory that the man jumped back and forth in time to do his dirty work, the Major would have to be gone for a length of time that would inevitably be noticed. No, his guilt didn't seem very probable.

"That our murderer is a very confused man," she finally replied with a smirk.

The Major's face reddened. " 'Our murderer.' Since when do proper young women involve themselves in such ugly matters as murder?"

Mac's temper spiked. "When the *men* who run this place won't even see fit to warn their female employees of a demented killer who gets his jollies killing women."

Shock, anger, indignation and reproach—she clearly read each emotion in the alternating shades of apoplexy that crossed the Major's thin face. Finally his expression settled into . . . discomfort.

"You are unaccountably well informed for being here for so short a time," he said stiffly.

Mac had expected him to rip her a new one. From past experience, she knew the signs too well. Instead, he had managed to surprise her with a guilt-ridden tone. She eyed him warily. "I heard things and put two and two together. My mama didn't raise an idiot."

The Major coughed discreetly. "I suspected as much. However, this does not change the unfortunate circumstances."

A cold fist knotted Mac's stomach. "What unfortunate circumstances?" But even as she asked, she knew. Jane had ratted on her and the Major was obligated to take action.

"You were found to be in attendance with a man without a proper chaperon. That is immutable grounds for dismissal." His military bearing wilted. "I am sorry, Miss McAllister, but I cannot allow such indiscretions to remain unpunished." He paused and the starch returned to his spine. "You are dismissed from your position."

Mac's shoulders slumped. It wasn't as if she hadn't suspected this might happen. If he knew about that *really* big indiscretion in the Garden Room, she doubted he'd be so regretful. She'd broken the rules and she'd been caught. Nothing new there. Only there were damned few options in this time as opposed to her own.

Self-pity reared its ugly head. Why was it always the woman who had to pay the price? She crossed her arms and fixed a glare on the Major. "What about Mr. Yates? Will he be summarily dismissed from the Chesterfield also?" Before he could reply, she laughed, a cold harsh sound. "Oh, but of course not, he's a man, and men are expected to sow their wild oats before they settle down, right?" She elbowed the Major and winked.

The Major's face reddened and Mac wouldn't have been surprised to see smoke erupt from his ears. "Miss McAllister, your impudence is hardly becoming. Please accept your dismissal with at least a modicum of dignity."

Mac took a deep breath and her anger fled with the exhalation. Exhaustion stepped in to claim the area vacated by her ire. "I'm sorry, Major. I understand why you have to do this, but that doesn't mean I have to like it."

He nodded stiffly. "Since you are Miss Sparrow's cousin, it is doubly difficult to . . ." He cleared his throat. "What do you intend to do now?"

She shrugged. "I think I'll try my luck with the newspaper in Hope Springs. I used to do a little reporting."

The Major scrutinized her. "I have been a friend of Edward Banks, the owner of the *Hope Springs Times* for many years. Perhaps I can put in a word for you."

Mac's mouth gaped and she abruptly closed it. "You'd do that for me?"

The man's lips remained firmly set, but his eyes held the barest twinkle. "You are a unique individual, Miss McAllister, and I believe you would be a better reporter than a maid."

Mac grinned. "Damned straight I would be. Thank you." Impulsively, she hugged his ramrod-straight body. "You won't regret this, sir."

She stepped back and the Major raised his chin. "I already do, Miss McAllister."

But she saw the fondness glimmering in his eyes and her own vision grew blurry. Who would've thought the by-the-book Major had a weakness for smart-assed women?

"You may spend the rest of today and tonight here, but I'm afraid you will have to vacate your room by nine o'clock tomorrow morning," the Major said.

That was twenty-four hours more than Mac had assumed she'd get. "Thank you," she said sincerely.

"You may go now."

Mac bobbed her head once and scurried out of the ballroom where the morning inspections were conducted. On her way to the room she shared with Erin, Mac considered her options. There were damned few of them. If she didn't get a job at the newspaper, she hadn't a clue what other avenue was open to her.

The other obstacle was clothing. The only clothes she owned were those she'd worn from her own time period. She couldn't possibly go to an interview in those. The editor would probably be scandalized.

*Damn it!* Why had she involved herself in Jared's investigation? Why couldn't she have let sleeping dogs lie? The murders in this time eerily resembled those in hers, but didn't history often repeat itself?

Why in the world had she suggested going to Jared's room to discuss the crimes? Had a part of her wanted a repeat of their lovemaking? Sex was fine and dandy, but she had never let it rule her head before. Men followed their dicks; women followed their brains. So why was she thinking about Jared and getting hot and bothered?

It was Jared's fault. *Everything* was Jared's fault, from seducing her to losing her job.

The more she thought about it, the more her temper notched upward. Soon her anger pulsed in time to her heartbeat. She changed directions and ran up the stairs, holding her skirt a scandalous twelve inches above her ankles. Since it was Jared's fault, he was going to have to buy her some new clothes. It was the least he could do.

She arrived at his door and pounded. "Open up, Yates. Now!"

The sound of turning doorknobs and creaking doors told Mac she had an audience, but she didn't give a damn. What could they do—fire her?

*Been there, done that.* The only thing she needed was the damned T-shirt.

Using a fisted hand, she hammered even harder. "Let me in, Yates. Now!"

The door swung open and the air in Mac's lungs whooshed out, leaving her gasping like a landed trout.

Jared Yates, shirtless, barefoot and wearing only a pair of trousers with the top button undone, stood framed in the doorway. Curling light hairs covered his chest with the thickest swatch smack-dab between his pectorals and tapering down to a line that disappeared into his waistband. Mac had no trouble recalling what lay at the end of that line, hidden now by wool trousers. His biceps looked as though he spent most of his time in a gym, but Mac knew they were authentic, formed by bona fide labor.

The epitome of temptation grabbed her arm and yanked her into his room, closing the door swiftly but quietly behind him. He took hold of her upper arms and his blue eyes blazed above ruddy cheeks.

"What the devil are you doing?" he demanded.

Mac wanted to reply, but her tongue was so dry it stuck to the roof of her mouth. The room had seemed bigger and the bed smaller yesterday. Now, the bed loomed close, inviting her and Jared . . .

"Mac, are you all right? You don't look very well."

Jared's voice changed to concern, though there was still a large measure of impatience mixed with it.

"I, uh, I'm fine," she managed to stammer out. Her fingers curled around his muscled forearms, which were rock solid. Like the rest of him.

"What're you doing here?"

Mac tried to think past the lust that had tossed all coherency out the window. Her nose tingled with the overpowering scent of shaving soap and the underlying trace of male sweat. Leaving her brain behind, she swayed toward him and her nipples brushed his chest.

"First contact," she murmured.

Jared groaned and the vibrations went straight to Mac's belly to mix with the undulating pool of liquid heat. The ripples moved outward and downward until Mac had to press her thighs together, which only heightened her excitement.

"If your goal is to torture me, it's working," Jared muttered.

He swooped down to capture her lips with bruising intensity. His cheeks were freshly shaven, and Mac lost herself in the cool satin against her skin and the kiss that depleted any remaining brain cells.

She wrapped her arms around his neck, pressing herself into him, wanting—needing—to feel his hard angles. He complied with a growl that twisted the coiled tension in her belly even tighter. He nibbled at her earlobe and moved down her neck, leaving teeth marks in his wake. Mac's knees buckled, but Jared caught her and carried her to his bed—his really big bed.

Some sane part of Mac laughed at her loss of control, but she didn't give a damn, not when Adonis was doing his best to make her forget her name. She tilted her head back, giving him full access to her neck. He continued to nuzzle her as she felt his fingers undo the buttons on her dress. Cool air heralded his success and she squirmed until the garment was removed from her arms and slipped down to her waist. Jared left her neck to trail a line of damp kisses to her breasts. He pulled a camisole-covered nipple into his mouth.

"Jared," Mac whimpered, unable to articulate anything more.

Her hands abandoned the back of his neck and slipped between their bodies. Jared shifted enough that she could find the buttons on his pants, and after a few moments of frantic frustration, she managed to release them. Slipping her fingers inside the front of his pants, she encountered the coarse hair surrounding his arousal and she couldn't help but grin—no underwear.

"Were you expecting me?" she murmured.

"Mmmhmmmm," came Jared's reply, muffled by one of her nipples in his mouth.

Mac ran a fingertip up and down the silky smooth skin that covered his steely erection. "Ahh, Jared," she said huskily.

The musky scent of him invaded her senses and her breathing grew more ragged. She traced a line of kisses across Jared's brow, but it wasn't enough. Her body was growing taut, spiraling upward in anticipation of the release that was coming too fast.

She wanted to make it last. *Had* to make it last. She wanted to taste him as he'd tasted her.

"Roll over," she said, barely recognizing the hoarse voice as her own.

Jared raised his head and gazed at her with heavy-lidded sexy eyes. "What?"

She gave him a push that sent him rolling off her to settle on his back. Mac scrambled to her knees as quickly as her voluminous clothes allowed. For a moment, she could only stare at his perfect body. Broad shoulders, curling chest hairs over red-flushed skin, lungs pumping up and down with shallow rapid motions, trim waist and a penis that remained undaunted by her perusal. She gave in to the urge to touch him and his erection jerked in her palm. She leaned close and kissed the tip tenderly.

Jared groaned and buried his hands within her hair, as if to both hold her still and make her continue. Her own body was ready with slick heat and constant pulsing, but she was determined to give Jared back what he had given her two nights ago. She reveled in the taste and feel of his hard length.

Jared clutched her hair almost painfully. "Oh God, what're you doing?"

She swept her tongue up and down his arousal. Jared's breathing became little pants and Mac released him. She wanted to feel him within her.

She paused momentarily, remembering the lack of a condom or any other kind of birth control. But if she hadn't gotten pregnant their first time together, she doubted if she would now this late in her cycle. Besides, her body wasn't going to accept no for an answer. It craved a repeat of two nights ago, the indescribable high followed by boneless satisfaction.

Tossing caution aside, Mac lifted her skirts and threw a leg over Jared to straddle his waist. His hands immediately settled on her thighs, kneading her skin gently.

"What—?" Jared began.

Mac leaned down to silence him with her lips and eased his mouth open with her tongue. While their tongues intertwined, Mac raised her hips and shifted back until her damp folds settled over him. Slowly, wanting to enjoy each incredible inch, Mac lowered herself onto him. Jared's groan was silenced by their fused mouths, but Mac could feel it all the way down to where their bodies were intimately joined.

She flexed her inner muscles, watching Jared's eyes widen in surprise. His penis jerked within her and she inhaled sharply, almost losing her hard-fought control. She raised herself, feeling the slow withdrawal of Jared's length, but stopped before she lost him completely; then she moved her body downward, swallowing him once more.

Jared clutched her hips, his fingers digging into her skin, but it only increased Mac's pleasure as he guided her body up and down. She ended their kiss and sat up, feeling him move even deeper within her.

"Jared," she cried with a groan.

"Oh, Mac, you're so hot, so wet," Jared whispered hoarsely. "So damned beautiful."

The movement of Jared within her and against her sensitive flesh, as well as his murmured endearments, brought her close to the edge. She wanted to let go, to dissolve in a million pieces, but the desire to see Jared lose himself first stopped her. She stared at the wall behind the bed and tried to count the number of roses in the floral wallpaper to postpone her orgasm. Biting her lower lip, she didn't know how much longer she could delay the inevitable.

Mac knew the moment Jared began to lose control and her gaze darted back to his face, which twisted into ecstasy. His strong hands held Mac still as he raised and lowered his own hips. With a loud groan, he emptied himself deep within her. The flood of slippery warmth and the look on Jared's face sent Mac over the edge, her voice joining with his in a chorus of moans and gasps.

The explosion receded and Mac's muscles experienced meltdown. She fell forward onto Jared's chest and buried her face in the damp curve of his neck and shoulder. The feel and smell of him brought with it the overpowering illusion of security and comfort. And another emotion Mac refused to examine.

"Jeezus, Mac, if you're trying to kill me, you damn near succeeded," Jared said, a teasing note in his voice.

"If I were trying to kill you, I'd come up with a more creative method, like shooting you or something," Mac retorted.

Jared's arms slipped around Mac's waist and he held her snugly against him. He kissed her forehead. "That sounds more like the Mac I know."

*And love.*

Mac's mind supplied the added words and she scoffed at the absurdity. Jared loved her as much as she loved him, which meant there wasn't any love involved here. Just some good old-fashioned debauchery, which was the way Mac liked it.

They lay quietly with their legs entwined, ignoring the rest of the world. Some minutes later, a crow's caw startled Mac back to awareness. She didn't want to peel herself from Jared's body, but she had no choice. Today was her last day at the Chesterfield and there were things she had to do to prepare.

She began to ease upward, but Jared's embrace tightened.

"I'm not letting you go until we talk," Jared said, his voice rumbling through Mac via his chest.

"We have nothing to talk about." Mac struggled to escape her human bonds, but he didn't release her.

"Why did you come to my room?" Jared asked.

"To clean your plumbing?" She waggled her eyebrows.

Jared playfully swatted her backside. "Why?"

Mac took a deep breath and dropped her forehead to his shoulder and muttered, "TheMajorfiredme."

He frowned and thought for a moment. "Did you say the Major fired you?"

"Actually, I said the Major fired *me*."

Jared lifted Mac off him and sat her down with her back against the headboard. After buttoning his trousers hastily, he joined her.

"The Major fired you so you came to my room to, well, to do this one last time?"

Mac rubbed her brow where a headache had decided to set up shop. She hoped it wasn't another migraine. "No offense, big guy, but I didn't have this in mind on my way here."

Confusion darkened Jared's crystal eyes. "Then why?"

"What was I supposed to do when you answered the door looking like"—she motioned to his body—"that?"

At first he appeared disconcerted, then he smiled crookedly. "So what you're saying is you couldn't resist me?"

Mac flounced off the bed and whirled around to face him, hands planted on her hips. "Why do I even bother? I swear, every single male ever created thinks the universe revolves around him."

Jared shifted off the bed and stood. "You're the one who came to my room and practically attacked me."

"Like you didn't enjoy it."

"I didn't say that. I was just shocked." He stared at her, his perceptive gaze making her nervous. "You were fired. What are you going to do now?"

Mac deflated like a punctured balloon. "I'm going to try to get a job at the newspaper office in Hope Springs. The Major said he'd put in a good word for me."

"And if you don't get it?"

Her backbone snapped back into place. "How should I know?"

"Can't you sell some freelance stories or something?"

"Not when I don't have any written, and now I don't even have a place to write them."

Jared dragged a hand through his tousled hair, and Mac's attention was riveted to the rippling muscles in his shoulder and arm. When did she suddenly start noticing rippling muscles?

*The moment I spotted Jared Yates.*

Mac punted that notion out before it could score a field goal. "I just came up here to tell you I was leaving tomorrow," she lied. How could she demand money after what they had just done? She would feel too much like a prostitute. But worse, Jared might think that was why she had jumped his bones. "So I guess I'll be seeing you around."

She turned to leave, but Jared caught her wrist and pulled her back.

"Just like that?" he demanded, his face only inches from hers.

Mac's heart threatened to leap out of her chest even as her hormones stood up and took notice. Again.

*Shit.*

"Look, we had some great sex, but that's all it was. You don't owe me a ring and I don't owe you a commitment. We're both adults and we each have our own lives to live. Let it go at that, Jared." Mac was surprised her voice remained so steady.

"What if I want to see you again?"

"For a quick romp in the sheets?"

Jared's face flushed a deep red. "We don't have to unless you want to."

The way her body was homing in on Jared's told Mac she would want to again, but she couldn't risk losing her control. She'd lost control two more times than she should have already. "We do need to keep in touch, but strictly to work on catching the murderer."

Jared nodded without hesitation. "Exactly. I'll let you know if I turn up anything, and I'll expect you to do the same."

"If I get that job at the paper, I'll have more of a pulse on the town and the people around here. Maybe something will turn up." Mac was pleased with her logical excuse to see him again.

They remained standing close, their bodies nearly touching as their breath mingled. A muffled voice in the hallway startled them out of their reverie and each took a step back.

"I'd better go and pack," Mac said.

Jared, still clad in only his trousers, nodded. "I suppose. When are you leaving?"

"Tomorrow morning. I'll catch the first train into town."

"That's at eight o'clock. I'll meet you in the lobby at seven-thirty and walk you down."

"You don't have to."

"I *want* to," Jared said softly.

Mac wanted to lose herself in the tenderness of his eyes, but the risk was too great. "Okay. I'll see you in the morning."

She wrapped her hand around the doorknob, but a larger hand came down upon hers as Jared's too-sexy chest pressed against her back. "What is it now?" she demanded impatiently.

His eyes twinkled. "You might want to redress yourself."

Mac glanced down to see the top half of her maid's uniform hanging from her waist and her nipples peaking against the damp rings on her camisole. Her face flaming, she tugged the dress up, surprised when Jared helped her. With shaking fingers, she buttoned the bodice.

"Better?" she asked sharply.

Jared shook his head and smiled languidly, sending little spokes of desire spinning through her. "I liked it better the other way, but the other guests might not approve."

Mac rolled her eyes and after a quick check of her appearance, she left temptation behind. She hurried through the hallways and took the back stairs. Once safely ensconced in her room, she leaned against the door and tilted her head back.

The combined scents of their lovemaking rose to tickle her nose. She'd never lost control like that before and the feeling left her both frightened and fascinated.

Just as Jared Yates both frightened and fascinated her.

# FOURTEEN

Later that evening in her room, Mac shook her head at Esme Sparrow. "I can't accept all these clothes."

"Nonsense," Esme said with a wave of her hand. "You have no clothing other than those inappropriate trousers from your time. That dress and the skirts are too long for me. If you take them, it will save me spending my evenings sewing."

"Right," Mac said, meaning she didn't believe a word of Miss Sparrow's rationale. "So what about the cape and shoes and underwear?" she asked, motioning toward the items scattered across the bed.

"Consider them Christmas presents from your cousin."

Mac skimmed her hand along the forest green dress that hugged her curves as if made for her and shook her head. "It wasn't your fault I was fired. You don't have to feel obligated to give me this stuff."

Miss Sparrow sighed and dropped to the edge of Mac's bed. She plucked at a loose thread on the quilt. "On the contrary, Trish, I do take a certain amount of responsibility for your discharge. I should have stressed more firmly the importance of obeying the rules of this time period." She lifted her gaze. "Yet I understand you cannot be who you are not."

Jared's question drifted back to Mac: *Who are you?*

Mac plopped down beside the woman. "I don't know who I am anymore."

Esme shook her head and clasped Mac's clenched hands. "Come, come, Trish. You are one of the most strong-willed women I have ever had the pleasure to meet."

Mac tried to stifle a snort and failed. "Pleasure? We both know my short stay here could hardly be called pleasant for either of us."

"Perhaps not, but you have done well for being thrust into a strange world without benefit of friends and family."

Mac eased her hands away from Esme's, suddenly made uncomfortable by the contact. She had grown too close too quickly to these people, especially Jared. Standing, she put more distance between herself and Esme. "The truth is I didn't have many friends in my own time. It was always hard for me to get close to anyone." She shrugged. "You let someone in and they're bound to hurt you, simple as that."

Esme didn't appear surprised by Mac's admission. "What of your family?"

"Nobody but my father and he barely knows I exist." Again the sharp talon of betrayal drew blood. Mac massaged her brow and barked a weak laugh. "My one goal in life is to best him at his own game."

"And after you do?"

The softly spoken question startled Mac. "What do you mean?"

"After you've bested him, what then will you do with your life?" Esme asked patiently.

"I—I hadn't thought about it."

"Perhaps you should ponder it with the time you have remaining here."

"I don't have time to ponder that little mystery of life," Mac said, her uncertainty making her snappish. "I have to find a job."

"What of a position at the *Hope Springs Times?*"

"Who says the editor will hire a woman?"

"He will," Esme assured with the same maddening calm. "Both the Major and I have already given him glowing recommendations."

Mac couldn't understand why two people who hardly knew her would do that. "Does the Major know I'm from the future, too?"

Esme was obviously startled by the question. "No. I am the only one aware of your, shall we say, travels?"

Mac nodded, relieved. "You said I could return to my own time at the next solstice if I complete some mysterious task, right?"

"That is correct." Esme's gaze flickered away from her. "There is one more condition also."

The whisper of unease in Mac graduated to a shout, but she kept her voice deceptively soft. "And that is?"

"The only clue that I can impart at this time is to ask you to remember clearly what you were doing the exact moment you were brought here."

"What—?"

"This is something you must remember on your own." The stubborn glint in Esme's eyes told Mac she'd get no more information.

Mac paced with long strides, her frustration making her head pound with the rhythm of her footsteps as she tried to remember that night and what had led to her being transported across more than a century. She could recall in startling detail the murder and her blowup at Sheriff Longley, but the events after that were blurry. She had been following someone and there had been snow—a lot of snow—and she'd been forced to find shelter. She'd found the ruins of the old hot springs resort, but after that her memory was hazy.

"But I can't remember everything." It sounded suspiciously like a whine, but it couldn't have been—Mac had never whined in her life.

"It will come back to you in due time," Esme reassured her.

"Easy for you to say. You're not the one with a black hole in your memory."

With a sigh of resignation, Mac glanced about the room she'd shared with Erin. Mac had told her roommate about her dismissal earlier that evening in the dining hall. Erin had been surprisingly upset. Both she and Louise were genuinely angry at Jane for being the catalyst behind Mac's dismissal; the fact they cared had puzzled Mac.

Esme approached her and withdrew an envelope from her skirt pocket, which she handed to Mac. "Here, my dear."

Bewildered, Mac closed her fingers around it. "What is it?"

"The money you earned working here. It should be enough to buy a train ticket into Hope Springs as well as pay for room and board for a week."

Mac clasped the envelope tightly. "Thank you, Esme."

"No need to thank me. You earned it." Esme smiled. "You will do well, Trish. You are a fighter."

"I've had to be."

Esme peered at her, her eyes seemingly too ancient for a woman only a year or two older than Mac.

"A good soldier knows when to fight and when to compromise," Esme said quietly. Then, before Mac could back away, she hugged her. "Listen to your heart, my dear," she whispered, then withdrew. "I shall visit you the next time I travel down to Hope Springs."

The head housekeeper scurried down the hall, her small bustle swinging in almost businesslike precision to her determined footsteps. Mac watched until she disappeared around the corner, feeling more than a twinge of trepidation. Esme Sparrow was Mac's lifeline to the future, the only person who understood— and she'd left her, just like everyone else in Mac's life.

*Get a grip, Mac. It's not like she's* real *family.*

She mechanically removed the dress Esme had given her and hung it in the armoire. The other clothes she folded carefully and placed in the suitcase Esme had also given her.

Even though the woman wasn't related, Esme felt more like family than anyone had since Mac's mother died. Unexpected anguish struck Mac and her eyes filled with moisture.

She had been nine years old when their roles had been reversed: Mac had become the parent and her mother the child. For a year, her mother had lived in a world that drifted between reality and fantasy until one day she'd just stopped breathing.

Tears rolled unheeded down her cheeks. Her mother's death, though merciful, had thrown Mac from one foster home to another.

Through moisture-laden eyes, she turned in a slow circle as she contemplated her room. It was just one more in a long line of rooms she'd lived in—one she'd lived in for far less time than many others. So why did she feel so terrible leaving it behind?

Mac sucked in a shaky breath and rubbed away her tears. This wasn't her home and these people were nothing more than ships passing in the night.

*Oh God, I've sunk to using bad clichés.*

"Pull yourself together, Mac. Think of this as the adventure of a lifetime," she said aloud, then grinned crookedly. "Complete with a dashing hero."

Thinking about the Pinkerton detective, Mac's momentary despair faded. He would be here in the morning to walk her down to the depot. Her excitement in seeing him again had nothing to do with the little flutter in her heart.

Nothing at all.


Jared's stomach was tied in knots as he strode down the hall to Mac's room. He'd hardly slept the night before as he'd tossed and turned in the same bed where Mac had boldly made love to him. The frustration his memories had evoked had made sleep impossible.

He paused in front of Mac's door, suddenly uncertain. What did he say to a woman who had thrown his world off balance? He shouldn't have told her he'd escort her to the train depot. No, he wanted to see her again. The problem was he wanted to see *a lot* more of her.

He tried to find something to think about to make the blood retreat from his groin. Cold waterfalls . . . with Mac standing under the falling water, naked and beckoning. His breath caught in his throat.

Okay, that wasn't going to work.

He searched for something else to waylay his thoughts. What about the telegram he'd received that morning from his mother? She was nearly begging him to return home to celebrate the arrival of the new year with the family—every single one of his six sisters, their husbands and children.

His erection wilted. Completely.

Jared took a deep breath and knocked. It was answered almost immediately and for a moment, he could only stare at Mac. Instead of a uniform, she wore a dark green dress with an ivory bodice that fitted her curves like a snug glove. His gaze rested on her breasts, remembering the taste and feel of them.

If his renewed hard-on could talk, it would be giving its rendition of the Rebel yell.

"Hello, Yates," she said.

Her tone made it sound as if they were acquaintances rather than lovers. Obviously, she hadn't been lying when she'd said what they had done was nothing more than sex.

All right. It wasn't like their relationship was some kind of strange courtship. Neither one had plans to marry.

"Good morning, Mac," he said, cursing his husky undertone.

Her lips turned downward into a familiar scowl, but all Jared could see was her mouth coming down to encircle his . . .

"Morning maybe, good no," she muttered.

He couldn't help but smile. "Get up on the wrong side of the bed?"

She met his gaze solidly. "Maybe the wrong bed."

So she had been thinking about it, too. "Maybe so," he said. "I wouldn't have thrown you out of mine."

Mac's eyes darkened. "I know."

How did she manage to turn around and fluster him when he was trying to fluster her? "I'll carry your bags down," he said gruffly.

"I can do it. There's only one," she said.

Jared gritted his teeth. "I don't mind. The fact is, I feel guilty about what happened."

"What 'what' happened?"

The glint in her eyes made him want to spank her or kiss her. Maybe both. He ignored the jibe. "I tried to talk to Payne, but he wouldn't budge. The only thing he said was that you would have no trouble finding other employment."

"It seems he and Esme put in a good word for me at the newspaper office."

"So they know you're a reporter?"

"I didn't tell them, but that doesn't mean they didn't find out. I should've been more discreet."

Jared laughed at that impossibility. "You, discreet? It'll never happen, Mac."

She shrugged. "You're right. Who am I kidding? I'm about as discreet as a man in a lingerie shop."

*Would you model the underclothing personally?* Ignoring that mental picture *and* Mac seemed the better part of valor. He glanced into the room. "Let me get your bag and I'll walk you down to the depot."

"Suit yourself."

Electricity sparked through her veins as Jared stepped past her, brushing her breast with his arm. The pheromones were alive and kicking.

Jared picked up her suitcase and returned to the hall to wait while Mac tugged on the heavy cape Esme had given her. She picked up her backpack and closed the door behind her. A foreboding tickled her consciousness. As pragmatic as she appeared, Mac believed in fate and that whatever happened did so for a reason. If destiny brought her here, there was a reason for it. She just had to find it.

"Are you all right?" Jared asked gently.

Why did he have to spoil their relationship by being so solicitous? "Just dandy for someone who got fired from her job, kicked out of her home and can't continue her story investigation because she doesn't have any money."

Mac expected him to get angry, but he didn't. Instead, he brushed the backs of his fingers against her cheek in a light caress.

"I'm sorry, Mac," he said. "If there was any way I could make things right, I'd do it. You know that, don't you?" His clear blue eyes held her spellbound.

She nodded as she swayed toward him, intent only on kissing those sensuous lips. Needing to taste and feel them one more time.

Jared suddenly stepped back. "We'd better go or we'll be late."

Mac lowered her gaze to hide her humiliation.

*Where did that sudden urge to jump his bones come from?* If Jared had accepted her unspoken invitation they would be doing it like bunnies again, only this time it would be on the hallway floor.

"All right." She was proud that her voice didn't waver.

Their footsteps thudded dully on the carpeted floor as Mac followed Jared. She tried to keep her attention off his backside, but her eyes seemed to have an agenda all their own. Who was she to argue with them?

Once outside in the bright sunshine Mac moved up to walk beside Jared. The silence stretched into minutes but Mac didn't mind. It gave her time to think, to prepare her arguments for the newspaper owner. Of course, maybe Esme and the Major's recommendations would be enough to land her the job.

"I'll wait here while you buy your ticket," Jared said as he stopped on the depot platform.

Mac glanced around, trying to find the ticket office. Jared placed his hands on her shoulders and turned her one hundred and eighty degrees. He pointed over her shoulder to the office.

"I knew that," Mac muttered.

"Go," he ordered.

"Sheesh, give a girl a break here." She smiled though, and Jared's eyes twinkled in response.

Hurrying over to the ticket window, Mac felt Jared's warm gaze on her. Confusion clouded her thoughts and she pressed it aside. She didn't have time to think about the Pinkerton or the feelings he breathed to life within her. Their brief fling was over almost before it had begun.

Mac pulled some money from her backpack and bought her ticket. She returned to Jared who was staring off into the distance.

"I have it," Mac said when Jared didn't acknowledge her.

"Agnes Ledson has clean rooms at a reasonable price." He turned his head to look at Mac. "As long as you don't mind a woman who's half Seminole as your landlady."

Mac frowned in bewilderment. "Why should I mind?"

Jared leaned back to scrutinize her. "Most people don't care for persons of mixed race."

"I'm not most people."

A corner of his lips quirked upward. "No you're not, are you?" He sobered. "Tell her I sent you."

Mac nodded. Nervousness writhed in her stomach, drying her mouth and making her sweat. This was worse than before her first interview.

"What—" Jared began.

"How—" Mac asked at the same time.

"You first," they both spoke together, then laughed.

Jared extended his hand toward her. "Ladies first."

"How long will you be staying at the resort?"

"Another week, maybe two. I have to follow up on some things from this last murder."

"What things?"

Jared slipped his hands in his jacket pockets. "I'm waiting for the lists of passengers who were on all the trains that came into Hope Springs or the resort from the twenty-first to Christmas Eve. I'm also waiting for word on the train schedules from San Francisco."

Guilt assailed Mac. The latter was a dead end. The killer didn't come from San Francisco. She remained silent, however. He couldn't find out she and probably the killer were from the future. She doubted the pragmatic Jared could handle such an absurd claim. To be fair, if their roles were reversed she knew she wouldn't believe it either.

"If you think of anything else, I'd appreciate your letting me know," Jared said.

"You'll be the first." Her heart pounded in her breast, urging her to ask him if he'd visit her. How pitiful would that sound? "What were you going to ask me?"

Jared cleared his throat nervously. "I, uh, I want you to let me know if, uh, you miss, uh, your—" He coughed. "What we did . . ."

Comprehension dawned on Mac. Her handful of boyfriends in her time wouldn't have even thought to ask, much less worry that they might have fathered a child. For them, it was the woman's responsibility, not the man's. But not Jared Yates. Responsibility was his middle name. "Don't worry. I'll let you know one way or another," she finally said.

"All right. Good. That'll work."

Mac nearly laughed at his relief that she understood without him having to actually say the "p" words—

period and pregnant. The knowledge that she might have conceived should have brought panic, but it didn't. Maybe because deep down she knew she hadn't. Or was there another reason, one she didn't wish to dwell on?

The train whistled three times in preparation to leave.

"You'd better get aboard," Jared said, guiding her toward a car with a light hand against her waist.

He handed her the small suitcase, and they stood facing each other awkwardly.

"Thanks for walking me here," Mac said with forced lightness.

"It was my pleasure."

"Gallant to the end." She favored him with a cheeky grin. "Next time you're in town, drop by the newspaper office."

"Awfully certain of yourself, aren't you?"

"I have to be."

She stared at him as he stared back at her and the embers of attraction flared to life.

"Aw hell," Mac muttered.

She dropped her suitcase and backpack and wrapped her arms around Jared's neck, pulling him down for a kiss. Their lips met, mouths opened and tongues mated. Pure unadulterated lust steamrolled through her veins. Jared was enjoying himself, too, if his lengthening arousal was any kind of measure.

*About eight inches worth.*

The train's whistle blew more impatiently and Mac struggled to extricate herself from Jared's arms and mouth. Their lips were the last to disengage.

Mac grabbed her carpetbag and backpack, then hurried aboard just as the train started moving.

"I'll be down soon," Jared called out.

"I'll be there," Mac shouted back.

She felt like the star in some romantic movie, but it didn't stop her from waving at Jared until she could no longer see him.

Pausing just inside the train car, she looked around and déjà vu made her shiver.

*Looks as though you're right back at the beginning of the movie, Mac.*

# FIFTEEN

If the interview at the newspaper office went half as well as acquiring a room at Agnes Ledson's boardinghouse, Mac would be in like Flynn. Agnes had turned out to be a middle-aged widow who treated Mac like a long-lost relative after learning Jared had sent her. The woman's Native American heritage could be seen in her high cheekbones and still thick black hair that she wore in a bun at the back of her neck. She'd given Mac a bright airy room in the corner with nobody around her. It was perfect and the price was right.

In spite of Mac's overabundance of clothing, a north wind kicked up her petticoats, making her shiver. She was half tempted to return to her room and don her blue jeans beneath the dress. If she hadn't been so desperate to get the job, she would have done so without a second thought.

Agnes had given her directions on how to get to the newspaper office, which was one block over and two blocks up in the growing town. The brisk walk chilled Mac's cheeks and nipped at her ears, which her ugly and completely useless hat did nothing to protect.

She paused in front of a glass window with bold

dark letters painted on it: *Hope Springs Times, Edward Banks, Editor.* Mac shaded her eyes with one hand and leaned close to look into the office. Uncharacteristic doubts assailed her as she questioned her sanity in applying for a position here. The newspaper business in the nineteenth century was a world apart from the media of her own time. She had spent a summer working in Colonial Williamsburg playing the part of an early newsman, but that had been for show rather than practical application.

"You don't have any other options," she murmured to herself. "Necessity is the mother of invention. Or at least the mother of desperation."

Mac needed this job.

She sucked in a lungful of brisk, fresh air . . . and promptly began to cough. Vaguely aware of the door opening, she was surprised to feel large hands steering her into the newspaper office. The odor of ink and paper tickled her nose, adding to her fit.

She finally overcame her coughing spasm and wiped her tearing eyes. When she could see, she looked up at shrewd brown eyes peering at her through wire spectacles perched on a bulbous nose. This man had to be the *Hope Springs Times* editor. It seemed there was a prototype for editors extending as far back as the 1800s.

"Miss McAllister?" The man's voice was as gruff as he looked.

"Mr. Banks?"

"Good. The introductions are out of the way." He moved back to the old-fashioned press and began to set type in the frame. "Spell presidential."

Mac blinked. "P-r-e-s-i-d-e-n-t-i-a-l."

"You're hired. You can hang your coat over there."

He motioned to a rack by the door where a single
jacket hung.

Stunned, Mac remained rooted in place, then her
suspicious nature took over. "Just like that? No interview? No background check?"

Banks didn't look up from his task. "You want to
be in the newspaper business, I need an employee. We
both get what we want." He spared her an impatient
glance. "Don't make Esme and Reg out to be liars."

*Reg?* That had to be the Major. She squelched a
grin. The name fit him like a Speedo. *Don't even go
there.*

"You going to stand there all day or get to work?"
Banks demanded, his attention once more moving between his adept fingers and the piece of paper sitting
in front of him.

His blunt voice spurred Mac into action and she
quickly removed her cape and added it to the coatrack.

"Grab an apron and some sleeve guards or you're
going to ruin your dress," Banks ordered.

Mac spotted the items and donned the apron. She
studied the sleeve guards a moment, then tugged them
on over her forearms.

"Now what?" she asked, covering her apprehension
with pure bravado.

Banks inclined his head toward another tray with
metal letters. "Pull those and start the setup for the
next page."

The press was similar to the one she'd used at Williamsburg where she'd learned how to typeset. She
hadn't been especially fast, but she understood the ru-
diments and could sling type without looking like a
complete idiot.

She leaned over the table and began her task. As
she lifted the previous type out, she placed them in

their correct places in the smaller boxes surrounding her. All she had to do was remember the alphabet. Not too much of a feat, though she did find herself reciting the letters under her breath to remember if *S* came before *R* or after.

After the frame was emptied, she looked around. "Where are the articles for this page?"

Banks motioned toward his desk, which overflowed with sheets of paper. "There."

Mac stifled a grimace. "Any idea which one of these hundred sheets is the right one?"

The editor glanced sharply at her, but a faint twinkle made it to his eyes before being squelched. "The latest one, Miss MacAllister."

"It's Mac," she fired back. She pawed through the mountain of papers and latched onto one with December twenty-sixth written across the top. " 'Sleigh Overturns on Main Street,' " Mac read aloud. She clamped a hand over her mouth to stifle her laughter. "Earth-shattering stuff, huh?"

Banks glowered at her. "I am the editor, you are the typesetter and maybe, just maybe, sometimes a reporter. Understood?"

He sounded exactly like Mac's first editor. She'd been fired from that position after three days. She couldn't afford to lose this job, so she bit her lower lip and took the paper over to her station to begin the tedious chore of setting each individual letter of the article.

"It was a councilman's," Banks suddenly said.

"What?" Mac asked in confusion.

"The sleigh that overturned. It was Councilman Thurman's. He tried to shut me down one time because I printed only what he told me, word for word."

Humor glinted in his dark eyes. "It didn't matter that he'd been a few sheets to the wind."

Mac caught on immediately. "Payback time?"

"You're quick, Mis—Mac. I like that." He threw her an approving, but fleeting smile. "Back to work. We have a paper to put out."

Mac saluted. "Aye, aye, sir."

Banks grumbled something about uppity females, but his eyes twinkled above his spectacles.

They worked in companionable silence with only an occasional question from Mac. Though she hadn't enjoyed her job as a historical typesetter, now she was grateful for the experience. She worked much slower than her boss, but she would have been clueless without the knowledge garnered from that summer employment.

The afternoon dragged on as Mac struggled to read Banks's scrawl. She reined in her impulse to correct his style and change the purple prose to precise journalistic terms. She'd read enough about the history of newspapering to know that conciseness was often ignored for melodrama and sensationalism.

Mac was vaguely aware of Banks's turning on the gaslights as dusk descended on Hope Springs. She glanced out the window and spotted snowflakes playing kamikaze against the glass. Sighing, she hoped it didn't become too heavy. All she needed was a blizzard to slog through to her new temporary home.

Sometime later, Banks announced, "Time to call it a day."

Mac straightened her spine slowly. After two cracks, three sharp twinges and an assortment of "ows" and "uggs," she managed to stand erect. She glanced at her employer and noticed how his backbone remained slightly curved, his shoulders hunched. "This doesn't get any easier, does it?" she asked.

"This business is for fools," he muttered.

"So why do you do it?"

"Same reason you do, Mac. There's ink in our blood."

She couldn't argue with him there, but she didn't plan on being merely a typesetter forever either. "When do I get assigned my first story?"

Banks shrugged. "You bring me a story and I'll read it. If it passes muster, I'll print it."

"Passes muster, huh? I'll bet you and the Major served together in the military."

"Nothing gets past you." He settled himself in the chair behind the desk and leaned back, but kept his astute gaze aimed at Mac. "You haven't done this much, have you?"

Mac froze. She needed this job and would beg, borrow or steal to keep it. "I'll get faster."

"You'd better." The sparkle in his eyes belied his abrupt tone. "Reg said you'd only worked at the Chesterfield for five days before being fired."

"He told you that?"

"I asked, he answered. We've been friends for more years than you've seen."

Mac almost laughed aloud. If he only knew how many years she'd seen in the past week. "Did he tell you why I was dismissed?"

"Yes, but he also said you were a scrapper and he knew that's what I needed. I don't have time for simpering females or milksop men." As if to make his point, he pulled open a drawer in his desk and drew out a brown bottle and a glass. "You aren't one of those temperance females, are you?"

"Hardly."

"Good." He unscrewed the cap and splashed a generous amount of liquor in the tumbler. "You drink?"

Mac grinned. "Do you know a reporter who doesn't?" She plopped into the only other chair in the office and it squeaked in rebellion.

Banks's chuckle sounded rusty as he passed the drink to her. He touched the bottle's neck to her glass. "To a long and rewarding partnership."

"I'll drink to that." Mac tasted the whiskey and was relieved that it wasn't rotgut. Or what she imagined was rotgut. She drank half of the contents, enjoying the warmth and tingle that lined her throat and belly. "I'm a damned good reporter, Mr. Banks. Why don't you just give me an assignment so I can prove it?"

Banks held the bottle as he studied her. "I heard you already had an assignment."

Mac stilled instantly. Had Jared told him? "Oh?"

"Don't play coy, Mac. It doesn't suit you and insults my intelligence. This town and the resort have peacefully coexisted ever since the Chesterfield was built, but with the murders, there have been some in town who think that if the resort wasn't here, we wouldn't have the killings."

Mac pondered the new information. It was the same in every town, whether in this time or her own. Although the resort had given the townsfolk jobs, they didn't hesitate to blame the ills of society on it.

"If you can get an exclusive from Yates about the murders—all of them—that would be front-page news," Banks said.

The bribe was damned tempting, but she knew Jared. "He wouldn't do it."

"Maybe you could persuade him."

She could persuade him to make love to her, but an interview was something else. Unless she combined the two. She could seduce Jared—the most enjoyable part of the assignment—and then afterward, when he was mellow and relaxed, she would ask. It might just work.

Except she didn't want to use him. It didn't seem fair.

*And fair is being stuck back in the dark ages?*

"I'll think about it," she finally said.

"Don't think too long. The latest murder is still fresh enough to make everything involved with it timely." Banks eyed her thoughtfully. "Where are you from?"

"A long ways away."

Banks continued to study her and she forced herself not to squirm. "I don't care about what you've done or where you've been," he said. "I only care about the present and the job you do for me. You do a poor job and I'll fire you. You do a good job and you'll have a position here for as long as you want."

Mac lifted the tumbler to her lips and cursed her hands for trembling. She swallowed the remaining whiskey in one gulp. Her eyes teared, but the burn was soothing. "I won't let you down."

"I hope not." Banks waved his hand in a shooing motion. "You're done for the day, Mac. Come back bright and early tomorrow morning."

"How bright and early?" Mac asked suspiciously as she stood.

"Eight o'clock."

Mac sighed in relief. "I'll be here."

"I know you will." Then Banks turned his attention to the mountain of papers on his desk.

Mac removed the apron and sleeve guards then tugged on her cape. "Good night, Mr. Banks."

He spared her a brusque smile. " 'Night."

She left the warmth of the office for the cool evening air. Fortunately, the snow had stopped falling. She shouldn't have been surprised by how late it was, but then she hadn't planned on starting the job so quickly either.

Technological differences aside, she had felt comfortable in the newspaper office. The smell of ink and paper wasn't so far removed from her own time and Mr. Banks seemed to be a decent boss. All in all, she could think of many worse positions she could be in, including cleaning toilets at the Chesterfield.

She owed the Major and Esme big time.

Her steps lightened as she walked down the boardwalk, past the general store, which was just closing, the Dolly Day saloon with tinny piano music and men's voices spilling out, and a darkened lawyer's office. Things were working out almost too well after the strangeness of finding herself in this time period. At the newspaper office she would have a pulse on the town and on those who lived in and around it. She should be able to discover what her secret mission was while doing a job she loved.

However, the cynical twenty-first century Mac was waiting for the other shoe to drop—nothing was this easy. There had to be some catch someplace.

*The other condition to getting home.*

Esme had sprung that one on Mac without warning. What if Mac's memory of the night she'd time-traveled never returned? How was she to know what else had to be done?

She had nearly six months to recall the lost memory. Surely that would be enough time.

It damned well better be because she didn't intend to spend the rest of her life wearing Mother Hubbard dresses and stupid hats.

* * *

The following days passed swiftly for Mac as she grew more comfortable setting type and doing the other odd jobs around the newspaper office. However, there was little time for anything besides work, and the only people she spoke to were Mr. Banks and her landlady. She even missed ringing in the new year, 1893. She'd fallen asleep at ten that night, her back and shoulders aching after printing the weekly paper that day.

But Mac was proud of her first edition, even if it was only four pages long and nearly half of it was advertisements. She hadn't written a story yet, but that would be the next step.

Mac entered the office on New Year's Day to find Mr. Banks already there as he worked to finish folding the remaining papers.

"I was wondering when you were going to drag yourself in."

"And here I thought I had the day off," Mac shot back, pulling on the apron and sleeve guards over the black skirt and white blouse she'd taken to wearing like a uniform.

"The only days a newspaper man has off are those days when there's no news."

Mac froze. "Has there been another murder?"

There shouldn't have been, but the serial killer was never far from her thoughts. There seemed to be a loose pattern to the murders, but that didn't mean he'd stick to it. Psychos were by definition psychotic, which meant reality had no place in their lives. Mac suspected the killer was making up his own rules as he went.

Banks tilted his head down and gazed at Mac over his glasses frames. "No. Were you expecting one?"

Mac lifted a pile of unfolded newspapers from the stack Banks was working on and found a spot on his desk for them. She sat down and started to fold them in half. "Not really." She could feel her boss's eyes drilling a hole in the back of her neck.

"What do you know about the killings?" he asked.

Though Mac liked and respected her boss, she had no illusions about him believing her wild hypothesis. She'd be without a job again. "I know the woman killed the other night was number five. I know she and the other four women didn't deserve to die." She finally looked at Banks. "And I know that the bastard who killed those women is out there laughing at us."

He stared at her a moment, then nodded slowly. "This old reporter's instincts are saying the same thing." He continued to fold the papers silently. "Yates is in town. Ran into him this morning."

Mac caught her breath. Why hadn't he come to see her? "Oh?" she asked, careful to keep her tone neutral.

"He said he had to check out a few things. I asked him if he was willing to give me an exclusive story."

"And what did he say?"

"Said that it would violate his principles." Banks chuckled. "Hell, everyone knows newsmen have no principles."

"The story is everything," Mac said, her mind agreeing but her heart uncertain.

"Damn right it is. You and I know that. People like Yates don't."

"You mean, principled men like Yates?"

Banks stabbed her with a sharp gaze. "Which side are you on, Mac?"

"My own," she replied. Though she had used some less-than-aboveboard techniques to get her stories back in her time, she'd never violated a trust. She probably knew everything Jared did about the murders, but her conscience balked at writing the story. Jared had shared his information for one reason only: to increase their odds of catching the murderer. He'd also exacted a promise from her not to use his information in a news story.

Harsh silence filled the office as Mac waited for Banks's explosion. But he only continued to ready the papers for distribution.

Two hours later they finished.

"Get your coat on," Banks said.

"You're firing me for answering with the truth?"

Banks smirked. "I'm not firing you." He handed her a pile of papers. "Get out there and sell these. It's part of your job description."

Though relieved, Mac hadn't hired on to be a street vendor hawking newspapers. "I didn't see it listed in the fine print," she grumbled.

He removed his spectacles and rubbed his bloodshot eyes with his thumb and forefinger. "I know you wanted the job to write stories, but I need you to set type. I'm willing to give you a shot as a reporter, but if you're not willing to do what you have to . . ."

She'd never been accused of slacking before. In fact, she was often criticized for pushing too hard too fast. She'd had to in order to move ahead of her male colleagues.

Was she getting soft? When had Jared Yates become such a sensitive subject for her? She had slept with him twice, but that had no bearing on her job. He was a source; she was a reporter. She had an obligation to report the news—to hell with emotional entanglements.

"I'll get your story from Yates," she said, then smiled sweetly. "He'll never know what hit him."

She set the papers down and donned her cape, then headed to the door with the newspapers nestled in one arm. She paused suddenly. "How much do I sell these things for?"

Banks barked a laugh. "A nickel."

She squared her shoulders and headed out.

An hour and a third supply of newspapers later, Mac spotted Jared. His long-legged stride and broad shoulders were easily recognizable from across the street.

She stepped off the boardwalk. "Hey there, Yates," she called.

He paused, turned toward her and his face lit with a smile. As they met in the middle of the street, Mac struggled to keep from launching herself into his arms.

Jared didn't share her restraint and embraced her. "Hey there yourself, Mac," he said, his breath whispering across her ear.

Surprised, she hugged him back, enjoying the brief intimacy.

He stepped back but kept a gentle hold on her arms and studied her. Her face warmed under his perusal and when she realized she was probably blushing like a teenager, she cocked her head. "Like what you see, mister?"

His lips turned upward in a sexy grin. "Careful, I might take that as an invitation."

"And if it is?"

"Then I'd have to take it under consideration." He eyed her as though she were dessert—a sinfully rich silk chocolate pie. He released her. "You're looking good, Mac. The newspaper job must be agreeing with you."

"For the most part."

"Do you want to take a break, maybe have some coffee?"

Mac glanced at the two papers left in her hand. "Let me sell these first."

Jared dug into his pocket and took her hand. He placed a dime on her palm. "Consider them sold. Let's go someplace a little less public."

"Don't tell me you're shy, Yates," Mac teased. She leaned closer. "Because I *know* you're not." Passion flared in his light blue eyes and Mac laughed, recognizing the expression. "You and me both, but maybe we should start with coffee."

"Good idea," Jared murmured.

He guided her into a small café with red-checkered tablecloths. A candle was placed in the middle of each table, though at this time of the day, none were lit. Mac experienced an odd sense of déjà vu, then realized why. The restaurant looked more like one found in her time than here in the late nineteenth century.

"The police chief's wife owns this place," Jared said, taking Mac's cape from her shoulders. "Nice apron."

Mac glanced down. She'd forgotten she still wore the ugly thing, but she didn't care. The maid's uniform she'd worn at the Chesterfield had been worse. "Are you embarrassed to be seen with me?"

"No."

The single word held a husky undertone that curled her toes. "Good."

Jared took care of her wrap and sat down across from her. "What would you like?"

"Are you paying?"

Jared grimaced. "I remember the last time I answered that. You had one of everything on the menu."

"Not quite. But I would have if I had had room." She leaned toward him. "Especially if I'd known how much energy we were going to use later."

Mac wondered just how far his cherry-red blush descended. . . .

worried that. You had one of *my* men with you, so that
that name, but I would have if I had had room."
She rolled her eyes. "I once told you I'd known how
much trouble you were going to give me..."
Marnie gave Grant hell for the detour and lined up
again.

# SIXTEEN

Jared had known he'd see Mac again. He'd planned
on it.

He *hadn't* expected the powerful desire that swept
through him when he had embraced her. He had
missed her but hadn't realized how much until that
moment. He'd also missed matching wits with her, always wondering what she'd say or do next. She was
a puzzle and he hadn't a clue how to make the pieces
fit. As a Pinkerton detective, he was bothered by her
unpredictability, but as a man it intrigued him.

Now, sitting in a public place with the object of his
fascination across the table, Jared was uncertain how
to bring up the matter that had brought him into town.

He cleared his throat. "I don't think we have to
worry about that this time." He ignored Mac's feigned
pout. "Coffee and cake?"

"That'd be fine," Mac said. She glanced around, her
keen eyes missing little. "I'd like to meet her."

Jared lost track of the conversation. "Who?"

"Chief Garrett's wife. Not many women own a restaurant in this time."

*In this time?*

"She cooks in the evenings. I'll have to bring you
here for dinner some time. She calls herself a chef

and some of the dishes she prepares I've never seen anyplace else."

A crease appeared in Mac's brow. "Is that so?"

Studying her thoughtful expression, he leaned back in his chair and laced his fingers across his belly. "What is it?"

She blinked and her wayward gaze returned to him. "What's what?"

"I was just wondering why you got so quiet."

"Did you think an alien had taken over my body or something?" she asked.

He doubted it was an alien, but with Mac he couldn't be sure of anything. Of course, the thought of taking over her body did hold a certain amount of appeal. "Something."

She laughed. "Did anyone ever mention how cute you are when you blush?"

"My mother," he muttered.

A waitress arrived at their table bearing two glasses of water and delaying Mac's comment. Jared was certain she had one.

"What would you like to start with?" the redhead asked.

"Coffee," Mac and Jared said at the same time.

"And I think I'll just have one of Corinne's poppyseed muffins," Jared added.

"What other kind of muffins do you have?" Mac asked.

"Lemon, strawberry, peach, orange marmalade, and carrot," the waitress replied.

"I'll take carrot."

"That's a poppyseed and a carrot muffin and two coffees," the waitress reiterated.

Jared and Mac nodded and the girl retreated.

"This reminds me of a place I used to go to back

home," Mac commented. "It was this little coffee shop with an old jukebox in the corner and those candles that melted over the wine bottles on the tables."

It sounded as if Mac were speaking a foreign language. He'd never heard of a jukebox or candle wax on wine bottles. "Where was this?"

She picked up her napkin and made a show of spreading it across her lap. "Back home."

"San Francisco?"

"Close enough." She rested her clasped hands on the table. "So have you found out anything new about the murders?"

It was obvious Mac didn't want to talk about her childhood or where she came from. She had been adamant about them sharing *only* their bodies. Jared should have been happy with just that.

So why did he want more from her?

"I received the lists of passengers from the railroad, but I'm sure they're not very accurate. There were fewer than a hundred names among the five lists." He paused. Even if it wasn't part of his job, he needed to learn where Mac had boarded the train. "You weren't listed as a passenger the night you came in."

If he hadn't been watching for her reaction, he would have missed her guilty gaze sidle away.

She shrugged. "As you said, bad bookkeeping."

Jared couldn't let this one go. She had ridden up to the Chesterfield on the same train as he. He tried to remember if he'd seen her before the conductor had caught her without a ticket, but couldn't recall. Somebody like her would have been hard to miss. "When did you sneak aboard?"

"In town."

She didn't even flinch. Jared suspected it was because she was an accomplished liar.

AT MIDNIGHT                                219

"You said you were a reporter from San Francisco.
Was that a lie, too?" He felt as though he was con-
ducting an investigation with a hostile witness, but he
was suddenly tired of all her half-truths and outright
omissions.

"I'm a reporter," she stated, her eyes glittering as
if daring him to refute her.

"Are you? I sent telegrams to twenty different
newspapers, including the *San Francisco Register,*
asking about a reporter named T. A. McAllister. Not
a single one had heard of you." He didn't try to hide
his angry disappointment. "Why the hell don't you
just tell me the truth?"

"Because the lies are easier to believe," she
snapped. She took a deep breath and closed her eyes
momentarily. When she looked at him again, she had
regained her composure. "Let it go, Jared. Please."

She had never pleaded with him before and he
found himself disconcerted by her entreaty. He had
no reason to trust her, but he wanted to. "I'll let it go
under one condition. Someday I want the truth, all of
it."

He could almost see her mind racing before she
finally nodded. "Someday you'll wish you'd never
asked," she said quietly.

Her dark premonition sent a shiver down his spine.
His grandmother used to say that sense of foreboding
was someone walking over your grave. If that was the
case, Mac had just walked over his.

The perky waitress returned with their coffee and
muffins, but Jared found his appetite had deserted
him.

"Have you eliminated everyone on the lists?" Mac
asked curiously.

"All but three, and they're women so I'm not too

concerned. By the evidence, I'd say it's a man we're looking for." Jared scowled, wishing he had been able to garner at least one viable suspect from a week's worth of work.

"More than likely. A woman might have been able to do it, but odds are against it. Do you have any leads?"

Jared gave up his pretense of trying to eat his muffin and pushed his plate away. "None. If he holds true to form, he won't kill again until June."

*"If* he continues with the same pattern."

"You're saying he won't?"

"What I'm saying is I'm not a mind reader," Mac said irritably.

Jared had made the same mistake on Christmas Eve, not expecting the murderer to kill until after the holiday. He sighed. "I know. I'm sorry." He clenched a hand into a tight fist. "It's just that he's gotten away with murder."

"Literally," Mac murmured. "And if it's the same man, he's killed at least ten times that we know of."

The somber woman across the table little resembled the person he'd originally met on the train. Her cocky attitude had disappeared in the wake of the brutal murders. He had accused her of only caring for her story, but he had been wrong. The women's deaths had gotten past her defenses, too, leaving a driving need to find and expose the killer so the victims' souls could rest in peace.

"Have you learned anything new?" he asked.

"Nothing." The single word held a multitude of meanings, including disgust and anger.

He settled his hand on hers and closed his fingers around it, giving it a gentle squeeze. She'd never struck him as fragile until this moment. "We'll get him, Mac. I'm not giving up."

"And you think I am?" she demanded.

The firebrand returned and Jared smiled as he shook his head. "You're not a quitter, Mac. As long as you can breathe, you won't give up."

She glanced at him with a puzzled look and dropped her gaze. Drawing her hand out from under his, she picked at her carrot muffin. "Are you in town long?"

"Just for the day."

"Oh."

He frowned at her un-Mac-like answer. "Just 'oh'?"

She raised her head and really looked at him. "What do you want, tears and gnashing of teeth?" She lowered her voice. "You were good, Jared, but not that good."

Jared's mouth gaped, then he snorted. "That's not what you said the first time."

Her eyes twinkled. "I didn't think either one of us did much talking either time."

Her frank words reminded him he should ask her if . . . Even with six sisters, he had a hard time discussing *that*. "Are you, uh, with child?"

The impish grin was his only warning. "You'll be happy to know that my period arrived precisely on time and there will be no pitter-patter of little Yates's feet in nine months." Her smile grew. "I know, too much information. Get over it, Yates. You're a big boy now."

Between his embarrassment and humor, Jared didn't know if he should laugh or walk away ducking his head. He opted for the laughter, glad to see Mac's wicked humor had returned. "Don't you have any sense of propriety?"

"No. I figure if everybody would just say what they meant instead of tap dancing around a subject, we'd be a lot better off." She tipped her head, appearing coquettish and sexy at the same time. "For instance, I was going to suggest that if you were spending the night in Hope Springs, you could share my room. I wouldn't toss you out of my bed."

Jared choked on the piece of poppyseed muffin he'd just swallowed. Mac leaned over and pounded his back.

"I'm all . . . r-right," he managed to say in between Mac's slaps. "It went down wrong."

Mac watched him with a too innocent expression. "The muffin or my offer?"

Jared wiped at his tearing eyes with the napkin. "Both," he replied hoarsely.

"As I said, I speak my mind." She sipped her coffee as she continued to watch him above the rim.

Jared knew he should ignore those sultry eyes, but he couldn't pull his gaze away. The promise in her expression and his own body's traitorous leanings combined to cloud his judgment. He opened his mouth to accept her offer, then abruptly closed it. What was wrong with him? They'd averted disaster so far, but Jared couldn't take the chance again. "I can't. I have to get back to the resort."

"What time does the last train leave?"

"Eleven-thirty."

"That gives us plenty of time after I get off work at the newspaper office."

She licked her lips, drawing the attention of the part of him below his belt. He could remember too well the feel of her against him, on top of him, around him. Shoving the images aside, he shook his head.

"We can't risk it. If somebody should see me, your reputation would be ruined."

Mac sighed. "You're right. It'd be a foolish risk to take since I need this job so badly."

Surprised she didn't continue arguing, Jared felt a twinge of disappointment. "Good. That's settled then. There's nothing wrong with just being friends."

"That's right." Her eyes glittered with evil mischief as she leaned forward. Beneath the table, her fingers climbed up his thigh and he twitched at the close proximity to his groin. "Being friends is so much better than being lovers," she said with a voice that could've melted a glacier.

Jared quickly stood, nearly toppling his chair and tossed a few coins on the table. "We should get going."

Mac rose, her eyes twinkling. "Whatever you say, Jared."

He kept his gaze averted as he helped her with her cape. If he looked at her, he was afraid he would weaken and give in.

He escorted her back to the newspaper office.

"Here." Mac shoved the two newspapers at him. "You bought them. They're yours."

"I'll take them back to the Chesterfield and leave them in the lobby."

"Make sure to read page two first."

"Just page two?"

She grinned. "I typeset it."

"I'll make sure and pay close attention then." He paused. "Good-bye, Mac."

"See you around, Yates." She put her arms around his neck and hugged him. "If you have time, my offer for tonight still stands," she whispered.

Then she released him and fled into the office, leaving Jared's arms empty.

Mac cursed at the press as she tried to clean the black ink from her fingers. If she had any technological sense, she would build the first computer and damn the time-continuum consequences. She didn't have to worry about violating some Prime Directive.

She had worked on typesetting a long article all afternoon. Once she had finished, she scanned the type and realized she'd missed an entire paragraph in the middle of the story. If she'd had a computer, all she would've had to do was cut and paste and it would have taken five minutes, tops. As it was, she had to remove half her type, add the missed paragraph and replace what she'd spent nearly two hours doing earlier.

She glanced at the Regulator clock on the wall—seven-oh-five. Another spate of swearing was interrupted by Mr. Banks's arrival.

He took one look at her and hastily retreated behind his desk. "I thought you were leaving early today."

She glared at him and her frustrated anger came tumbling out. "I planned to, but this 'little' article had different ideas. If you wouldn't use so many adjectives and adverbs, I would've been done hours ago."

"You don't like my writing?" he asked softly.

*Now I've royally screwed up.*

Mac tossed the stained towel off to the side and attempted a little more tact. "I wouldn't say that. It's just that you get a bit verbose at times."

He narrowed his eyes. "What do you mean?"

"Your journalistic style can use some tightening up. For example . . ." She snatched a piece of paper from the mountain on his desk and read aloud, " 'Thomas Medford, though usually a good-natured sort of fellow, had an apoplectic fit today when he spied John Taylor skulking around his farm. It appears that John Taylor was attempting to steal some of his prize chickens. Taylor was apprehended by Chief Garrett the same day.' "

"What's wrong with it?" Banks demanded.

Mac rolled her eyes. Reading it had almost made her gag. "You report the news, you don't comment on it. Try this. 'John Taylor was arrested for attempting to steal chickens from Thomas Medford's farm.' "

Banks wrinkled his nose. "Too plain."

"But it gets the point across in a fourth of the words, and when we're typesetting, that makes a big difference."

"But people want the entire story, not just the facts."

Mac sighed in resignation. "Then write a book." It took her longer than usual to remove her apron and sleeve guards as her fingers cramped painfully. "I'm going home." She paused by the door but didn't turn around. "Do you want me to come back tomorrow?"

"Why wouldn't I?" Banks asked, surprised.

Mac faced him. "I thought you'd be pis—uh, angry at me for criticizing your work."

"Jeezus, Mac, if I couldn't take a little constructive criticism, I sure as hell wouldn't be here today."

The weight on Mac's shoulders slid away. "Thanks, Mr. Banks." She opened the door.

"Mac?"

"Yes?"

"I'll think about what you said. Typesetting all those words is a pain in the ass as well as the back, and if we can do it in fewer words, we should try." He held up a hand. "Not that I want to eliminate all commentary, but maybe cutting back would help."

Mac grinned, grateful he'd at least think about it. "Yes, sir."

Through his gruff mask, Mac could see a fond twinkle. "Get out of here."

She grinned. "Good night, Mr. Banks."

He merely nodded.

Mac hurried down the boardwalk, wondering if Jared would be waiting for her. She'd left the invitation open, but he'd been resolute about watching out for her reputation. It wasn't like she cared—in a little over five months, she'd be gone.

After a quick hello to Agnes who was in the parlor, Mac flew upstairs. She opened her door and found her room . . . empty. Her heart plummeted. If he had decided to come, he would have been there.

The day's work and her disappointment caught up with her and she sagged onto the bed. A long hot bath would feel like heaven, but she wasn't sure if she had the strength.

She fell back against her pillows and closed her eyes. It would be so easy to fall asleep. She drifted for a few minutes, allowing her imagination to run wild with Jared and herself starring in her little fantasy, which included a Jacuzzi, wine, soft music, moonlight and nothing else.

The smell of her own body odor mingled with ink ended her erotic daydream. She wrinkled her nose. No doubt about it, she *needed* a bath. Groaning, she pushed herself upright. At least she didn't have to go down the hall to a community washroom. Agnes had given her the only room with a private "water closet."

Mac started the hot water running into the claw-foot bathtub and grabbed the scented oil she'd splurged on, but only added a few drops. She stripped as she moved back into her room, tossing her shoes in a corner and dropping her undergarments on the floor. She took the time to hang up her skirt and blouse so she wouldn't have to press them the next morning.

Finally naked, Mac stepped into the tub and the water rose to just above her breasts. Using her toes, she turned off the faucet, then leaned her head back against the tub. The scented oil slicked the water surface and gave off the aromatic scent of hyacinths. Closing her eyes, Mac breathed in deeply through her nose then exhaled through her mouth. As she did the breathing exercises, her muscles relaxed and her body slid lower into the comfortably hot water.

She allowed her mind to wander, hoping it would take her back to the fantasy she'd been having about Jared. Instead, it reminded her of the front-page story Mr. Banks had urged her to write—an exclusive from Jared about the murders. Her muscles tensed again. By writing the story, she would be seen as a reporter instead of a typesetter. She *craved* that recognition, just as she had in her own time.

Being a reporter was her life.

If she was a reporter, she wasn't a homeless waif with a father who didn't care. She wasn't a burden on the welfare system.

She wasn't a poor little girl with a loony mother.

The key to getting back to her time could be writing the story. By doing so, she could save a young woman's life that might otherwise be snuffed out by the killer.

Could she afford *not* to write the article?

How much more information would she need? She had read all of Jared's notes and could probably come up with a story based on what she remembered. The only problem was she'd promised Jared she wouldn't print any of the information until the killer was caught.

*So what's the plan, Stan?*

Mac opened her eyes and stared at the droplets slipping from the faucet into the water. Seduce and persuade. She pictured a red-lipped whore. Was she willing to prostitute herself for a story?

She heard the soft snick of a door closing and her heart skipped a beat. Muffled footsteps approached the bathroom. Fear sliced through her—was it the killer?

The door swung open slowly and Mac froze.

"Hello, Mac."

It took a moment for Jared's husky voice to penetrate her paralyzing fear. She gasped and sank deeper into the tub as she closed her eyes. "Thank God."

She heard him move around to the side of the bathtub and knew when he knelt beside her.

"Are you all right?" he asked, his hand cradling her face.

Taking a deep breath, she opened her eyes to find Jared's concerned visage less than a foot from her. "I-I didn't realize it was you."

He appeared puzzled only for a moment. "I'm sorry, Mac. I didn't even think that I might frighten you." He framed her face between his palms, leaned forward and kissed her damp brow. "I'm sorry."

With the terror gone, Mac was acutely aware of her nakedness and Jared's nearness. She didn't care why he'd changed his mind, only that he was here with her now. Staring into his nearly translucent blue eyes, she felt the inescapable attraction growing between them.

"Let's start over. Hello, Jared," she said, intending

to imitate Bette Davis's throaty voice. Instead, it sounded like a croak.

*A frog instead of a sex goddess. That's the way to seduce a man, Mac.*

"Hello, Mac," Jared said, playing along. "Were you expecting company?" His husky voice was like silk across her skin.

She traced a wet trail along his jaw with her fingertip. "No. I usually leave my door unlocked with a trail of clothing leading to the bathtub where I'm stark naked and waiting for some stud to make mad passionate love to me."

His smile stole her breath. He stood and disappeared behind her, then pressed his lips to the nape of her neck. She shivered. His large hands massaged her shoulders. Her nipples peaked, rising above the water's surface.

He kissed the side of her neck and slid his tongue up to her earlobe which he worried gently between his teeth. Exquisite sensations traveled down to Mac's toes.

"Oh God, Jared, that feels so nice," she murmured.

"Just 'nice'? I'm going to have to do something about that," he teased.

He nibbled a path around her neck and Mac instinctively leaned her head back, giving him full access to her throat. All thoughts ceased as Jared rendered her little more than a limp doll with his drugging nips and kisses.

Mac reached behind her to wrap her arms around Jared's neck. He drew away from her and she nearly groaned at the loss of his provocative caresses.

"You're getting me all wet," he said and she could hear the smile in his voice.

"I think that's my line." She settled deeper into the

water. "Why don't you join me, big guy? The water's just right."

She heard the catch in his breath and imagined his gaze stroking her like his lips and hands had done a few moments earlier. Her own breath stuttered and flitted in and out more quickly.

"It's too small," he said, giving the tub a measuring glance.

She sat up and turned, laying her palm against the front of his trousers. "No, just right."

"Shameless." His rich chuckle crawled right into Mac's unguarded heart.

Resting her crossed arms on the tub, she settled her chin on them to watch Jared remove his clothing. He glanced at her and his nostrils flared with arousal.

"Enjoying the show?" he asked.

"Immensely."

Once he was naked, he stood almost shyly. "I've never bathed with a woman before."

"Who said anything about bathing?" Mac winked and reached for him.

# SEVENTEEN

Lying on top of Jared with her head pillowed on his damp chest, Mac merely listened to his steady heartbeat, allowing it to calm her racing pulse. His fingers carded through her short blond hair. If she were a cat, she would have been purring.

"I think we needed a bigger bathtub," Jared said, laughter in his voice.

Mac raised her head to gaze into his relaxed face. "How's your head?"

"It's fine. Besides, the pleasure far outweighed the pain." He chuckled. "I didn't think what we did was possible."

"I was a contortionist in another life," Mac said in a bantering tone.

He kissed her forehead. "Nothing about you surprises me anymore."

She drew back in mock indignation. "Are you saying I'm no longer a mystery?"

Jared trailed his fingertips down the side of her face, cupped her chin and tenderly pressed his lips to hers. "Never. Even if we're together a hundred years from now, I have a feeling you'll still be an enigma."

She would be around in a hundred years, but Jared wouldn't.

"Good, I'd hate to be predictable," she said flippantly, hiding her sudden attack of melancholy.

Mac felt his laughter in the motion of his chest beneath her. "No worries there," he said, running a fingertip down her arm.

Mac closed her eyes, losing herself in his gentle caress. Back in her time, it was "slam, bam, thank you, ma'am." Jared was her first lover who enjoyed cuddling after the main event was over, and she found herself liking the intimacy. A lot.

*Her time.* Her contentment slipped away with the reminder that this was only a visit and Jared was only her temporary lover. With the mood broken, she attempted to get out of the tub without accidentally kneeing Jared in a vulnerable spot. He took hold of her arms and helped her up. She stepped out onto the soaked floor.

"I found all the water that disappeared from the tub," she said, keeping her voice light.

Jared grimaced as he stood. "Agnes won't be happy."

"Who says she's going to find out?" Mac passed Jared a towel. "Here. Cover yourself up before I lose control."

"Again." Jared grinned, but did as she said. His gaze skimmed over her and Mac shivered, causing her nipples to pucker into little pebbles. "I would suggest you do the same."

Mac grunted, but grabbed the other towel and wrapped it around her, covering herself from breast to thigh. Jared stepped out of the tub, then clasped Mac's arm to guide her out of the bathroom, ensuring she didn't slip.

"I'll take care of the mess in there," Jared offered.

Mac shook her head. "I'll do it after you leave."

She sat on the bed, her back against the headboard. She patted the mattress next to her. "Join me?"

"I don't think that's a good idea," Jared said as he remained standing by the bathroom door.

"Why?" Mac asked with playful innocence.

He leveled a quelling gaze at her. "You know why. You. Me. Bed."

"And here I thought you were exhausted from your 'bath.' "

Jared shook his head but smiled. He sat beside her as he kept his towel in place with a firm hand. Mac quickly eliminated the space between them and settled herself close to his side, an arm resting on his waist. The towel over his groin moved.

"Behave yourself," Jared said.

"Me or your towel?" Mac teased.

"Both." Jared wrapped his arms around Mac and she snuggled against his chest, their towels the only barrier between their bodies. He settled his chin on her head. "I tried to stay away, Mac."

"Why?"

"To prove I could."

"That's a stupid reason."

He kissed her crown. "You're right. It *was* a stupid reason."

Mac detected an increase in his heartbeat. "What's wrong?"

"When I came in, you thought I was the killer, didn't you?"

She shivered with remembered fear. "Yes." Suddenly she remembered the man she'd seen the night of the murder in her time. Her breath caught in her throat and she opened her mouth to tell him that she may have seen the killer. Abruptly she clamped her lips together. What could she tell Jared—that she may have spotted the killer over a hundred years in the future? Right before she traveled back to this time?

Even if she could come up with a lie to go along with the truth, she had a feeling Jared would insist that she needed protecting. Though the thought of having him around twenty-four hours a day was a pleasant one, she couldn't chance it. She was here for a reason and she doubted it was to make love to Jared Yates every day, although the idea had merit.

"I'm sorry I frightened you." His breath huffed gently in her hair.

Her arm tightened around his waist. "Don't worry about it. You more than made up for it." She dropped a kiss onto his chest. "I'm just glad you changed your mind."

"You're a hard woman to ignore."

"And you're such a sweet talker." She brushed her palm across the crinkly hair in the center of his chest. "I'd like to do a story for the *Times* about the murders."

Immediately, his body stiffened just as she knew it would.

"What kind of story?" he asked.

Mac wished she could take back her words, but this might be the last chance she had of getting his approval. "I could write a helluva story with all the information you have on the murders along with what I know." She paused, knowing she had to strike quickly. "Someone might read it and remember seeing somebody."

Jared lifted his head from hers. "It also might scare the killer off so I'd never catch him."

"If we scare him off, maybe he won't kill another woman."

He shifted Mac away from his chest to look into

her face. "Do you really believe a newspaper article will stop this cold-blooded killer?"

"What have we got to lose?"

"The murderer," Jared said, his jaw clenched so tight Mac wondered if his teeth hurt.

"You don't know that."

"Neither do you."

Mac stared up at Jared's granite expression. "There isn't that much that was in your notes that isn't already common knowledge."

"I thought we agreed you wouldn't use all the information until the murderer was caught."

She shifted uncomfortably. "Mr. Banks would like a story covering all the murders."

"What did Banks do, bribe you with a front-page story?"

Mac blinked, startled by his insight. Should she lie? No, he'd already seen the truth before she could hide it. "I wouldn't use the word *bribe*."

Jared's laughter was harsh. "You newspaper people are always so good at semantics. You can twist words around to make them mean anything you damn well please."

"What if there's a chance the information will help someone remember?" she asked. "Or make the next victim stop to think before she goes out alone? I think it's a risk worth taking."

Jared surged off the bed and grabbed Mac's shoulders. "That bastard killed my fiancée. I want him so bad I can taste it. Do you know that every morning I wake up and wonder if today that bitter taste will finally go away?"

Mac had known he'd loved his fiancée, but she had believed he was over her. Obviously she was wrong.

The knowledge sliced more deeply than it should have.

Her temper flared. "You don't care if he kills another woman. You just want revenge."

"And you just want a story." He stared at her as though she were a frog in a dissecting tray. "What we did here, did it mean anything to you? Or were you just doing your job?" He didn't hide his bitterness.

He made what they'd done seem dirty and sordid, but she hadn't meant it that way. What she and Jared had shared was something Mac hadn't felt before and suspected she'd never feel again. It was clear Jared didn't feel the same way toward her.

She lifted her chin. "I guess I didn't do my job very well, did I?"

Pain flashed across his handsome features and Mac nearly capitulated to her own hurt.

Jared shook his head as his eyes darkened. "No, you did it too well, Mac."

He returned to the bathroom as she remained rooted in place. When he came out fully dressed five minutes later, she still hadn't moved.

"I'm going back to Staunton in a few days. I won't be stopping by again," he said curtly.

"What about the case? What if I learn something new?" Mac managed to ask above her heart's thundering.

"You can send a telegram to the Pinkerton office there." He paused. "I'm usually traveling so it may be days or weeks before I get back to you."

She nodded, unable to speak past the lump in her throat.

He turned the doorknob but didn't open the door. "Write your damn story if it's so important to you,

but don't ask me to condone it. I can't." He jerked
the door open.

"Will you be back in June?" Mac asked.

Without turning, he replied, "Yes, but don't expect
me to come calling. I plan to catch a murderer and
you damn well better not get in my way."

Then Jared was gone, the door's slam echoing in
the void he left behind.

Mac's trembling legs buckled and she dropped to
her knees. Her eyes burned, but there were no tears.

Jared had left her, just as everyone else she'd ever
cared about. It didn't matter. She still had her newspaper job and that was all she needed. All that she
had ever needed. She'd write the story about the murders and maybe some good would come of it.

It was that hope that gave her the strength to dig
out her notebook and pen from her backpack and begin writing.


"Damn, this is good stuff, Mac," Banks said, grin-
ning around a cigar. "I figured the murders were connected, but you drew it all together like a good book."

Mac wearily brushed a strand of blond hair from
her brow. "The only problem is this book doesn't have
an ending."

"It doesn't matter. This is going to sell newspapers."

Impatience surged through her. "It *does* matter. The
next murder will probably happen in June, which
means some innocent woman will die. Or don't you
care about that?"

Banks aimed his smelly cigar in her direction.
"Don't you know a good reporter doesn't get emo-
tionally involved?"

"Once upon a time I believed that, Mr. Banks." She rose from the chair in front of her boss's desk and moved to stand by the window, her arms crossed as if she could ward off the chill within her. "Do you want me to start setting type on the story?"

"Why are your petticoats all ruffled, Mac? I thought you wanted this chance."

"I did, but I didn't realize how costly it would be."

"It's Yates, isn't it?"

Mac continued to stare out the window and was surprised when her vision of the street blurred. "He's a good detective. I don't want this story to hurt his chance to catch the killer."

"Sit down."

"I have to—"

"That wasn't a suggestion," Banks said.

She drew her arm across her eyes and crossed back to the chair she'd recently vacated. "What?" she demanded with a surly growl.

"First thing is to get rid of that tone of voice. Then we talk."

Mac closed her eyes and tried to relax with her deep-breathing exercises. She could hear the editor's impatient grunts, but surprisingly, he didn't speak. Finally she achieved a modicum of relief from her tense muscles and taut nerves. "All right. I'm ready," she said, opening her eyes.

"When did you fall in love with Yates?" Banks asked.

Her muscles went back into overdrive. "I don't love Jared."

Banks merely continued to stare at her silently.

"Maybe he and I got together a few times, but the sex didn't mean anything."

Banks's face turned brick red. "Did I ask for details?"

On firmer ground, Mac smiled sweetly. "Didn't you want specifics?"

"No." Banks struggled to regain his aplomb. He took a drag of his cigar and exhaled slowly. "I think it's pretty clear that you and Yates had more than, uh, sex." He held up a hand as she opened her mouth. "I don't want to hear about it. The only thing I care about is your ability to do your job and if you're pining for Yates, your work is going to suffer."

Mac had never pined for anyone in her life. "I wrote the story. What else do you want from me?"

Banks stared at her a moment, then shook his head. "Nothing."

Mac stood. "Good, because I have work to do."

She was aware of Banks's gaze on her, but she ignored him. Jared Yates was history. Literally. Mac had a mission to complete then she could return to her time. Working at the newspaper office appeared to be the best route to accomplish that.

So what if Jared left? It wasn't as if she was planning a happily-ever-after with him. No promises were made, which meant no promises could be broken.

*Except for the one I made to Jared promising not to use the information he showed me for a newspaper story,* her conscience reminded her. However, his parting words last night had been such that she could write the article if it was that important to her. It *was* that important and she'd managed to hang onto some part of her shredded self-respect. She had resisted using the detailed notes from Jared's files—his personal conjectures on the killer and the two pertinent facts that were clearly the murderer's modus operandi. The first was the use of piano wire for each strangulation, and the second was the two distinctive twists of the wire that had ultimately killed the women.

As she set type for the story, she wondered if Jared would read it or merely condemn her, believing she had broken his trust.

It didn't matter. He had said good-bye and Mac knew what good-byes meant.

They meant forever.


As Mac's job expanded to both reporter and type-setter, winter gave way to spring. Green grass replaced brown and leaves fattened up the trees and guaranteed a shady place as the sun grew hotter. Birds that had migrated in the fall returned to build nests and start new families.

When the first day of May dawned, Mac dragged herself out of bed, her vivid dream still haunting her.

*Cold. Wet. Snow.*

*Have to find shelter. The ruins of an old building loomed and she entered tentatively, half expecting the remaining walls to lose the fight against the blustery north wind. Once inside however, she was glad for the scant protection and sat down with her back against the strongest-looking wall.*

*A chest. She crawled toward it, surprised she hadn't noticed it when she had stumbled in. The dust-free wood appeared incongruous within its time-neglected surroundings. A master craftsman must have carved the flowers in the front, top and sides of the chest. The initials EMS were etched into the front below the fashioned flowers.*

*Her hands trembling, she raised the lid. She had expected a musty odor, not the rich cedar scent that arose from within. She noticed shiny objects nestled inside the chest, but the one that caught her gaze was a broken, rusted pair of handcuffs with some letters engraved upon them. Her fingers closed around the cuffs and she had to squint in the dim light to make out the barely discernible initials—EJY.*

*Then her world shimmered and disappeared.*

It didn't feel like any dream she'd ever had before. In fact, it felt more like a . . . memory. She squinted at the haggard face in the mirror, trying to find the answer.

She had been holding the handcuffs when she took her unscheduled trip into the past.

*That's what Esme wanted me to remember.*

But why?

She had to speak with Esme. Find out why the handcuffs were so important.

Mr. Banks had asked if she wanted to attend the May Ball at the Chesterfield this evening, but she'd declined. She would tell him she changed her mind and accompany him so she could see Esme.

Now if only they had a mall where she could do some last-minute shopping.

Mr. Banks alighted from the coach that halted in front of the ballroom entrance. He turned to lend Mac a hand. With the weight of the powder blue gown she'd managed to find and the numerous skirts beneath it, Mac had to accept his assistance or she would have found herself on the ground in an undignified heap.

Once standing safely on solid earth, Mac tried to take a deep breath, but the corset Agnes had insisted she wear made that impossible. Panic swelled, but the moment passed and Mac forced herself to breathe shallowly.

"Are you all right, Mac? You look like you buried your face in a keg of flour," Mr. Banks said.

She glared at him. "No, I'm not okay. I hate dressing up and I especially hate corsets." She no longer censored her speech around her boss, having become friends as well with him. For a nineteenth-century man, he was amazingly open-minded . . . about some things.

"Then why did you change your mind and come with me?" he asked in exasperation.

"Because I have to speak with Miss Sparrow about a confidential matter."

Banks eyed her curiously but didn't interrogate her. After Jared had left Mac had found sanctuary in the newspaper office working for the deceptively gruff-looking man. As long as she was there, she could forget about the Pinkerton. But the moment she returned to her room, one look at the bathtub and the memories returned with a vengeance. It was probably good that she'd agreed to go to the ball—she could get away from the memories for an evening. The only problem was the resort carried its own memory bombs.

Banks handed an invitation to the stiff-necked man at the door to the ballroom. Standing too straight and not cracking a smile, the man appeared to have been trained by the ever-correct Major.

"How about first things first?" Mac asked, snatching a glass of champagne from the tray being carried past.

"I prefer something a little stronger."

They moved through the throng toward one of the bars, greeted by many of the businessmen in town who knew the editor. Most ignored Mac, but she couldn't help but cast them mocking smiles. Even though she'd done stories on some of them, she was still below their station.

At the bar, Banks ordered bourbon while Mac watched the swirls of color and listened to the artificial laughter people typically used at snobbish galas. She caught sight of a hook-nosed matron trying to pawn off her daughter on a blushing boy. A paunchy man stared with unconcealed interest at a woman's cleavage until his wife elbowed him in the side. Mac grimaced in sympathy and cheered the woman for her powerful right elbow.

"Edward."

The familiar voice caught Mac's attention, and she spotted the Major striding in their direction. She found herself smiling at the familiar swagger and soldier-perfect posture.

"Hello, Reg," Banks said as he greeted his friend with a hearty handshake.

"I'm glad you could attend," the Major said. He glanced at Mac, and instead of the expected censure, Mac saw fondness. The Major took her hand in his and kissed the back of it gallantly. "I see the newspaper business agrees with you, Miss McAllister."

"Better than the toilet business," Mac quipped.

The Major's expression slipped momentarily. "Ah, yes, I'd forgotten about your unique wit."

Banks chuckled. "Unique is the right word to describe her, Reg. I never did thank you for sending her my way."

"It was entirely my pleasure," the Major said dryly. Mac nudged him with her elbow. "I'll bet it was."

"Trish," a woman's voice called.

She glanced around and caught sight of Esme moving toward them. It had been over a month since Esme had been down to Hope Springs. Mac and Esme hugged briefly.

"It is wonderful to see you again, Trish," Esme said in her proper British accent. She turned to Banks. "And you, too, Mr. Banks. I am so very glad you could make it to the ball."

"Mac insisted I come," Banks growled and winked at Mac.

Esme smiled. "I rather doubt that. I believe Trish stated before the Valentine's Ball that she despises such social affairs."

"Despise might be a little weak," Mac said. "Abhor is closer to the truth."

"Then you won't mind if I leave you here with Esme to commiserate while Reg and I go argue about old battles?" Banks said.

"No, that's fine. You two behave yourselves," Mac said, anxious to speak to Esme alone.

The Major appeared affronted, but Banks only shook his head in amusement. "I'll find you when it's time to leave," the editor said.

She watched them weave their way through the crowd and smiled.

"You're fond of Mr. Banks," Esme commented.

"I guess. He's a pretty good boss." She winked at Esme. "And he puts up with me."

Esme smiled and led her over to a relatively secluded area. They took advantage of the empty chairs and sat down.

"How're things going at the resort?" Mac asked.

"Business has been a bit slower than normal, thanks to your article."

Though there wasn't any accusation in Esme's voice, Mac felt compelled to justify the story. "It was only the truth."

"I know that, dear. Most of the employees—including the Major, even though he can never admit it aloud—were grateful for your insights." She sighed. "It was only the owners who weren't so pleased."

"I don't care about them. It's you and all the other women who live and work here that I wrote the story for," Mac stated. She knew she should ask Esme about the handcuffs, but found herself procrastinating. "How are Erin and Louise?"

"Doing well. Louise has found herself a beau."

Mac pictured the shy blonde and smiled. "Are they serious?"

"They announced their engagement yesterday. The wedding will be in three weeks."

Mac chuckled. "They didn't waste any time."

"Time is too precious to waste, Trish. You of all people should understand that."

Mac's laughter died in her throat. She couldn't put off her question any longer. "I had a dream last night, Esme."

"Oh?"

"I think it was more a memory of the night I time-traveled." Mac's palms grew slick. "I found this chest in the ruins of the Chesterfield and there was a pair of broken handcuffs in them. I picked them up and the next thing I knew I was here."

Esme smiled. "Then you must have those same handcuffs in your hand on the summer solstice in order to return to your time."

Mac had suspected Esme's explanation. "Where are they? Whose are they?"

Esme laid her palm on Mac's arm. "You will know when the time is right."

Mac groaned. "I solve one mystery and get another. Isn't there anything about this time jump that's easy?"

"Anything worth having is worth fighting for."

Mac's treasonous thoughts took her to Jared. Was he worth fighting for? "Have you seen Jared lately?"

Esme hesitated and Mac knew the answer. The hurt tore the breath from her lungs. "I guess he pretty much hates me, huh?"

Esme laid her palm on Mac's arm. "No, he doesn't hate you, my dear. He is disappointed in you. There is a difference."

"Then he didn't read the story. If he had, he'd know I didn't print everything."

Esme's eyebrows shot upward. "Why?"

"Because I made him a promise." Mac rubbed her brow. "Was he all right when you saw him?"

She nodded slowly. "He appeared well, though I believe he may have lost some weight and he didn't smile nearly as often or as easily as before."

Puzzled, Mac glanced at Esme. "Before what?"

"Before he fell in love with you."

The words were delivered in such a calm voice that Mac wasn't certain she'd heard correctly. "What?"

"He loves you."

The orchestra's music dimmed as the ballroom itself zoomed in and out of focus. Mac's temples throbbed as Esme's words echoed in her mind, but she forced a laugh. "And I thought *I* had an imagination."

"I know you do not want to believe it."

"How can you be so certain? He never said anything to me."

"He does not realize it either," Esme said.

Mac hadn't felt this off-balance since she realized she was in the nineteenth century. "Then how do you know?"

Esme laughed, a soft tinkling sound. "It is obvious, just as it is obvious you are in love with him."

The air whooshed from Mac's lungs even as she tried to laugh at the absurdity of Esme's claim. "I'm not sure what you're seeing here, Esme, but it's definitely not love. I don't plan on falling in love now or ever. It's not in my game plan."

"The only problem is, love follows its own game plan, Trish." Esme rose and waved to a man across the room. "I must go. It was so very nice to see you again. If we do not run into each other again this evening, I will stop by the next time I'm in Hope Springs." She leaned over and gave Mac a quick hug. "Good-bye, my dear."

Stunned, Mac watched Esme weave through the dancing couples until her vision blurred. Moisture on her cheeks made her wipe the back of her hand across her face. Tears? It couldn't be. Trish McAllister never cried, because there was nothing in the world worth crying over.

Nothing except love.

# EIGHTEEN

The morning after the ball Mac awakened cautiously. Her head pounded and she scowled at the rotten taste in her mouth. She scrubbed her face with her palms, barely suppressing a groan of self-induced agony.

*Note to self: Never drink champagne again.*

After Esme had left her, Mac had decided to see how many glasses of champagne it would take to forget her words. She'd forgotten nearly everything else *but* the damn words.

*It is obvious, just as it is obvious you are in love with him.*

"Shut up!" The moment the words were out of her mouth, Mac gripped her head and fell back against the pillows.

The only good thing about today was she didn't have to go in to work at the newspaper office. Mr. Banks had imbibed a bit himself and Mac was certain they had made quite an impression as they'd left the ballroom. Her only question was what *kind* of impression?

She groaned silently. This was almost as bad as her migraines. Maybe she should try some of those headache powders the doctor had given her months ago.

At least she wouldn't end up trying to pull Jared down into bed with her this time.

Damn. She was back to the subject she was trying hard to forget existed.

A soft knock on the door startled her. "Yes?"

"I've got breakfast on the table, Mac," Agnes said from the hallway.

Mac's stomach roiled and rumbled at the same time as if it couldn't make up its mind whether to be sick or hungry. "I'll be down in five minutes."

"I'll keep it warm." Agnes's footsteps faded away.

Mac pushed off her covers with her feet and carefully shifted to a sitting position. Bile rose and fell in her throat and she swallowed convulsively. Her head felt as though somebody had poured a bucket of sand in it. It had been a long time since she'd tied one on like this.

When she thought she could move without the room tipping over, she eased her feet off the bed and planted them on the floor. It seemed to anchor her and she stood with only a moment or two of fading vertigo.

Ten minutes later she could pass for a human being if nobody looked too closely at her pale face and bloodshot eyes. As she walked down the hallway she ran her hand along the wall, and going down the stairs she kept a death grip on the railing. The smell of frying meat and eggs, and of coffee, assailed her at the bottom of the steps, but she staunchly forced the nausea aside. Coffee would help and the food wouldn't hurt.

Agnes, bless her heart, didn't say a word but set a plate of food in front of her. If she ate fast, maybe she could convince her stomach everything was fine and dandy.

*Fat chance.*

Mac sipped her coffee first and didn't wait for the rebellion to begin, but shoveled the eggs mixed with sausage into her mouth, alternating with bites of toast. The first signal to make it to her brain arrived after she'd cleaned off her plate. Two minutes of controlled breathing managed to get the queasiness under control. In fact, she thought she might even survive.

Agnes appeared and refilled Mac's coffee cup. "Better?" The woman's dark eyes sparkled with mischief.

"Miraculously."

Agnes laughed and sat down on the other side of Mac. "How was the ball otherwise?"

Mac tried to remember the details but found her memory was fuzzy. "I think I danced." She dropped her head to her folded arms and groaned.

"Isn't that what a person is supposed to do at one of those fancy doings?"

"Not if the person doesn't know how to dance." Mac raised her head and squinted at Agnes. "I talked to Esme. She said Jared was at the resort three weeks ago."

Agnes nodded. "He was. He stopped by to visit."

"Why didn't you tell me?"

"He didn't come to see *you*."

The chiding tone made Mac feel like a kid and she squirmed uncomfortably. "Did he ask about me?" As soon as her question was spoken, she wished she could retract it. "No, don't answer that. It's none of my business."

"He didn't ask in so many words." Agnes stood and picked up Mac's empty plate and silverware. "Would you like to dry the dishes?"

Mac knew when she'd been baited and hooked by

a pro. "Sure, why not." Snagging her coffee cup, she followed the older woman into the kitchen.

Mac retrieved a towel from the rack, glad for the routine task. Whenever she arrived home from work at a decent hour, she would dry the dishes for Agnes. The ordinary ritual was one Mac had come to enjoy as she and Agnes discussed their day.

Agnes slid a plate into a tub of clear hot water and Mac fished it out. She wiped it dry, then set it on the counter. Although she was bursting with curiosity about Jared, she remained quiet, waiting for Agnes to speak. Another dish, then the silverware. Mac snatched the flatware from the bottom of the tub.

"He worries about you," the landlady finally said.

Mac nearly dropped the hot silverware. "Sure. That's why he ignores me when he comes to Hope Springs."

Agnes paused with her hands buried in the soapy water and gazed at Mac with understanding eyes. "You hurt him."

The breath whooshed out of Mac's lungs and inhaling seemed impossible. Who would've thought three simple words could produce so much anguish?

She scrambled for air and finally found some. "I didn't mean to."

*Great excuse, Mac. Maybe you should accidentally kick his dog, too.*

Agnes returned to her task, her brow furrowed as if she wanted to say more.

"He doesn't understand how much my work means to me," Mac tried again.

Agnes took a deep breath. "Maybe you don't understand how much *you* mean to *him.*"

"*He* was the one who ran out of here so fast he left skid marks," Mac said.

"Fear does that to a person."

Mac bit her lower lip and finished drying the dishes. She hung the towel back on the rack and poured herself some more coffee.

Jared didn't seem like the type of man who was afraid of anything. He reminded Mac of one of those stoic heroes from a spaghetti Western, and just as in the movies, the cowboy rode away leaving the girl behind.

She shook her head. She had more important things to worry about, mainly what her mission was and where to find handcuffs with the initials EJY on them. After nearly five months she should have some idea what she was supposed to do. Maybe some flickering candle at the end of a black tunnel.

*Wrong analogy.*

Mac glanced up to see Agnes had disappeared from the kitchen. She wondered if the woman was angry with her. Agnes had a soft spot for Jared and if she thought Mac had hurt him, she might not be all that inclined to remain on friendly terms with her.

A jab in the vicinity of her heart made Mac realize how much she admired the widow who'd made a life for herself against the odds. Being part Native American and a female in this era wasn't an easy path to follow, yet Agnes had forged her own successful trail. Her story would definitely be one worth writing.

Excited by the prospect, Mac hurried into the parlor, hoping Agnes would be there. The sound of the piano told Mac her guess was right. She entered the bright room and paused to watch Agnes's fingers float across the ivory keys and to listen to the melody floating from the piano wires.

*Piano wires.*

Why did the killer use them? Why not just plain wire? Or rope? What was the significance?

The answer was close. She could feel it in her gut.

Agnes ended her song and Mac applauded as she crossed the room. She used a finger to play a couple of keys and smiled wryly. "I envy people who have the gift of music. I'm musically challenged."

Agnes smiled. "I could give you piano lessons."

"I'd like that." Then Mac remembered she had little time left in this world. "But not right now. I'm pretty busy."

Agnes's fingers skimmed over the ivory keys, playing a lighthearted tune. Mac suddenly had an image of another woman with brown hair playing the piano. She blinked, dispelling the remnants of the odd vision.

"How does a piano work?" Mac asked.

Agnes paused and the lively notes ended. "The keys correspond to a hammer, which strikes a certain string. That produces the note we hear."

"If I had a piano wire in my hand, would someone be able to tell me what note it was?"

"I don't believe so. There are different size wires, but the same sizes serve different chords. It depends on how tight the wire's pulled and where the hammer hits it."

Mac's hopes plummeted. She had hoped that maybe by identifying the wires, it would give a clue to the murderer's identity.

Agnes ran through some scales. "However, if you were to find a piano that was missing the same wire you had, then you could identify what notes it was used for."

Mac had no idea where to start looking. The piano could be in the future or it could be in this time period.

Even then, the wires had probably been replaced since the murders started two years ago. "Thanks, Agnes."

"You're welcome, Mac. Are you thinking about those poor murdered women?"

"Actually, I was thinking about the person who strangled them. I'm going for a walk. Do you need anything at the store?"

"No, thank you."

Leaving the parlor, Mac ventured upstairs to retrieve her cape. She would take a walk and get some fresh air. Maybe stop at the store and see if anything new had come in. Mr. Banks had asked her to pick up another bottle of whiskey for his desk drawer two days ago. She had her keys to the office with her so she could accomplish that task even though she was officially off work.

As she strolled down the boardwalk, she greeted the people she passed. Hand-selling the papers had brought her into contact with many of the townsfolk and though she didn't know all their names, she did recognize their faces.

She arrived at the general store first and wandered in. When she had first shopped here, she'd been dumbfounded by the lack of variety. Growing up in the twentieth century with shopping malls and big retail stores had spoiled her. It was downright humbling to realize how little she actually needed to live. There were no electronic games or CDs or boomboxes or portable televisions, yet she'd grown accustomed to not having them and found she didn't miss them anymore.

Her admitted obsession was books, which were expensive, but she always liked examining and handling them. Today there weren't any new ones and she wandered back onto the street. The next stop was the Dolly

Day, the usual place to pick up a bottle of whiskey since Mr. Banks had an account there. Because it was still early, Mac found the saloon empty except for Levon, the manager and piano player.

She walked over to the upright piano. Levon had his head buried inside it.

"Lose something?" she asked.

Levon jerked up, his head bumping into the piano's lid, which was held open at an angle. He rubbed the offended spot as he scowled at Mac. "Son of a bi— What the hell are you doing here so early, Mac?"

Levon had been rude since the first time she'd met him and Mac had learned it wasn't personal. He was an asshole to everybody. "Good morning to you, too, Levon. Is your piano broken?"

Levon grumbled some choice words, then replied, "Four wires are missing."

Mac's heart skipped a beat. "Did they break?"

"Near as I can figure, someone cut them clean through." He shook his head and growled an epithet. "Who the hell would want some damned piano wires?"

*Someone looking for their next victim.*

Mac struggled to keep her voice calm and steady. "Has this happened before?"

"Not since I started working here about six months ago."

"So you didn't lose one like right before Christmas?"

"Nah. I'd remember with all the requests for carols and crap like that."

Mac swallowed a chuckle. Those were her sentiments exactly. "How did you know these four were missing?"

"Because when I tried playing a request last night, I couldn't."

"What was the song?"

" 'Beautiful Dreamer.' I used to like playing Stephen Foster songs until I started working here. Did you know this place is named after one of his songs?"

Mac frowned. The only song she could remember by Foster was "Camptown Races." " 'Dolly Day' is the name of a song?"

Levon nodded. "Not one of his better ones if you ask me, but the boss musta liked it."

Mac glanced around. "I've never met the owner."

"He's around. Comes and goes in between his gambling trips."

"So he's a gambler?" She conjured the vision of Mel Gibson in *Maverick*.

"Pretty good one, too. Never short on cash."

Mac nodded, her mind returning to the missing piano wires. "Who had the opportunity to do this?"

Levon scratched his thinning hair. "I suppose anybody who comes in here. It isn't like I guard it."

There hadn't been a wire stolen before the murder on Christmas Eve, and the fact that the next killing shouldn't be for another six weeks suggested that Mac's theory was full of holes. Still, she had that little tingling at the back of her neck that said two and two weren't equaling four.

She was missing something important. "You said you needed those keys to play 'Beautiful Dreamer'?"

"Yep. Seems to be one of the favorites. Even the boss likes it."

"I've heard it a couple times myself," she said vaguely, searching for an elusive memory. Did it have to do with something in the future? Or was it something she'd seen or heard since she arrived in the nine-teenth century?

Thrusting the frustration aside, she had Levon get her a bottle of whiskey and add it to Mr. Banks's tab.

"Do you have new wires to replace the ones that were stolen?" she asked.

"No. I have to order them from Richmond." He granted her a curt smile.

She waved and left the stale liquor and sawdust smell of the saloon behind. Pausing on the boardwalk, she tilted her head back to gaze at the sign that read Dolly Day.

Her gut instinct told her she was on the right track, but which direction did the track go? She shivered despite the cool day and glanced back at Levon who had his head back in his piano. Could he be the killer? Or was it someone who frequented the Dolly Day? The answers to her questions were close.

She should send a telegram to Jared. But what would she tell him?

*I have this theory that our killer is murdering women because of a song.*

She snorted. He'd get a good laugh out of that.

Her breath caught in her throat as she remembered something Dan had told her. At first it hadn't seemed important, but now Mac knew the significance.

She sank down onto a chair in front of the saloon. Sweat popped out on her brow and her hands trembled. The forensics report had stated that the wires used for the murders in her time had been manufactured at least a hundred years before, but appeared to be almost new. It was a riddle no one had been able to solve. Until now.

The piano wires had been brought with the killer from this time period. Any doubts that Mac had about the murderer being the same both here and in the future were dispelled. The missing piano wires at the Dolly Day were too coincidental.

She rose and crossed the street to the telegraph office. She had to tell Jared. He would help her investigate. Between the two of them, they might be able to figure out the mystery and catch the murderer. And if that was her mission, then all she had to do was find a pair of handcuffs and she could leave this world behind for good.

Her step faltered. She would also be leaving Jared behind.

Forever.


Jared entered the Pinkerton Detective Agency in Staunton, glad to be back after four weeks of working on a case in New York, then ten days of visiting his mother and sisters in Harrisburg. Yes, he was definitely glad to be back in his own office.

He noticed that the walls had been painted and two burned-out gaslights replaced while he'd been gone. They must have had visitors from the home office.

He greeted Jim Styles, another Pinkerton who worked out of the Staunton office, and smiled at Mrs. Sullivan who had been the secretary for as long as Jared had been there.

Mrs. Sullivan lowered her reading glasses, allowing them to hang by the chain around her neck. "Mr. Yates, it's nice to have you back. How was your trip?"

He shrugged. "The usual. My mother demanded that I quit my job here, then she broke into a well-rehearsed spontaneous fit of crying."

Mrs. Sullivan shook her head. "Bring her here to

the office and I'll have a woman-to-woman chat with her."

"A woman-to-barracuda chat," Jared amended. "Thanks, but I don't want to chance losing you. This office would fall apart without you."

"You say the nicest things, Mr. Yates." With a smile, Mrs. Sullivan opened a drawer and pulled out a file filled with papers. "These are the missives and telegrams that have accumulated since you've been gone."

Jared opened the file and flipped through the papers. "Anything important?"

"Mostly the usual, although there are three odd telegrams from a woman requesting information about a case you're working on. I checked her out and learned she was a reporter."

Jared's breath caught in his throat. "Who was it?"

"Miss Trish McAllister. She works at the *Hope Springs Times.*"

"Are the telegrams in here?" he demanded.

"The bottom of the pile. I assumed she was merely trying to gain information for a story. Do you know her?"

Jared nodded, his blood heating as he recalled how well he knew her. Even after all this time, he could still remember their lovemaking with startling clarity. "I met her while I was at the Chesterfield over the holidays." He headed to his office. "I'm going to try to catch up on the paperwork."

"Yes, sir," Mrs. Sullivan said, falling back into her professional capacity.

Jared closed his door and dropped into the chair behind his desk. He sighed and stared at the file of papers. Was Mrs. Sullivan right? Was Mac only using him to try to get another exclusive?

Restless, Jared stood and crossed to the window to look down on the bustling town. He raked a hand through his hair.

"Damn you, Mac," he swore aloud. "Damn you for making me care, then throwing it all back in my face."

When he left Hope Springs in January, he had expected to get over Mac within a week or two, but he hadn't. If anything, his feelings had grown. He had missed her every day for the past five months and four days.

The trip he'd taken to Hope Springs earlier had been hell. He'd caught sight of Mac twice, and each time it felt like somebody had twisted a knife in his gut. Her hair had grown out and she moved with a poised confidence no other woman he knew possessed. She had done well at the newspaper office and folks in town tended to like her despite her straightforwardness.

As illogical as it was, he had been relieved to learn she wasn't seeing another man. The thought of her sharing her bathtub with someone else brought piercing jealousy.

His mother had even noticed his preoccupation and had asked him about it, but he had managed to deflect her questions. Mac and Mrs. Everett Jared Yates the Second had absolutely nothing in common.

His gaze fell to his desktop where the file with the telegrams lay. Taking a deep breath, he returned to his chair and opened the file. He quickly set aside the top papers and found the three messages from Mac. The first one dated three weeks ago read: *Urgent! Have new information on the case. Involves the piano wires. Mac.*

The second one, dated one week later, was just as

frantic: *Important! Are you there? Need background on Levon Handler. Mac.*

Wasn't Handler the manager of one of the saloons in Hope Springs? Was he involved in the murders? Jared had talked with the man on occasion and though brusque, he had seemed decent enough. Did Mac think he was the killer?

The last one was dated May thirty-first, ten days ago. *I know you're angry with me, but lives are in jeopardy. Mac.*

He reread the three telegrams. Mac must have stumbled onto some clue, but damned if he could figure out what it was by her cryptic messages. He opened the bottom drawer of his desk and pulled out a box that held five brown envelopes, each marked with a date corresponding to one of the murders. He stared at them, wondering if they held the key. Mac had mentioned the piano wires and he assumed she had stumbled across something involving them. Though she had lost his trust, he recognized her keen intellect. She wouldn't have contacted him unless it was important and he was going to find out what it was.

He poked his head out of the office. "I need a train ticket for Hope Springs. For the day after tomorrow, preferably in the morning."

After so many years of working in a detective agency, Mrs. Sullivan didn't even blink. "Yes, sir. I'll have it for you within an hour."

He gave her a quick smile. "Thanks."

Jared retreated to his office. He'd spend the rest of today catching up on his work and tomorrow he'd check into Levon Handler. It would be a long day of checking public records, but at least it would give him something concrete to work on. He'd planned to return to Hope Springs anyway since the killer would be striking soon if he held to his June twentieth pattern.

He picked up the five envelopes, wondering what Mac had unearthed. He wouldn't be getting the answers until he returned to Hope Springs.

And this time, he wouldn't settle for anything less than the whole truth.

Mac finished typesetting the story she'd done on Agnes Ledson and breathed a sigh of relief. Tomorrow, the paper would have to be printed, folded and distributed. Usually she and Mr. Banks printed the papers one day, then folded and sold them the next, but Mac had gotten behind in the schedule. Of course, it didn't help that Mr. Banks had come down with a fever and chills. Fortunately, the doctor didn't think it was too serious, but the editor would be out of commission for three or four days, leaving Mac to finish the paper alone.

She rolled her shoulders, grimacing at the stiffness. How was she going to work the press tomorrow if she could hardly move this evening? Mac had been at this job long enough to know when she was this sore, the next day she would be lucky if she could drag herself out of bed without some heartfelt groans.

Though it was nearly eight o'clock, it was still light out. The days were lengthening, moving toward the solstice, the longest day of the year.

And the day she could return to her own time, provided she passed the tests.

Solving the murder had seemed a possibility when she thought she'd discovered an important clue with the stolen piano wires. But she hadn't heard back from Jared and the investigation she'd conducted had yielded nothing. She'd surreptitiously asked Mr. Banks about Levon Handler, but he admitted to not knowing him very well. She expanded her questioning and included trying to determine if someone who frequented the Dolly Day might have stolen the wires. Mac had no idea where to turn next.

It was pretty damned likely that she would live out the rest of her life here. That likelihood didn't hold the same desperate fear it had over five months ago. Mac had grown accustomed to the town and actually liked knowing her neighbors and fellow townsfolk. There was a certain amount of comfort to be taken in that kind of stability—it was something she'd never known in her own time.

But if she did figure out the puzzle and was able to return to her time, she would do so without looking back. Regrets, however, were another matter.

She sat down in Mr. Banks's chair and reached into the drawer that held the whiskey and now two glasses, one for each of them. She poured herself a shot but set the bottle on the desk. Placing her legs on the desktop, she crossed her ankles and leaned back to take a sip of the fiery liquor.

Closing her eyes, she enjoyed the hot trail down to her belly and waited for the whiskey to do its job. Her muscles tingled and loosened, melting away the stress. God, she loved the contentment she felt after a long productive day. The only thing that would've made it perfect would have been for a man to be waiting for her at home with two glasses of wine and a steaming bathtub.

No, not any man.

*Jared.*

Her satisfaction disappeared like smoke curling into

fog. He hadn't even acknowledged that he'd received her telegrams. Did he hate her that much?

Esme and Agnes both said he cared for her, but they didn't know . . . They didn't know that Mac had broken a trust for the sake of a news story. She forced herself to really look around the office, to see the typesetting equipment, the press, the rolls of paper and bottles of ink. Had it been worth it? Had her job been worth all the nights she'd spent alone since Jared left?

A tear trickled down her cheek and she savagely wiped it away. Exhaustion. That was the only way she could explain her maudlin emotions.

Somebody walked past the front window and Mac's breath caught in her throat. She would have sworn it was Jared, but it couldn't have been. Hell would freeze over before he made an effort to see her again. She'd ensured that.

The door opened and a man stepped in, his impossibly light blue eyes settling on her.

"Hello, Mac," Jared said quietly.

Mac blinked, expecting the apparition to disappear. It didn't.

She held up her empty whiskey glass. "Join me for a drink? It's not every day hell freezes over."

# NINETEEN

Jared wondered if he looked as shocked as he felt. He expected Mac to do the unpredictable, but seeing her with her legs propped on top of the desk and a bottle of whiskey was almost too much for even him to grasp.

"Whiskey sounds good," he said. "Mind if I sit down?"

"Be my guest." Mac dropped her feet to the floor, which was just as well since Jared wouldn't have been able to carry on a coherent conversation with the view he had from his side of the desk.

She retrieved another glass and splashed some liquor into each of them, then handed him one. She raised hers. "For old times' sake."

Jared clinked his glass against hers and downed the whiskey in two gulps. He would need the fortification to get through whatever came next.

"I received your telegrams," he began. He cleared his throat. "I was out of town when they came in."

Something flickered in her curtained eyes, but it was gone before he could identify it. "So you did get them."

He nodded, feeling a need to explain. "I was working on a case in New York and got roughed up a bit so I took some time off to go home and visit the family."

"You were hurt?"

"Not badly. Bruised ribs and a helluva shiner." He laughed, but it sounded shaky even to his ears. "My mother used it as an opportunity to point out how dangerous my job is."

"She's right."

Her sharp tone startled Jared. She was the last person he expected to find fault with his chosen career. "I'm a big boy. I can make my own decisions."

"I *know* you're a big boy." Her seriousness evaporated and her eyes twinkled. "Intimately."

Jared's body responded to her velvet tone. How could he have forgotten how one word from her silky lips could make him as randy as a tomcat? He shifted in his chair, trying to alleviate the pressure in his groin.

"You said you had some new information about the piano wires. You also said you needed to find out more about Levon Handler," Jared said.

She narrowed her eyes. "That's right. What did you find out?"

He shook his head. "First, I need some answers."

She leaned forward as if to seize the bottle of whiskey, but sighed and sank back into her seat without touching it. "Fire away."

"What about the piano wires?"

"I had a hunch. The killer is methodical, murdering the women with the exact two twists of the wire each time. The woman is always young, pretty, single, so he isn't randomly picking anyone to kill. It only makes sense that he uses the piano wires for a reason, too.

"So I started wondering why. I was listening to Agnes play the piano one day and it hit me. The wires might correspond to notes, which produce a song that is for some reason significant to the killer."

"So what has this got to do with Levon Handler?"

"The day I sent you the first telegram, I happened to stop by the saloon to get another bottle of whiskey. Mr. Banks has me pick up a bottle whenever he's running low. That day Levon said he'd just had four piano wires stolen." She paused to let the significance sink in. "Who would want to steal piano wires?"

Jared stared at her, amazed and unaccountably proud of her intuitive leap. There was definitely a sharp mind behind her eccentricity. "Somebody who's using them to murder innocent women."

"Got it in one." She flashed him a smile. "So if we accept this line of reasoning, then the killer was in town a month ago and he might still be here now." She raised her open hands and shrugged. "For all we know, he could be living in Hope Springs. I had you check into Levon because he was the most obvious suspect. Now it's your turn."

Jared reached into the inner breast pocket of his suit coat and withdrew a piece of paper. "I couldn't find much on him. He was born in Richmond and attended college there. He left school after a year, then pretty much dropped out of sight."

"So there's no information on him between then and now?" Mac demanded.

He shrugged. "It's not like there are a whole lot of ways to keep track of people."

"What I wouldn't do for a computer with Internet access," Mac mumbled.

"A what?"

She shook her head. "Forget it. It's just my sleep-deprived mind rambling."

He studied her closer and found telltale lines of exhaustion around her eyes and the corners of her lips. Her face appeared paler than usual, but it was hard to be certain since it had been some time since he had seen her. "Is everything all right?"

She shot him a crooked grin. "Mr. Banks is sick. I have a paper to get out tomorrow. There's a killer stealing piano wire for his next victims. And the solstice will be here in less than a week."

"The solstice is when the last two killings have occurred," Jared said thoughtfully.

"You know, you're brighter than you look, Yates."

Irritation made Jared frown, but when she stood and stretched, pulling her apron taut over her breasts, his annoyance disappeared.

"I'm going back to my room to get some sleep. I've got a long day tomorrow," she said.

"What about the murderer?" Jared forcibly drew his attention away from her curves.

"What about him? I gave you what I had and in the month it took for you to reply to my telegrams, the trail has gotten cold," she said bitterly.

Guilt assailed him and he spoke sharply, "I told you, I was out of town. I didn't even know about any of this until two days ago."

"You're forgiven," she said flatly.

She removed her apron and sleeve guards as Jared watched, his emotions in a turmoil.

"You're a good one to be talking about forgiveness," he finally said.

Her complexion paled, but she lifted her chin and met his gaze evenly. "You're right. You're the one who should be asking for it."

Jared had been prepared to let bygones be bygones. Over the past months, he had come to understand that her job was just as important to her as his was to him.

He couldn't fault her for wanting to get a scoop. But he wasn't about to apologize for something that was clearly her doing. "I wasn't the one who broke my word."

Her nostrils flared and her eyes narrowed. "I'm going to lock up now."

He stood. "I'll accompany you. I'm staying at Agnes's this time."

"Suit yourself," she said after a moment's surprised hesitation.

Jared stepped over to the door to wait while she placed the whiskey bottle in a desk drawer then turned off the lights. The sunset lent a burned orange glow to the room, burnishing Mac's blonde hair. The faint scents of hyacinth wafted to him and it triggered the memory of making love in her bathtub. The same scent had surrounded them even as Mac's body had surrounded him, hot and sleek against his own.

"Are you going to spend the night here, Yates?" she asked impatiently.

Jared tried to toss off the remembered sensations, but his body wasn't ready to release them. He stepped out onto the boardwalk stiffly. Mac followed, locking the door behind her. They walked without speaking toward the boardinghouse and Jared missed her lively banter. The woman beside him seemed a pale ghost of the vixen whom he'd made love to so many months ago.

"Have you been to the Chesterfield lately?" he asked, needing to fill the awkwardness.

"Mr. Banks and I went to the May Ball. Esme told me you'd been to the resort." Mac kept her gaze aimed straight ahead.

"That's right." He couldn't tell her that he'd wanted to see her, talk with her. Make love with her.

"You could have stopped by the office. I wouldn't have attacked you in public."

A smile twitched Jared's lips. "Somehow I think you'd do whatever you wanted no matter where you were."

Her step faltered. "No matter *when* I was," she said softly.

The odd statement sent a shiver down Jared's spine. "What do you mean?"

She stopped abruptly and spun around to face him. "Exactly what I said. You didn't read the article I wrote, did you?"

The unexpected question brought a surge of justified anger. "Why should I? It was everything I asked you not to print."

Her smile was brittle. "Was it?" She whirled around and marched away.

Jared caught up with her in three steps and grabbed her arm, spinning her around. "Damn it, Mac. I've never known you to tiptoe around anything. If you have something to say, say it."

She glared at him. "You want me to speak my mind. Okay, Mr. Pinkerton Detective, here it is. If you had read the story I wrote, you'd know that I didn't break any confidences. The only information I used in my article was that which was already public knowledge. I merely pulled everything about the five murders together." She smiled coldly. "The only thing I did was piss off the resort owners and they lost some business. So if you want to hold on to that holier-than-thou attitude, go ahead. But for once in my life, I didn't put the story first." Her eyes glistened with moisture. "I put *you* first."

When Mac ran away this time, Jared didn't follow.

He remained frozen in place, hearing her words over and over again.

*I put* you *first.*

Finally, he continued on to the boardinghouse, his steps as heavy as the weight on his chest. All this time, he had thought she'd broken his trust. He had misjudged her.

But then, whom had he misjudged? The maid? The reporter? Or the lover? Who was Mac? Why was she so different from any other woman he'd met?


Mac's hopes of getting a good night's sleep had been dashed the moment Jared told her he was also staying at Agnes's boardinghouse. Knowing he was under the same roof made her restless—in both mind and body. Twice she'd gotten out of bed to pace the floor. Once she'd even put her hand on the doorknob to go to him. Even though they disagreed, she knew their bodies wouldn't let a misunderstanding stop the pleasure they could share.

Seeing Jared again had brought it all back in crystal-clear clarity. The pheromones were expected, but not the longing for his arms around her, holding her warm and secure after the loving was done.

*Loving?*

Her belly twisted with physical need, but she couldn't deny the ache in her heart that was just as powerful. She'd always laughed at the old adage that absence makes the heart grow fonder. In fact, she personally preferred the corrupted version about abstinence making another part of the anatomy grow harder.

She shook her head. She'd latched on to that one

after the boy who'd taken her virginity had said, "See ya later and don't wait by the phone."

She finished buttoning her blouse and tucked it into her simple black skirt. No corset and only one slip. Fewer clothes to lose if she and Jared should happen to . . .

No, she couldn't think about that. There were only six days left until the solstice, and she still had no idea what the hell she was supposed to do. If it involved the murderer, she was sunk. Levon was a dead end and trying to find the culprit who'd stolen the piano wire a month after it happened was laughable. In fact, when she'd gone to speak with Chief Garrett about the crime, he hadn't known anything about it. Levon hadn't even bothered to report it.

After making a few quick passes through her hair with the brush, Mac headed downstairs for breakfast. She paused on the bottom step, hearing Jared's low gravelly voice as he talked with Agnes in the dining room. She couldn't face him. Not yet.

Continuing to the door she called out with false brightness. "I'm running late, Agnes. Bye."

Mac made a clean escape. Five minutes later she unlocked the newspaper office and after putting on a pot of coffee, she donned her protective wear. Tucking her hair behind her ears, she sighed and set the press.

It was nearly noon when Mac's aching body demanded a break from the physical task of printing the paper. She groaned as she lowered herself into the nearest chair and inhaled the fresh air coming in through the open door. Her stomach growled, but she couldn't take the time to eat. Mr. Banks was counting on her to get the paper out on time.

Why should she care about some small town hokey paper? She should be spending every last minute trying to find the handcuffs and discover what she had to do in order to return to her time. But Mr. Banks trusted her to get the paper out and she had no intention of letting him down.

*Even if it means never showing your father how much better you are?*

"Shut up," she spoke aloud.

"I didn't say anything."

Startled, Mac glanced up to see Jared with a bag in hand standing in the doorway. "Look what the cat dragged in," she commented above the sudden thundering of her heart.

Jared stepped inside. "Have you looked in a mirror lately?"

"No need to flatter me."

He smiled and Mac's breath caught in her throat. She'd forgotten how lethal his smiles could be.

"What brought you into my web?" Mac asked irritably.

"I was worried about you. Agnes said she heard you pacing the floor most of the night."

"Great. A landlady who's a light sleeper. I'm fine. Just a little busy." She stood and returned to the press, hoping he could take a hint.

"I didn't sleep very well myself," Jared admitted. "I kept thinking about you, about your theory that the music might mean something to the killer."

"Fat lot of good it does."

"I talked to Levon this morning."

Her interest piqued, Mac turned to face him. "About?"

"He said he was starting to play 'Beautiful Dreamer' when he noticed the missing wires."

Mac nodded impatiently. "He told me."

Jared continued as if she hadn't interrupted him.

"The stolen wires were the twelfth, fourteenth, fifteenth and seventeenth notes of the song."

Mac's mind raced. "But the next murder would be number eleven, not twelve."

"What if the first victim was never found? Or maybe it was someone outside the normal pattern?"

"You mean like the real target?"

Jared smiled. "Got it in one."

The modern term coming from a nineteenth-century man made Mac grin, but the humor was short-lived. "What about the next notes? Why aren't they in order?"

"Because notes thirteen and sixteen are repeats of the notes before," Jared said triumphantly.

"Damn, you're good."

He winked. "I've heard those words before."

Mac felt her face redden with unaccustomed embarrassment, but she spoke with a cheeky grin, "And I meant them then, too."

The air in the office thickened and Mac's senses narrowed until they were focused completely on Jared—from the smell of his shaving soap to the specks of midnight blue in his light-colored eyes to the sound of his steady, even breathing.

"Agnes showed me the article you wrote about the murders," Jared said, breaking the spell.

Mac had to concentrate a moment to figure out the meaning of his words. She stiffened. "And?"

"Maybe I do owe you an apology," he said quietly.

She wanted to come back with a sharp retort, but her mind blanked. Jared was man enough to admit he was wrong. Could this man do anything else to shock her? "Maybe you do."

He didn't rise to the bait and spoke sincerely, "I'm sorry, Mac. I was wrong about you."

Instead of feeling vindicated, she felt an emotion she was unfamiliar with—shame. To cover her confusion, she turned away from Jared and fussed needlessly with the press.

A soft scuff behind her and a sense of a body close to hers alerted her to Jared's nearness. He clasped her shoulders and squeezed them gently. "What's wrong? I thought you'd be glad that I finally saw the error of my ways."

Mac could hear the effort he put into making his words teasing. It made her feel worse. "You were right the first time, Jared," she began. "I'm not a very nice person. I've been known to lie and break a promise to get a story."

His tender massage halted and she expected him to walk out the door immediately. She deserved nothing more. Instead, he turned her around to face him and raised her chin with a cupped hand. She closed her eyes, unable to bear his disappointment.

"Open your eyes, Mac," he said softly.

She couldn't stop herself from obeying his quiet words. The expected displeasure was absent from his handsome features and in its stead was a tenderness she'd never seen directed at her before.

"But you didn't do that this time. What I've heard around town is that you're trustworthy and dependable," he said as his thumb caressed her cheek.

"Are you sure you're not talking about a horse?" Mac managed to ask past the thickness in her throat.

Jared slowly shook his head, not allowing her to make light of his words. "You're also smart and beautiful and generous and—"

She held up a hand. "Maybe I should take you to the doctor's office."

He chuckled. "And funny."

If she didn't know better, she'd think Jared cared for her.

*Danger, Will Robinson. Danger.*

She sobered. "But that doesn't excuse what I've done in the past—before."

"Do you believe people can change?"

Did she? She'd been a cynic for years; she couldn't remember if she ever believed that a person could change his or her life around. She thought of the people she'd talked with in this town while she'd written the local news column. Many of them had started a new life here, leaving behind pasts darkened with tragedy or scandal or poverty.

"I've seen it happen," she finally admitted.

"Then why is it so hard to think that maybe you've changed?"

Mac considered the life she'd had in the future and how she had adjusted to the nineteenth century. She had made changes and it wasn't just the differences in the two worlds. It was the man standing in front of her. Jared had somehow changed her, made her a person she liked a little more than the woman she'd been six months ago.

"Are you sure you aren't a lawyer?" Mac asked, feeling a weight lift from her shoulders.

He threw back his head and laughed, and Mac took the opportunity to kiss his exposed throat. Jared's laughter died but a sexy smile replaced it. He lowered his smoky gaze and settled his mouth upon hers.

Mac collapsed against his strong chest and opened her lips to his, tasting him on her tongue. How had she lived five months without this man? How could she live the rest of her life without him?

Reluctantly, she drew away, glad when her legs

didn't collapse beneath her. "I have a paper to get out or Mr. Banks is not going to be happy with me."

He retrieved the bag he'd set on the desk. "Eat first."

She peeked inside and the smell of something wonderful wafted out. "From Corinne Garrett's restaurant?"

He nodded. "I thought you'd like it."

"It's one of my favorites." She waggled her eyebrows. "Among other things."

Jared removed his jacket and rolled up his shirtsleeves.

"What are you doing?" Mac demanded, wondering if he was about to take her sexual innuendoes seriously.

*I can only hope.*

"I'm going to help you keep your job."

She studied the determination in eyes that looked at her with so much affection that it almost frightened her. It was even more potent than the incendiary passion they had shared. "If you plan to help, you'd better put on Mr. Banks's apron and sleeve guards."

"Yes, ma'am."

"I like your attitude, soldier," Mac said as she winked.


Six hours later, Mac and Jared dropped into the two chairs. All the papers had been printed, folded and sold. Neither spoke for five minutes as contentment washed through their exhaustion.

"I wouldn't have been able to do it without your help," Mac admitted.

"I know."

Mac half-heartedly threw a pencil at him. "Nothing like a little humility."

He chuckled. "I'm too tired to be humble." He raised his head from the back of the chair. "Did I ever tell you how cute you look with ink smudges on your face?"

She groaned and buried her face in her hands. "Please, anything but cute." She raised her head to look at him. "Precocious children are cute. Puppies are cute. Ben Affleck might even be considered cute. If you insist on assigning me an adjective, gorgeous would be acceptable. So would lovely, elegant, graceful, charming, and I'd even let you get away with an adorable. But I am *not* cute."

Jared's shoulders shook with laughter. "Why do I even try?"

"Because you can't help yourself."

"Was it me or does this conversation make no sense?"

Mac thought about that a moment and realized her brain was too far gone for any type of strenuous activity. "I think we're both punchy from exhaustion and lack of food."

Jared scrubbed his face with his palms. "No argument there. If we're lucky, Agnes saved us some supper."

"I'm sure she saved *you* some supper." Mac rolled her eyes. "For some unknown reason, she likes you."

"You're just jealous."

She feigned a glare in his direction. "Nah. If she wants you, she can have you. Too much maintenance on your model."

"You're not from San Francisco, are you?" Jared suddenly asked.

"Where did that come from?"

"Answer my question."

His voice was low, almost hypnotic. But beneath the curiosity there was something else. Affection. Concern.

She rubbed the chair's armrests, feeling the cool wood polished smooth by someone's diligent hand. All the jagged edges were gone, but it was still possible to get a tiny sliver caught under the skin.

"I once told you the lies were easier to believe than the truth. That hasn't changed, Jared," she said quietly.

He pushed himself upright but there was no anger, only resignation as he gazed down at her. "Now *you* don't trust *me*."

She stood and her hand latched onto his muscled forearm. "It's not a matter of trust. It's a matter of believing."

His eyebrows drew together. "They're the same thing."

"No. I don't trust easily, but for some reason, I trust you." She laughed weakly. "I must be getting soft in my old age."

"You're soft, Mac, but in the right way." He feathered the back of his fingers down her arm and gooseflesh arose in their wake. "Marry me."

# TWENTY

The second the proposal left Jared's mouth, he regretted it. He hadn't planned on saying it, but that wasn't the reason for his regret. He didn't know how or when it happened, but he had fallen in love with the exasperating woman.

No, the reason he regretted his impulsive words was the panic in Mac's eyes. How often had she told him they only shared a physical attraction? But if it had simply been a case of sexual need, Jared could have taken care of that compulsion by visiting some willing woman at the Flower Patch. But he hadn't wanted anyone but Mac.

"Say something," Jared said, trying to keep his voice casual.

"Hell of an encore, Yates," she said flippantly, though he could see the rapid pulse in her slender neck.

That wasn't what he'd been expecting, but where Mac was concerned, expectations were rarely met.

"You should see my disappearing coin act," Jared said airily.

She pulled out of his arms and hugged herself as if chilled. "Better than the disappearing woman act."

"What're you talking about?"

She seemed to curl into herself. "I can't marry you, Jared. I won't be sticking around here much longer."

"Where—" His voice broke and he cursed his ill-timing anew. Had he frightened her so badly that she'd leave Hope Springs? "Where are you going?"

"Back home."

"San Francisco?" He couldn't stop the ugly derision that crept into his tone.

"Please, Jared, let's not make this any more difficult."

"No, I think you've made it about as difficult as it can be already." Jared tore off the printer's apron and sleeve guards and tossed them on the desk. He slung his jacket over his shoulder. "Good luck with your story. I'm sure it'll keep you warm at night."

He strode out, leaving a gaping emptiness. Mac shivered with the chill left in his wake, but inside she was numb. How had the day gone from perfection to disaster in the span of five minutes?

Did she love him enough to marry him? She thought of the stupid love songs her mother had listened to for hours on end. True love. Everlasting love. Inescapable love.

Love had made her mother lose her mind, then her life. Mac wanted nothing to do with something that destroyed a person's own self. To give so much power to another person was dangerous.

She had told Jared she trusted him more than she'd ever trusted another person, but that didn't mean wholly. Love and trust were too fragile to toss around like a kiss or even sex. For most men, the physical deed was enough. Why wasn't it enough for Jared? Why did he demand more?

Mac's heartbeat spiked and her breath came in quick spurts. She had but one goal in her life: to best her father at his own game and expose him to the world for the bastard he truly was.

*Then what?*

All Mac could imagine was her father's humiliation. There was nothing beyond.

Nothing but an eternity of darkness.


The bright sun of the early evening mocked Mac's gray mood as she walked back to the boardinghouse after work. Four days had passed since she had declined Jared's marriage proposal and her doldrums still remained. She hadn't even been this upset when an investigative story she'd spent five months on had been tossed into file thirteen.

She spotted a familiar woman a block away and shaded her eyes to identify Esme Sparrow carrying a basket she used to tote her purchases. Mac hadn't seen her for over two weeks, though she'd planned to visit her tomorrow. She'd asked for and received the next day off in preparation for her return to her own time.

Mac changed directions toward Esme as a man dressed in a fancy suit greeted her. Mac paused on the boardwalk to watch the two converse. Though she couldn't see Esme's face, she thought the woman was upset. Mac shifted her attention to the dapper man and frowned. It seemed as if she should know him.

Determined to find out why he appeared familiar, she continued walking. Mac was fifty feet away when the man glanced up to see her. He turned his head, said something to Esme and strode away in the opposite direction.

As Mac neared Esme, she noticed her pale face. "Are you all right?"

"Fine," Esme replied, her voice and eyes distant.

"Who was that man?"

Esme focused sharply on Mac. "Do you know him?"

"I don't think so, but he looked familiar."

Esme relaxed, but Mac had the feeling she remained tense beneath the surface. "That was Granville Foster. He owns the Dolly Day."

"So that's the elusive owner," Mac said thoughtfully. "Funny how he named the saloon after one of Stephen Foster's songs and his last name is Foster."

"Strange, isn't it?"

Mac eyed her closely, but Esme's gaze wouldn't meet her own. There was something else going on here. "How do you know him? He doesn't seem the type of man you'd associate with."

Esme's composure slipped, but she quickly righted it. "We knew each other as children."

Mac's suspicions were lighting up all across the board. "Here in Hope Springs?"

"No."

Mac waited, expecting her to expound but she didn't. Deciding a stalling tactic was in order, she smiled. "It's good to see you. I had planned to come up to the resort tomorrow." She leaned closer. "The solstice."

"That is why I came to town this evening. I had hoped to speak with you, too." Esme motioned to a little café.

They found a table in a corner with nobody near enough to overhear their conversation and ordered coffee.

"Have you determined what must be done?" Esme asked quietly.

"No, and I haven't found the damned handcuffs

either." Mac tamped down her frustration. "I'm not afraid to tell you I'm getting nervous."

"You still have a day."

"I've had nearly six months and haven't figured it out yet. Who says I'll be able to pull everything together before midnight tomorrow night?"

"Do you wish to return to your time?" Esme asked.

Mac glanced away, her thoughts taking her to Jared. She'd already estranged him though not without regrets. Mr. Banks would survive without her. Who else would miss her? Nobody.

"Yes," she replied.

Esme seemed to wilt before her eyes. "Then you shall have your answers."

Stunned, Mac asked, "You've known all along?"

"No, but you have." Esme rose. "I must return to the Chesterfield."

Mac couldn't let her leave. She needed more information. "You haven't had your coffee yet."

Esme laid her hand on Mac's. "Trust in yourself." Then she was gone.

*Everything always seems to come back to trust.*

The waitress arrived with two cups of coffee, and Mac motioned for her to set them both in front of her. "I need the caffeine kick."

The girl looked confused but attempted a smile before scurrying away.

Left alone, Mac leaned back and took a sip from the first cup. The brew was hot and bitter this late in the day, but she didn't mind. She tried to concentrate on her mysterious mission, but her thoughts kept returning to Jared.

She remembered the Garden Room and the moonlight that had made their lovemaking magical. The day she lost her job at the Chesterfield seemed an eternity ago, but her seduction of Jared that same day was clearer. So much clearer.

And the last time. The bathtub. Hot water. Hotter mouths and bodies straining together, sharing their ecstasy at the same moment in time. Each time they had made love, it had been better than the time before. If that was true, then surely the next time would kill them both. But it would be a happy ending.

*So what kind of ending are you looking for, Mac?*

If Esme was right, then Mac would be back in her own century in less than two days. Her Pulitzer story about a killer who leaped through time to choose his victims awaited. But would they believe her? Hell, she didn't even think Jared would believe her. How could she expect millions of strangers to believe her wild claim?

Mac entered the boardinghouse cautiously and listened until she was certain Jared wasn't nearby. She climbed the stairs, placing her toes on the part of the wood that didn't creak. She had never lived in a place long enough to get to know its secrets so well.

Once inside her room, she gave in to the sigh poised on her lips. One more night here. She should be celebrating. So why wasn't she?

Unwilling to dwell on it, Mac went into the bathroom and ran water to fill the tub. A hot bath would relax her muscles and allow her to sleep. She had a feeling she'd need all the help she could get tonight.

Mac counted the quiet chimes of the grandfather's clock in the parlor—ten . . . eleven . . . twelve. Midnight and she was still wide awake.

Only one more day until the solstice—one more day
to discover the answers that Esme assured her she'd
find. But that wasn't what made her toss and turn in
her lonely bed. It wasn't even the stifling summer heat
that made her feverish and restive.

Jared Yates lay less than fifty feet away, separated
only by thin walls and doors that opened both ways.
And this would be the last night the living vital man
existed in her lifetime.

Her perspiration-dampened body hummed with
need and tingled for Jared's masterful touch. Would
one last night be so terrible? Would he even want her
after she had turned him down? There was only one
way to find out.

She rose and pulled on her robe, tying the sash
around her waist. Though nobody else should be
awake at this hour, Mac cracked open her door and
peeked into the hall. Empty. She tiptoed out of her
room and down to Jared's. The doorknob turned easily
in her hand and she was inside his room.

Jared lay diagonally across the mattress, facedown,
with only a sheet covering his butt and legs. The
moonlight gilded his thick hair and smoothly muscled
back with silver light. He appeared vulnerable in re-
pose with one hand tucked beneath his pillow and the
other resting beside his head. His lips were parted
slightly and an occasional snore gently rumbled across
them.

How could she leave him?

How could she not?

Mac shrugged out of her robe, letting it drift to the
floor behind her. She fingered her nightgown and
without hesitation, drew it over her head to join the
other garment at her feet. Stepping out of the pool of
silk, she padded to the bed and lay down beside Jared.

Heat radiated from his lean body and she was instinctively drawn to it.

She breathed deeply, inhaling his masculine scent, imprinting it upon her for the lonely nights ahead. Then she dipped her head toward his shoulder and caressed him with her lips.

Jared moaned and shifted, but didn't awaken.

Mac continued her trail of kisses to his spine then downward to where the sheet hid him from her greedy eyes. With a trembling hand, she lowered the sheet, skimming her palm across one muscular buttock. The hard muscle flexed beneath her hand.

She couldn't deny the heat that licked through her veins, channeling toward her belly and pooling between her thighs.

"Jared," she whispered, the pain she'd been trying to hide rising from her heart and soul.

Jared's breathing changed, signaling his awakening. When he lifted his head to stare at her in shock, Mac merely kissed him deeply, fully, saying what she couldn't speak aloud.

They separated and Jared rolled onto his back, wrapping his arms around her and lifting her so she lay full length upon him.

"What are you doing here, Mac?" he asked softly.

She laid her forefinger on his lips. "Please. Don't talk. Just love me."

And Jared did all she'd hoped for . . . and more.


Later, Mac lay with her head on Jared's damp chest, her body slowly spiraling downward. It was time to leave. She tried to push herself up, but Jared's arms refused to release her.

"Stay with me tonight," he whispered.

And Mac did what he asked because she couldn't think of any other place she'd rather be . . . in any time.

Jared awakened slowly, his body languid and his mind tranquil, unlike most mornings when dark thoughts plagued him. A warmth against his left side and a weight upon his shoulder made him turn his head and open his eyes.

Mac's sleep-tousled hair and flushed face brought back the memory of the night's activities with startling swiftness. It hadn't been a dream. Mac *had* come to him in the middle of the night and they had made love, the first time with something akin to desperation after the months spent apart. The second time had been slower, each of them giving and receiving with equal measures of tenderness.

Why had she come to his bed? Why now after the past few days of trying to ignore each other?

She moved, her left leg sliding down his until her delicate foot rested upon his larger one. The feel of her silky skin gliding across him brought the blood rushing to his groin, causing his penis to stir.

This woman had become an addiction, one he would be loath to lose. But she was leaving unless he could convince her to stay.

She shifted again, her breath growing more shallow as she moved to wakefulness. He watched her, unable to look away, and was rewarded with the blinking of sleepy light brown eyes. For only a moment, they reflected panic; then it was gone and she smiled wryly.

"Morning," she greeted, then clapped a hand over her mouth and wrinkled her nose. "Sorry. Morning breath."

He chuckled. "If you can put up with mine, I can put up with yours."

"You're a brave man, Jared Yates," she said, lowering her hand.

He tightened his arms around her slim naked body. "No braver than you, Trish McAllister."

"Are you referring to my unexpected visit?"

"No, but I have to admit I wasn't expecting it."

She shrugged, the movement of her breasts against his side sending pleasurable sensations skating through him. "I wasn't either," she said.

"Then why?"

She settled her forehead in the crook of his neck and shoulder. "I wanted you."

The simplicity of her answer left him reeling. Women said "I love you," while a man, if he was honest, would say "I want you." Yet it was Mac who tried to keep the emotions from their lovemaking. Why? She cared for him, maybe even loved him as much as he loved her, but she couldn't admit it aloud. Could she even admit it to herself?

His lips caressed her hair. "I love you," he whispered.

She stilled and even her breathing stopped. Then she shot up off the bed before he could react. She turned her back to him as she tugged on her nightgown, covering her slender back, nicely rounded derriere and long legs.

"You don't have to leave," Jared said quietly.

"Yes, I do."

Her short answer told him what he already suspected. "Why are you running away?"

She donned her robe and, as she tied the belt, turned to face him. "It's what I do best."

Before he could come up with a reply, her gaze

latched onto his dresser and he followed her line of
sight to his handcuffs. She crossed over to them and
picked them up. Her eyes glazed and her mouth gaped.

"These are the ones," she whispered, then asked in
a stronger voice. "Are these yours?"

Puzzled, Jared nodded.

"Why are the initials EJY on them?" she demanded.

"They're mine. My first name's actually Everett.
My father has the same name so everyone called me
by my middle name, Jared." He rose from the bed and
noticed her gaze flicker to his groin. Her cheeks reddened and he bit back a smile. He donned his own
robe. "Why are my handcuffs so fascinating?"

She blinked. "I thought only cops had handcuffs."

"Most Pinkerton detectives do, too."

"Can I borrow them?"

"Why?"

"I need them."

"For what?"

"Please. I-I'll give them back to you tomorrow."

Every instinct told Jared to refuse her and he hadn't
survived this long in his line of work by ignoring his
gut feelings. "What do you need them for?" he repeated.

"You wouldn't believe me if I told you."

Raking a hand through his hair, he growled in frustration. "I'm getting damned sick of that excuse, Mac.
Tell me what the hell I won't believe."

She looked as if she was about to bolt. Just as Jared
got ready to lunge for her, her shoulders slumped. She
shuffled over to his bed and dropped down, looking
like someone who had just lost her best friend.

He lowered himself to the mattress beside her and
laid his hand on her clasped ones, which rested in her
lap. "Tell me, Mac. Trust me," he said quietly.

"I trust you, but you're not going to trust me after I tell you the truth."

Apprehension rippled down Jared's back, but he smiled gently, encouragingly. "Go ahead."

"I'm not from here," she began.

He smiled. "That's pretty obvious."

She turned to look him in the eyes and the desperation in hers tore the breath from his lungs. "You said I'm different. Well, there's a good reason for that. I'm not from here, not from this time. I shouldn't even be born yet."

Jared was trying to follow her rambling, but she had ceased to make sense. "What do you mean?"

"Remember the night on the train when we met?"

He nodded.

"That night the Piano Man Killer, the murderer who's been strangling those women, had taken another victim. I was there to cover the story and I happened to see a man watching us from the cover of some trees. I chased after him, but I lost him when the snow got too heavy. I took shelter in this old ruined resort called the Chesterfield."

Jared could hardly breathe as his heartbeat reverberated in his head. "You're saying you're from the future?"

"Got it in one." She smiled but it was a weak caricature.

"And the killer is also from the future?" he asked hoarsely.

"Or else he's from your time. It's hard to say unless we learn for certain who and when his first victim was."

Unable to sit still, Jared rose on legs that trembled. Yes, he had known Mac was different, but from the future? She had to be crazy. What other explanation could there be? Then why did she sound so sane?

Remembered snatches of conversation swirled through him. "Those women weren't killed in San Francisco, were they?"

She shook her head. "They were killed between Hope Springs and the remains of the resort in my time."

Maybe this was all a dream. Maybe he was still sleeping and had imagined Mac in his bed and now this deranged conversation.

"What do my handcuffs have to do with this?" He wanted to add "crazy story," but he restrained himself for her sake.

"I saw them in my time in a chest that was in the ruins. They were rusty and broken, but I could make out the initials. It was while I was holding them that I ended up here," she explained.

Jared took a deep breath. "So what you're saying is that you followed the killer to the Chesterfield, which in your time is nothing more than ruins. There you found this chest with my handcuffs in it and when you picked them up, you ended up on the train where we first met."

"Close enough." She frowned. "You don't believe me."

"So does all this have anything to do with why you slipped into my bed last night?" he asked, ignoring her comment.

She nodded and stood to face him. "June twentieth is the solstice and my theory is the killer is traveling between time periods with the solstices. I think that's how I got here, too."

Jared thought back to that night six months ago. "But that was December nineteenth."

"At midnight it became December twentieth," Mac said softly. "The winter solstice."

Yes, it had been after midnight when he had first seen her. Was he actually considering her story to be true? If so, he was no better off than she was.

"Look, I know this is a lot to swallow, but I can prove it."

She took hold of his hand and tugged him to the door. He didn't resist but followed her to her room where she released him and knelt down beside her bed. She leaned over, and if Jared hadn't been so dazed by her confession, he would have been able to appreciate the view of her shapely backside.

Mac withdrew a bag from beneath the bed and placed it on her mussed blankets. After rummaging around, she said, "Ah ha." In her hand she held a small purse, but it didn't look like any reticule Jared had ever seen before. Another moment of digging around and she produced an odd card and handed it to him. "This is my driver's license."

Jared stared at the shiny card with a small color image of Mac that appeared lifelike. He saw the town Staunton written there, as well as Virginia, then noticed her birth date. The date could be someone's idea of a joke. However, being a Pinkerton, he was fairly well versed in technological capabilities and knew this object had not come from this place.

Nor this time.

Jared sat down hard on the bed and Mac followed him, wrapping an arm around his waist.

*"Now* do you believe me?" she asked quietly.

He had dozens of questions clamoring in his head. "How does it happen? This time traveling?" he finally asked.

Mac shrugged. "I wish I knew. As I said, it's tied

to the solstice but damned if I can figure it out." She
paused. "Esme Sparrow knows. She knew I was from
the future when I first saw her at the depot that night.
She was the one who came up with the cousin story."

"Esme?"

Jared's voice nearly squeaked and Mac hugged him.
She could imagine how he must feel, to have his
whole world tipped. She didn't have to imagine—she
knew firsthand.

"She told me that for me to return to my time, I
had to accomplish two things. First, I had to find the
object I was touching the night I was brought here,
which I did." She held up the handcuffs she'd managed
to hang on to. "Second, I had to complete some unknown mission, which I've also figured out."

"What is it?"

Mac was pleased to see some color had returned to
Jared's face, making his dark morning whiskers appear
not quite as stark. "To catch the Piano Man Killer,
the murderer who's been killing innocent young
women in both of our times for the last few years."

Jared flinched. "How do we do that? I've been after
the son of a bitch for a long time and I haven't even
seen him."

Mac nibbled at the inside of her cheek. "I told you
I saw him, but I still haven't been able to remember
what he looked like. His face is blurry."

"Does he know you saw him?" Jared suddenly
asked.

Mac started, understanding exactly what Jared was
inferring. "I think so. But he's had six months to get
rid of me and he hasn't done it."

"Maybe he's planning on your being his next victim."

The naked worry in Jared's face brought moisture

to her eyes and she looked away before he noticed. "I don't think so. I'm pretty sure all the victims had something in common besides being young and pretty. They were all pure. Untouched."

"Virgins," Jared said.

Mac's somber expression eased. "And we both know I don't fit that criterion."

Jared's cheeks reddened. She loved how this big tough Pinkerton detective could blush. She also loved how he made her feel when they were in bed together, either making love or merely cuddling.

After tonight, he would find some other woman to share his bed.

Mac's heart skipped a beat and her throat grew thick. No, she wouldn't cry. She had anxiously awaited this day for six months—the day she could return to her own time, her own apartment. Her own empty bed.

Her hands fisted, but the metal handcuffs within her palm made her wince.

"So tonight if we can catch the killer and you're holding my handcuffs, you can return to your own time at midnight," Jared finally said.

She nodded, incapable of speech.

Jared stood and glanced down at his handcuffs, but he didn't reach for them. "I'm going to wash up and get dressed. I'll meet you in the dining room."

He started to the door, but Mac's hand on his arm stopped him. "What're we going to do?"

A kaleidoscope of emotions sifted through his eyes, but when he spoke, his voice was steady. "We're going to catch a killer, and then you can go home."

He stalked out of her room as Mac remained standing rooted in place. Isn't this what she wanted? Jared believed her and he was going to help her get back to her time.

So why did she feel like burying herself in her bed and not coming out until after the solstice?

# TWENTY-ONE

After a subdued breakfast, Jared and Mac sequestered themselves in Agnes's dining room and spread their notes across the table.

"What else can you tell me about the murders in your, ah, time?" Jared asked.

Mac would have smiled at his verbal stumble if she hadn't been so unsettled herself about everything. "Not much more than I've already given you. The dates of three of the murders correspond to the winter solstice. The two others occurred a week or two after the summer solstice."

Jared dug through a pile of papers and withdrew a sheet. "Two of the murders here were on the summer solstice, the other three a week or two after the winter solstice."

Mac arched her eyebrows. "Definitely a pattern."

"Another woman will be killed tonight." Jared's jaw clenched so hard Mac imagined she could hear his teeth complaining.

"Unless we can stop him."

Jared took a deep breath. "Unless we can stop him," he reiterated as if it was an oath.

Mac watched him in concern for a long moment and then dipped her head to study the notes she'd been able to pull together from her memory. "The piano wires used in the killings in my time were antique but not degraded."

Jared leaned forward. "Does that mean what I think it does?"

"If you're thinking that the killer carried the wires with him from this time, you're absolutely right."

"Which leads me to believe he's *from* this time and probably from Hope Springs or the resort."

Mac was encouraged to see that Jared didn't even falter with the time issue. "I'd say those were both logical assumptions." She picked up a pad of paper and a pen. "Let's come up with some possible suspects." She wrote Jared Yates at the top and crossed it off.

"What was that for?" Jared demanded.

"You were my prime suspect when I first arrived here," she said and waited for the inevitable explosion.

Jared narrowed his eyes and she could tell he remembered their conversation nearly six months ago. "All right, as long as my name's crossed off," he relented.

"Levon Handler," Mac said as she wrote his name.

Jared ticked off about a dozen more names as Mac dutifully jotted them down on their list. If they went with the theory that the killer spent half of each year in the respective time periods, then anyone who was seen in Hope Springs or at the resort between the end of June and the winter solstice could be eliminated. Two hours later they had crossed off everyone on their list.

By lunchtime, Mac and Jared were frustrated and no closer to the killer than they had been four hours earlier. Agnes served sliced ham and cheese as well as soup and Mac ate the meal though her churning stomach protested. While Mac helped Agnes with the dishes, Jared continued to study their notes.

"Well?" Mac asked as she returned to the dining room.

He shoved his fingers through his hair and shook his head. "Nothing." He jumped to his feet and began to pace. "We're missing something here, Mac. What the hell is it?"

She dropped into her earlier chair. "I wish I knew."

Jared stopped pacing as he kept his gaze locked with hers. "What if we don't find the killer before midnight?" he asked quietly.

"Then I'm stuck here." Mac kept her voice flat, uncertain how the prospect of staying here made her feel.

"Would that be so bad?"

*Not if I was with you.* The thought leaped unbidden to her mind and she quickly dashed it.

"You don't know anything about me, Jared," she said curtly.

"I know all I need to know. I love you."

Mac crossed her arms to hide her trembling. "I'm a bastard, Jared. My mother was unmarried and my father refused to have anything to do with me. Mom's mind started going when I was nine years old. I took care of her as long as I could. She died a year later. I was shuttled from one foster home to another, never staying in one place long enough to feel like I belonged. When I was thirteen, I decided to become a reporter." She gazed at Jared evenly. "Do you know why?"

He shook his head.

"Because my father was a nationally known reporter and newscaster, and I wanted to best him at his own game. I planned to do an in-depth story on our serial killer and use the national attention to tell the world what a son of a bitch my father is." She smiled coldly. "I used to dream of him coming to me begging for forgiveness and me laughing in his face." Her smile slipped. "I've spent over half my life working toward that goal."

"And that's the reason you want to return to your time?"

"Isn't it enough?"

Jared studied her thoughtfully. "I think you're the one who has to answer that question. All I can say is that I love you and I want to marry you."

*Damn him.* Mac didn't want to choose between her feelings for Jared and revenge against her father.

She stood. "We need to go up to the resort and warn the women either to stay inside tonight or to travel in groups of two or more."

Jared touched her arm, sending a shock of awareness rippling through her. "Think about it, Mac. Please."

Lost in the tenderness in his eyes, Mac nodded. "I'll think about it. But that's all I can promise."

"That's all I can ask."

Uncomfortable beneath his warm scrutiny, Mac said, "I'm going to run upstairs and get my purse, then we can catch the train."

Away from Jared, she regained her composure and remembered to put his handcuffs in her bag. She returned to the dining room to find Jared had donned a suit coat over his white shirt. As he adjusted his shoulder holster and gun, Mac allowed herself to savor his presence, so strong, handsome and courageous. Heroic, too.

*Keep this up and I'll start writing for Harlequin.*

When did she start believing in men in white hats?

The moment Jared had saved her from being arrested as a stowaway on the train the night she had arrived.

"Ready?" Jared asked, glancing at her.

She nodded and he guided her out of the boarding-house with a light but possessive hand on her back. As they passed by the Dolly Day saloon, Mac heard the strains of a familiar song. She halted and Jared nearly ran into her.

" 'Beautiful Dreamer,' " she murmured.

"That's right," Jared said, his confusion evident.

"I've heard it before."

"It's a popular song."

Mac shook her head, a memory teasing her. "No. Someplace else . . ." The answer hit her so hard she gasped. "Esme. The first night I was here, I stayed in her room. She was humming that song."

"She probably just likes it."

Mac thought back to the day she'd seen Esme with the owner of the Dolly Day. She spun around and gripped Jared's arms. "Granville Foster. Do you know him?"

Jared frowned. "Not well. He's not around much. He travels around to high-stakes poker games." Comprehension dawned. "Damn it, do you think—"

"C'mon, let's talk to Levon." Mac hustled Jared into the saloon.

The piano's chords died. "Mac, Yates, what the hell are you two doing here so early?" Levon asked in his typical brash manner.

"We want to ta—" Mac began.

"We would like to speak to Mr. Foster," Jared said, a polite Pinkerton smile in place.

"He left for Charleston this morning. Said he'd be gone for a while," Levon replied.

"Yeah, six months," Mac muttered.

"Maybe I can help you. I know the Dolly inside and out."

"Actually the questions were personal," Jared said. "Do you think we could take a look in his room?"

Levon rubbed his lantern jaw. "Mr. Foster doesn't like folks in his room." He squinted at them. "You looking for something in particular?"

"Not exactly," Jared said.

Mac poked him in the ribs with an elbow. "We think he could be the one who's been strangling young women," she said.

Levon's gaze bounced between her and Jared as though they were opponents in a tennis match. Finally he nodded. "All right, but I don't want either of you tellin' him I let you in."

He retrieved a key from the back room and led them up the stairs. After unlocking the door to Foster's room, he stepped inside.

"We don't need an audience," she said.

"But—"

"Mac's right. You have my word we won't steal anything," Jared said.

Grumbling, Levon backed out and Mac closed the door behind him. They set to work searching drawers and the armoire for anything linking Foster to the murders. Mac looked under his bed, but the only thing she found were some stray dust rhinos.

After nearly an hour, Mac threw her arms in the air. "It has to be him."

"We don't have any evidence backing our theory," Jared said.

Mac sighed and fell back on Foster's neat bed, only to hear the faint crackle of paper. She sat up abruptly. "Did you hear that?"

"What?" Jared asked.

Mac jumped off the bed and raised the mattress. "Help me, would you?"

Puzzled, Jared lifted the mattress and revealed a pile of newspaper clippings. Mac grabbed them and Jared lowered the mattress. Sitting side by side on the bed, Mac and Jared looked through the articles. All were about the murders.

And the newspapers were from both this time and the future.

"Gotcha, you son of a bitch," Mac said grimly.

Jared tugged one of the sheets from her hand and Mac glanced at the date at the top: December 21, 2000. She looked at her companion's pasty complexion and laid a palm against his cheek. "You aren't going to faint on me, are you?"

Jared grimaced. "I've never fainted in my life."

"You've never been hit in the face with the impossible before either."

He managed a sickly smile. "I believe you're from the future, Mac, but to see the killer has been there, too . . ." He rubbed his sweat-pearled brow. "Jeezus, this is going to take some getting used to."

Mac stood and grabbed his arm. "Come on. We have to get up to the Chesterfield and talk to Esme. She's our only link to this guy."

They were fortunate to find the next train to leave for the resort departed in ten minutes. They quickly bought tickets and boarded.

There were few passengers and Mac and Jared sat together toward the front of the car, reading the newspaper articles about the killings. Jared gave his attention to those from Mac's time and turned the sheets over to read the backs, too. Grocery ads and international stories only confirmed the impossible again.

"Are eggs really seventy-five cents a dozen?" Jared asked.

"On sale. Usually they're more expensive," Mac replied off-handedly. She felt his body stiffen beside her and turned her attention to him. "What is it?"

"I can't believe how in-depth these stories are. They even mention that the women hadn't been raped and, in fact, had been virgins. Isn't that a little too much information? Think of the poor women."

"They're dead, Jared," Mac said gently. "The press is dedicated to the truth in my time." She paused and shook her head. "Okay, maybe not all of the media, but we try to be as objective as possible."

Jared glanced at the byline on the story he'd been perusing. *"You* wrote this one."

Though it wasn't a question, Mac nodded. "I told you, I was covering the murders."

The rest of the journey was traveled in silence. Once they arrived, Mac and Jared didn't slow down until they reached the Chesterfield. They quickly tracked down Esme in the employees' dining hall, which was nearly empty.

"Trish, Jared. How nice to see you both," Esme said.

"We need to talk to you about Granville Foster," Mac said without preamble.

Esme's face paled. "What about him?"

Jared held out the newspaper clippings. "We found these in his room."

As Esme scanned the headlines of the articles, her face turned chalky white. Jared took her arm and led her to a vacant chair. "Sit down and breathe deeply."

Mac had the urge to give Esme a hug, a notion that seemed so out of character she almost laughed. But the urge didn't go away.

"What can you tell us about Foster?" Jared asked gently.

Esme set the clippings in her lap and clasped her hands together tightly. "We grew up in the same small town. His mother . . ." she paused as if gathering her courage. "His mother was a prostitute. She worked in one of the saloons and played piano and sang in addition to her other duties. Granville never knew who his father was and I don't believe his mother even knew. He grew up surrounded by these types of women and the life they led.

"I felt sorry for him in school since he was teased mercilessly. We became friends." Esme took a deep breath. "When we were older, he wanted more but my destiny did not lie with him. He said he understood why I wouldn't want to be tainted by him. After that, I didn't see him again until he bought the Dolly Day in Hope Springs."

"Was his mother's name Foster?" Mac asked.

Esme shook her head. "No." She smiled at a long-ago memory. "He always loved Stephen Foster's songs. His mother used to sing them as she played the piano. His favorite was 'Beautiful Dreamer.' " She blushed. "He thought of me as his 'beautiful dreamer.' "

Sickness rolled through Mac's belly. "What happened to his mother?"

"I believe she died about three years ago in Staunton. As I recall, she had been ill but I hadn't realized it was life-threatening."

"He killed her," Mac murmured. "She was his first victim."

"Pardon me?" Esme asked.

"We believe Granville Foster is our killer, Esme," Jared spoke gently.

"The man who strangled all those young women?"

"Women who were pure and untainted," Mac said.

Esme's hand flew to her mouth. "I never suspected."

"Do you think he found out a person could move from one time to another during the solstices?"

Esme's eyes widened and her gaze fell on Jared. "You know?"

He nodded. "Mac told me and it was hard *not* to believe after I saw the evidence."

"The solstices, Esme," Mac repeated.

Esme Sparrow nibbled on her lower lip. "I suppose it is possible."

Mac and Jared exchanged looks over Esme's head. "We asked Levon where Foster was. He said he'd gone to Charleston, but we think he's planning his next murder," Jared said. "Do you know where he might be now?"

"I'm not certain. We spoke only rarely." Esme paused, her brow crinkled in thought. "He did, however, mention a place he thought I might like to see someday. A waterfall about a mile from here."

Mac thought a moment. "There was a small waterfall in my time—a tourist trap."

"Do you think you can find it here?" Jared asked.

"I don't have a choice," Mac said grimly.

Jared curved his fingers around her hand and squeezed gently. "Then let's go."


Mac was exhausted from tramping in the woods around the waterfall. It would have been worse if she'd been wearing her long skirt, but fortunately, she and Jared had returned to the boardinghouse after talking to Esme. Mac had changed into the blue jeans and tennis shoes she had been wearing the day she arrived here. She'd left her winter coat behind but had thrown her backpack with the handcuffs tucked safely inside over a shoulder.

Jared, too, had exchanged his typical suit for brown trousers and a light blue shirt that matched his eyes perfectly. She had thought him handsome before, but now he was gorgeous, better than Harrison Ford and Mel Gibson combined.

They had spoken little as they scoured the general area where the previous murders had taken place. With no certain location, they were relying more on luck than skill.

Carrying a lantern, Mac was able to see only about ten feet in front of her. The same for Jared who walked beside her.

They paused in the darkness and Mac lowered herself to the ground, her back resting against the base of a large oak tree.

Jared checked his pocket watch. "It's already eleven." He dropped down beside her. "We only have an hour."

"Don't remind me. I have a feeling—"

A woman's scream shrilled through the air, rocketing both Mac and Jared to their feet.

"Where'd it come from?" Mac demanded.

"This way." Jared grabbed her hand and they ran through the brush.

Mac ignored the sting of the branches against her cheeks. She prayed silently, asking to be able to save one woman's life after so many had already died.

Another scream rent the night, this time closer. Jared increased his stride and Mac forced herself to keep up. Her lungs burned, but as long as she had air in them, she would run.

The sound of a scuffle told them they were close and Jared halted abruptly. Mac bounced against his back and only Jared's strong arms kept her on her feet.

"Stay here," he whispered hoarsely.

"But—"

"No arguments. Keep out of the way." He pressed a small revolver into her hand. "Use this if you have to."

Mac's fingers closed around the weapon even as righteous indignation flooded through her. He couldn't treat her like a child. But before she could find enough oxygen to argue, he was gone.

She tried to slow her breathing so she could hear what was happening. Dark shadows danced in the distance, but Mac wasn't sure if it was Foster and his next victim or a bush swaying with the wind. Then another shadow joined them and there was a brief tussle.

Mac surged out of her hiding place, Jared's words forgotten. He might need her help. Besides, she had his handcuffs. She also had his spare gun.

Her heart pounding in her breast, she burst through the undergrowth. And almost tripped over Jared who had a knee placed in the middle of a man's back as he lay stomach down on the ground.

"Is it . . . F-Foster?" Mac managed to ask in between pants.

Jared nodded and his scowl was evident even in the moonlight. "Didn't I tell you to stay back?"

She shrugged, forcing nonchalance into the gesture. "Have I ever listened to you?"

A slow sexy smile spread across Jared's face. "No."

"Damned straight," Mac said with a silly grin.

"Handcuffs?" Jared asked.

Mac dug into her backpack and handed him her

ticket to getting back to her time. After placing the small revolver in her backpack for safekeeping, she glanced at her wristwatch: 11:28 P.M.

"I'll get them back to you in time," Jared said quietly. "The resort is only five minutes away."

"Where's the woman?" Mac asked, suddenly realizing the intended victim was gone.

"When Foster released her, she ran in the direction of the resort." Jared towed the cuffed man to his feet.

Mac smiled in relief. "If she had that much energy, she should be fine." She glanced at Foster's feral expression and recalled where she'd seen him before. *"You* were the one I chased up the spur line."

"I was wondering if you remembered," Foster said, his voice as slick as oil.

"Why did you kill all those women?"

Foster shook his head. "I didn't kill them. I saved them. They remained chaste unto death."

"What about your mother?" Jared asked, unable to keep the hatred and revulsion from his voice.

Foster's expression slipped for a moment. "She deserved to die peacefully."

Mac shivered, shocked by the warped evil radiating from the killer.

"Maybe I should just 'save' you," Jared said, his lips pulled back in a snarl as he withdrew his revolver and stuck the barrel under Foster's chin.

Mac laid a hand on Jared's arm, feeling the tense muscles beneath. "He's not worth it, Jared. Your fiancée wouldn't have wanted you to kill him in cold blood."

He laughed, a harsh bitter sound. "You didn't know Sophia. She would've wanted me to avenge her." He paused, lowering his weapon. "I had every intention of killing him."

"So why didn't you?"

Jared shook his head. "I don't know."

Mac rubbed his arm. "Because you're decent and honest. And you're a good man, the best I've ever had the privilege to meet."

Jared cupped Mac's cheek in his palm. "No. The reason I won't kill him is that I don't want to disappoint you."

Before Mac could reply, Foster suddenly rammed his head up, catching Jared below the chin and sending him to his knees. Foster took off running as Mac sank down beside Jared, her heart thundering.

"Are you all right?" she asked.

He shook his head like a puppy that had just been kicked. "I'm all right," Jared said impatiently as he struggled to his feet. "Where'd Foster go?"

Mac helped him up and pointed in the direction he'd run. "That way."

Jared dashed away with Mac close on his heels. She wasn't going to stay behind this time. However, she found herself falling farther and farther back until she could no longer see Jared's broad shoulders ahead of her. Her breath tore at her throat and she stumbled as her toe caught on an exposed root. Flinging out her arms, she landed hard and the air whooshed out of her. Feeling a sense of déjà vu, she lay still for a moment, unable to draw in a breath. Then abruptly, air rushed into her lungs and she gasped loudly, her eyes tearing.

*Jared. I have to get to Jared.*

She pressed herself upright and continued running, hoping she was headed in the right direction. A stitch caught in her side and she had to stop. Bending at the waist, she panted. Her heart sounded like a bass drum had taken residence in her chest.

Finally she was able to straighten and she spotted Jared and Foster immediately. Foster had managed to get his handcuffed hands in front of him and in them he held a thick branch. Jared lay on the ground moving feebly as if he'd already taken a blow.

Though terrified, Mac dug into her backpack and her fingers closed around cold steel. Twenty-five feet away and she was no marksman, but Jared's life lay in the balance. She held the gun between her hands and raised it just as Foster lifted the branch above his head for the killing blow.

Mac swallowed hard and squeezed the trigger. The gun bucked in her hands, startling her, but she quickly focused on Foster who stumbled backward. He dropped the branch and landed atop it as he fell to the ground and lay still.

Mac raced over to Jared, falling to her knees beside him. "Jared, are you all right?"

He opened bleary eyes and managed a smile. "Now I am." He placed his palm against her cheek and she turned to kiss the palm gently. "Thanks, Mac."

"For the kiss or saving your life?" she quipped, a tear spilling down her cheek.

"Both."

Jared framed her face in his palms and settled his lips on hers. Mac opened her mouth to him, savoring his taste and heat. She wanted to crawl into his lap and assure herself he was alive and safe. Death had been so close . . . too close.

Jared broke the kiss and dug into his pocket. "It's time, Mac. You've done what you had to do."

She stared at him, wondering what he was talking about. He moved over to Foster's body and unlocked the handcuffs. "He's still alive. Just unconscious," Jared said.

In spite of his heinous crimes, Mac was relieved she hadn't killed him.

Holding up the handcuffs, Jared shook his head. "Looks as if he was about to get them apart."

He returned to Mac's side and she gazed at the links between the cuffs. One of them was almost cut through. Another few minutes and Foster would have separated them.

Just like she'd found them in the hope chest.

The blood left Mac's face and she plopped down on her backside. "My mission wasn't to catch the killer. It was to save your life." She buried her face in her hands. "You died."

Strong arms came around her, drawing her snug against his solid chest, and rocked her gently. "I didn't die, Mac. I'm right here beside you."

Mac raised her tear-blurred gaze to him. "You don't understand. When I found your handcuffs in my time, they were in two pieces. One of the links had been cut through. If I hadn't come back in time, he would've killed you and escaped."

"And I wouldn't have met you and fallen in love with you," Jared said huskily, brushing her damp hair back with loving hands.

The bell at the resort began to toll.

"Midnight," Jared whispered. He opened Mac's hand and laid the handcuffs within it. "I hope you write the best damned news story ever and your father finally sees what he's missed all these years: a wonderful, bright, intelligent, beautiful daughter."

Tears rolled unheeded down Mac's cheeks as she stared at the cuffs in her hand—her key to returning to her time. But was it home?

She lifted her gaze to Jared as the sixth peal tolled.

Her breath caught in her throat at the pure love blazing in his eyes.

Love, the one thing she swore she would never want to possess. Yet here it was in Jared Yates, a true hero in any time. A hero who would release her rather than hold her because he loved her too much.

A hero she loved with all her heart.

The tenth toll sounded, then the eleventh.

Mac tossed the handcuffs into the brush and launched herself into Jared's arms, knocking him to the ground. She lay atop him, gazing into clear blue eyes overflowing with love and desire.

"I love you, Jared Yates, so you damn well better make me an honest woman."

# EPILOGUE

*June 20, 1895*

Esme Sparrow knelt in front of her hope chest—the hope chest she'd been given years ago when her destiny had been revealed. She traced the chest's intricate carved floral design lightly, then raised the cover. Inside lay five shiny items: a gleaming pistol, a shiny five-starred badge, a polished brass nameplate, an unbroken gold chain and a pair of handcuffs, which she touched gingerly.

The nick in a link of the cuffs gave evidence to how close Esme had come to failing. If that link had been severed completely, so would the final link of her destiny have been broken and her own soul mate would never have been born.

She shuddered, not wishing to dwell upon such horrible consequences especially on the day she and her true love would pledge their lives and hearts to each other for eternity.

The five happily married couples, also brought together despite time's errors, would witness that which they had made possible. Even now, Drake and Gina's eight-year-old son, Jess and Corrie's six-year-old daughter, Delgatto and Emily's three-year-old son, and

Dimitri and Cynda's two-year-old daughter were mending the rent in time's fabric. The new life Jared and Trish had conceived seven months ago would add his pattern to the weave to complete the design—the lineage that brought to life her soul mate in the year of our Lord, 1969. He had been brought back with the winter solstice, but there had been no confusion. He had been waiting for her, just as she had waited a lifetime for him.

Esme gently lowered the hope chest's lid and straightened. She adjusted her flowing veil and smoothed the bodice of her wedding dress. Picking up the bouquet of white roses from the bed, she paused and plucked one flower from the bunch. She laid it atop her hope chest, a symbol of true and enduring love.

The past was fulfilled and the future set right before her. The present now beckoned to complete the circle.

# Contemporary Romance by
# Kasey Michaels

## __Can't Take My Eyes Off of You
   0-8217-6522-1                   **$6.50**US/**$8.50**CAN

East Wapaneken? Shelby Taite has never heard of it. Neither has the rest of Philadelphia's Main Line society. Which is precisely why the town is so appealing. No one would ever think to look for Shelby here. Nobody but Quinn Delaney . . .

## __Too Good To Be True
   0-8217-6774-7                   **$6.50**US/**$8.50**CAN

To know Grady Sullivan is to love him . . . unless you're Annie Kendall. After all, Annie is here at Peevers Manor trying to prove she's the long-lost illegitimate great-granddaughter of a toilet paper tycoon. How's a girl supposed to focus on charming her way into an old man's will with Grady breathing down her neck . . .

---

# Stella Cameron

"A premier author of romantic suspense."

\_\_The Best Revenge
0-8217-5842-X
$6.50US/$8.00CAN

\_\_French Quarter
0-8217-6251-6
$6.99US/$8.50CAN

\_\_Key West
0-8217-6595-7
$6.99US/$8.99CAN

\_\_Pure Delights
0-8217-4798-3
$5.99US/$6.99CAN

\_\_Sheer Pleasures
0-8217-5093-3
$5.99US/$6.99CAN

\_\_True Bliss
0-8217-5369-X
$5.99US/$6.99CAN

---

Call toll free **1-888-345-BOOK** to order by phone, use this coupon to order by mail, or order online at **www.kensingtonbooks.com**.

Name_____
Address_____
City_____ State _____ Zip _____
Please send me the books I have checked above.
I am enclosing                                          $_____
Plus postage and handling*                              $_____
Sales tax (in New York and Tennessee only)              $_____
Total amount enclosed                                   $_____
*Add $2.50 for the first book and $.50 for each additional book.
Send check or money order (no cash or CODs) to:
**Kensington Publishing Corp., Dept. C.O., 850 Third Avenue, New York, NY 10022**
Prices and numbers subject to change without notice. All orders subject to availability.
Visit our website at **www.kensingtonbooks.com**.